SMALLBONE DECEASED

MICHAEL GILBERT

with an introduction by
MARTIN EDWARDS

D1328928

This edition published 2019 by
The British Library
96 Euston Road
London
NW1 2DB

Originally published in 1950 by Hodder & Stoughton, London

Cataloguing in Publication Data
A catalogue record for this book is available
from the British Library

ISBN 978 0 7123 5297 0
eISBN 978 0 7123 6469 0

Typeset by Tetragon, London
Printed and bound by CPI Group (UK) Ltd, Croydon CR0 4YY

CONTENTS

INTRODUCTION

Smallbone Deceased was first published in 1950, and few British detective stories during the rest of the Fifties came close to matching it in terms of quality. This was Michael Gilbert's fourth novel, and the first in which he drew extensively on his first-hand knowledge of life inside a London law firm. The book blends in masterly fashion an authentic setting, pleasingly differentiated characters, smoothly readable prose, and a clever puzzle.

The opening scene, set at a dinner in a Holborn restaurant, offers a witty introduction to partners and staff of Horniman, Birley and Craine, "the Gordon Selfridge of solicitors, different departments to suit all tastes and purses". Several of those present will shortly become suspects in a murder case when a dead body is found at the firm's premises at Lincoln's Inn, concealed within a hermetically sealed deed box. Also in attendance is Henry Bohun, "the very newest thing in solicitors", a brilliant and slightly mysterious young man with a flair for amateur detection.

When the novel first came out, its publishers (Hodder & Stoughton) hailed it as "a connoisseur's piece", and they were not exaggerating. Unfortunately, the book appeared before the Crime Writers' Association (of which Gilbert became a founder member) was formed, and thus there was no opportunity for the story to compete for a CWA Dagger, although its quality was recognised by reviewers in Britain and the US. In *A Catalogue of Crime*, Jacques

Barzun and Wendell Hertig Taylor described it as Gilbert's "master-work", while Julian Symons included the book in *The Hundred Best Crime Stories* (1958). Similarly, H.R.F. Keating included it in his own survey of the "hundred best" crime and mystery novels, published in 1987. Three years later, the CWA featured the novel in its own "hundred best" list, and so subsequently did the Mystery Writers of America.

Keating described the book as a fine example of the classic detective story—two floor plans are supplied in the finest Golden Age tradition—and went so far as to compare the plot with "Agatha Christie at her best; as neatly dovetailed, as inherently complex yet retaining a decent credibility, and as full of cunningly-suggested red herrings". He pinpointed as an incidental pleasure Gilbert's "depic-tion of Britain's immediate post-war years, with an electricity cut playing a notable part in the establishing of alibis", and his stylish, urbane way with words, while arguing plausibly that touches of real-ism in the narrative "make you feel this ingenious tale is a good deal more closely related to real life than your average detective story".

Gilbert had begun his crime writing career with *Close Quarters*, a detective puzzle in the classic style of the Golden Age whodunit, and followed his debut with two lively thrillers—an early sign of the determination to keep trying something different that became his trade mark as a crime writer. Chief Inspector Hazlerigg played a part in each story, as he does in *Smallbone Deceased*. This is not, however, a novel which concentrates on police procedure.

Henry Bohun's sleuthing is an even more significant component of the book than Hazlerigg's official investigation. Bohun is a like-able and memorable individual who featured in no other novels. Intriguingly, he had made his debut in Gilbert's very first published story, "Weekend at Wapentake", which appeared in (of all journals)

Good Housekeeping on 16 October 1948; in that story, he was already a partner in the firm. An appendix in John Cooper's collection of Gilbert radio plays, *The Man Who Couldn't Sleep*, reveals that Bohun appeared in a total of nine short stories and a six-part radio thriller.

Hazlerigg looks rather like a farmer: "the only remarkable thing about this generally unremarkable person was his eyes, which were grey, with the cold grey of the North Sea." He seemed destined to become a major series character, but although he featured in nineteen short stories as well as six novels, eventually he made way for a host of freshly created protagonists, both professional detectives and amateurs who stumble across crime. Gilbert's career as a novelist lasted for more than half a century—his final book, the aptly titled *Over and Out*, was published in 1998—yet throughout that time, he kept ringing the changes, and never wrote a long series featuring a single "great detective". This reflects a splendid determination to avoid the formulaic, but it may also explain why, for all the critical acclaim he received, he never quite became a household name. Crime fans have a taste for series, and for characters whose cases they can follow over a long period of time.

Michael Francis Gilbert (1912–2006) was born in Billingshay in Lincolnshire, and studied law at London University. He also had a spell as a teacher at a cathedral school, which supplied him with the background for his first novel as well as funds to complete his legal education. The Second World War interrupted his work on *Close Quarters* as well as his attempts to establish himself as a solicitor, but in 1947 he joined a highly respected Lincoln's Inn law firm, Trower, Still and Keeling, becoming a partner in 1953; he remained with the practice until his retirement in 1983. His clients included Raymond Chandler, who became a close personal friend; when, towards the end of his life, Chandler was drinking heavily and struggling to cope after the death of his wife, Gilbert made strenuous efforts to help the great American novelist to resolve the financial difficulties he was facing.

The Swedish Academy of Detection made Gilbert a Grand Master in 1981, and the Mystery Writers of America followed suit six years later. He earned the CWA Diamond Dagger in 1994 to recognise his outstanding contribution to the crime genre, and was appointed a CBE in 1980. In all, he wrote thirty novels and 185 short stories, as well as work for radio, television, and stage. He served as Chair of the Crime Writers' Association, and was a proud member of the Detection Club for more than half a century. He was one of the leading lights of British mystery fiction throughout the second half of the twentieth century, and—to borrow a lawyer's phrase—there can be no reasonable doubt that his best books deserve to be ranked as crime classics.

MARTIN EDWARDS
www.martinedwardsbooks.com

SMALLBONE
DECEASED

"There is no point in concealing the fact that London solicitors work in certain well-known and well-defined areas; nor would much purpose have been served by giving these fictitious names. The fact, however, that a number of regrettable incidents are supposed to have taken place in Lincoln's Inn must not be interpreted as any reflection on the many and reputable firms who practise there: nor must any mention of the officials or functionaries of that Inn be taken as a reference to the present holders of those offices."

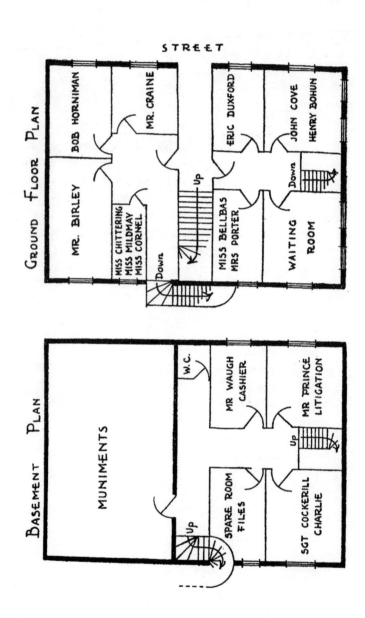

"One hundred and ninety thirdly (and lastly) Professional Gentlemen, as solicitors, attorneys, proctors, engineers, architects, medical practitioners, artists, literary men, merchants, master manufacturers, scientific professors, and others not engaged in manual labour, farming of land or retail trade, are considered to possess some station in society, although the Law takes no cognizance of their ranks *inter se.*"

Precedence: from *Dod's Peerage*, p. 434.

CHAPTER ONE

Parties to the Deed

First will be set out the Parties, each by his full name and address and by a Description, as, Lieutenant-Colonel in His Majesty's Grenadier Regiment of Foot-guards, Solicitor to the Supreme Court of Judicature, Clerk in Holy Orders, Butcher, or as the case may be and (where of the female sex) wife, widow, spinster or feme sole.

I

"THE THOUGHTS OF ALL PRESENT TONIGHT," SAID MR. Birley, "will naturally turn first to the great personal loss—the very great personal loss—so recently suffered by the firm, by the legal profession and, if I may venture to say so without contradiction, by the British public."

No one did contradict him; partly, no doubt, owing to the fact that Mr. Birley was personally responsible for the salaries of the greater number of those present, but also because the principal speaker at a staff dinner very rarely is contradicted; Mr. Birley, therefore, proceeded.

"It is difficult to speak without emotion of such a loss. Abel Horniman, our founder and our late senior partner, was a man whose name will be long remembered. Even those who are not qualified to appreciate the worth of his legal—ah—laurels, will remember him in connection with those innovations in office management which bear his name. The Horniman Self-Checking Completion System, the Horniman Alphabetical Index—"

"The Horniman High-Powered Raspberry," said John Cove to his neighbour, Mr. Bohun.

"—Abel Horniman was not only a great lawyer, he was also a great business man. Some of you will remember his boast: 'In thirty seconds,' he used to say, 'I can lay my hand on any paper which has come into this office in the last thirty years.' How many firms of solicitors, I wonder, could say the same? In this age of slipshod methods, of rule-of-thumb litigation, of printed-form conveyancing, how salutary it is to stop and think for a few moments of the career of a man who learned his law the hard way, a man who had perfected himself in every branch of a solicitor's work, a man who asked nothing of his subordinates that he could not himself do better—and yet"—Mr. Birley unwound this long relative clause with the ease of a practised conveyancer—"and yet a man who, as we know, was quite prepared to offer freely to his partners and his staff the fruits of his knowledge and his hard work."

"If he'd offered me a tenth of the money he made, I shouldn't have said no to it," observed Mr. Cove, desisting for a moment from his attempts to hit Miss Mildmay, three places away on the opposite side of the table, with a bread pellet.

"A grand old lawyer," went on Mr. Birley. "The founder and the inspiration of his firm—of our firm—perhaps I may say of our happy family—Horniman, Birley and Craine."

Sustained applause.

In the Rhodian room of the Colossus restaurant in Holborn one long and three shorter tables were set in the form of a capital "E", and round them were gathered some fifty men and women ranging in age from an exceedingly venerable party with a white beard, who was sleeping fitfully at one end of the top table, down to three young gentlemen of fifteen-plus (of a type normally described in police reports as "youths") who had collected at a point furthest from the eye of the chairman and were engaged in a game of blow-football with rolled-up menus and a battered grape.

Miss Mildmay looked up as a bread pellet struck her on the cheek and remarked in a clear voice: "If you hit me again with one of those things, John Cove, I shan't type any more of your private letters for you in office hours."

"Delilah," said John.

Henry Bohun was engaged, meanwhile, in a mathematical computation the answer to which seemed to puzzle him.

"How do they fit them all in?"

"Fit all what into what?" said John Cove.

"Into the office. When Birley was showing me round this afternoon I counted twelve rooms. One was obviously a waiting-room. That leaves eleven. If the partners have a room each—"

"Oh, these aren't all *our* people," said John. "Very few of them, in fact. We control three other firms, you know. Ramussen and Oakshott in the City, Bourlass, Bridewell and Burt in the West End, and Brown, Baxter and thingummybob in some impossible place like Streatham or Brixton—"

An indignant glare from a young man with long hair and a pillar-box red tie warned John that he was speaking perhaps a trifle loudly for the promotion of that happy family feeling which Mr. Birley had just commended.

"Oh Lord," he went on. "There's Tubby getting up. I do think all this speechmaking is a mistake."

Mr. Tristram Craine rose to reply to the toast of "The Firm". He was a plump little person, in appearance two-thirds of Charles Cheeryble to one-third of Lord Beaverbrook; in fact, an extremely sharp solicitor.

What he said is not important, since one after-dinner speech tends to be very like another. However, it afforded an opportunity for Henry Bohun to take a further quick look round the table in an endeavour to identify some of the people with whom he was going to work.

He himself was the very newest thing in solicitors.

He had qualified precisely three days previously and joined the firm only that afternoon. His single close acquaintance so far was the flippant Mr. Cove. Birley and Craine he knew, of course. The other reverend parties at the head table were, he suspected, the Ramussens, the Oakshotts, the Bourlasses and the Bridewells of the confederate firms.

There was a dark-haired youngster, wearing heavy horn-rimmed spectacles and looking a little out of place among the augurs. He suspected that this might be Bob Horniman, the late Abel Horniman's son. They had been to the same public school, but Bob had been three years his junior and three years is a long time when it marks the gap between fourteen and seventeen.

Mr. Craine unconsciously resolved this uncertainty for him by saying: "And I feel we should take this opportunity of welcoming our new partner, our founder's son, who steps forward now to take his father's place." (Applause.)

The dark young man blushed so hotly and took off and wiped his spectacles with such unnecessary gusto that Henry concluded that his guess had been correct. He also reflected that to have a great man for a father was not always an entirely comfortable fate.

"A Richard for an Oliver," said Mr. Cove, reading his thoughts accurately.

"Pardon?" said the young lady on his right.

"Granted as soon as asked," said Mr. Cove agreeably.

Then there was that man with the rather sharp face and the unidentifiable, but too obviously old-school tie—he'd seen him somewhere about the office. The girl next to him was a good looker, in a powerful sort of way. She was the possessor of auburn hair and very light blue eyes, elements which may be harmless apart but can be explosive when mixed.

"He died," said Mr. Craine—apparently he had reverted to the founder of the firm—"as I am sure he would have wished to die—in harness. It scarcely seems a month ago that I walked into his room and found him at his desk, his pen grasped in his hand—"

"It really is rather an inspiring thought," murmured John Cove, "that the last words he ever wrote should have been 'Unless we hear from you by an early post we shall have no option but to institute proceedings'. There's a touch, there, of the old warrior dying with his lance in couch and his face to the foe."

After Mr. Craine had sat down the old gentleman with the white beard, who proved indeed to be Mr. Ramussen, awoke and proposed the health of Mr. Oakshott, whereupon Mr. Oakshott retaliated by proposing the health of Mr. Ramussen; whereafter the Bourlasses and the Bridewells and the Burts toasted each other oratorically in a series of ever-decreasing circles. Even the despised Mr. Brown succeeded in putting in a word for Streatham before Mr. Birley, by pushing back his chair and undoing the two bottom buttons of his waistcoat, signified that the ordeal was at an end.

As people got up from the table and the more informal side of the evening began the junior members of the four firms, who up to now had sat in strictly anti-social groups, began to intermingle a little, a certain nice degree of stratification being observed. Partner opened his cigar-case to partner, managing clerk took beer with managing clerk, and secretary exchanged small talk with secretary. Someone started to play the piano and a pale costs clerk from the Streatham office sang a song about a sailor and a mermaid which would certainly have been very entertaining if anyone had been able to hear the words.

Bohun, as a newcomer, was beginning to feel rather out of things when he was buttonholed by a dark-haired, horse-faced woman of about forty-five whom he recognised.

"Miss Cornel, in case you've forgotten," she said.

"You're Mr. Horniman's—I mean, you were Mr. Horniman's secretary," he said.

"Still am," said Miss Cornel. Sensing his surprise she explained. "I've been handed down. I've been devised and bequeathed. I'm young Mr. Horniman's secretary now."

"Bob Horniman."

"Yes. I believe you knew him, didn't you?"

"I was at school with him," said Bohun. "I didn't know him very well. He came ten or twelve terms after me; and we weren't in the same house, you know."

"Never having been to a public school myself," said Miss Cornel, with a dry but not unfriendly smile, "I've no idea what you're talking about. However, come and meet some of the staff. I won't waste you on members of the outside firms because you probably won't see them again until next year's office party. Here's Miss Chittering now. She works for Mr. Birley, and Miss Bellbas, who works for Mr. Duxford and also for John Cove, God help her."

She waved forward a hipless off-blonde and a startlingly vacant-looking brunette, neither of whom seemed to have much to say for themselves.

"And why should Miss Cornel consider it such a penance to have to work for Mr. Cove?" asked Bohun helpfully.

The brunette Miss Bellbas considered the matter seriously for a moment or two and then said: "I expect it's the things he says." This seemed to have exhausted the topic, so he turned to the blonde.

"And how long have you been with the firm, Miss Chittering?"

"So long," said Miss Chittering coyly, "that I never admit to it now, for fear people might start guessing my age."

She looked at Mr. Bohun as if inviting him to indulge in some daring speculation on the subject, but he refused the gambit and said: "I understand you work for our senior partner, Mr Birley. That must be quite a responsibility."

"Oh, it is!" said Miss Chittering. "Have you met Mr. Birley yet, Mr. Bohun? That was him who made the first speech tonight."

"Yes," said Henry. "Yes, I heard him. Quite an inspired orator," he added cautiously.

Miss Chittering accepted this at its face value. "He's very clever," she said, "and such an interesting man to work for, isn't he, Florrie?"

"Frightfully," said Florrie. "I can never understand a single word he says. But then, I don't think I was really cut out for the law. Oh, thank you."

This was to John Cove who had appeared alongside and was contriving, with an expertness which suggested considerable practice, to carry four pink gins.

"You mustn't believe a word of it," said John. "I don't know what we should do without our Miss Bellbas. To watch her spelling 'cestui que trust' and 'puisne Mortgage' by the light of pure phonetics—"

"Really, Mr. Cove!" said Miss Chittering.

"But never mind, Miss Bellbas. What are brains beside beauty?"

"Well, what are they?" asked Miss Bellbas, who seemed to be a very literal-minded girl.

"Fully to explain that," said John, "I should have to take you to a secluded corner for a course of private instruction."

"Really, Mr. Cove," said Miss Chittering. "You mustn't talk like that. Mr. Bohun will be thinking you mean what you say. Tell me, why didn't you recite for us this evening?"

"The committee, I regret to say, censored both my proffered contributions. Well, ladies, we mustn't be keeping you from your admirers. I see old Mr. Ramussen has one of his ancient but inviting eyes on you already, Miss Bellbas—" He piloted Henry away: "Come and meet Sergeant Cockerill."

"Who?"

"Sergeant Cockerill, our muniments clerk, desk sergeant, post clerk, chief messenger, housekeeper, librarian, butler and tea-maker in chief. The Admirable Crichton in person."

Despite his title, Sergeant Cockerill proved to be a most unmilitary-looking person. He was a neat spare man and had something of the look of a Victorian Under-Secretary of State, with his stiff, chin-prop collar, his correct deportment and his intelligent brown eyes.

Bohun found, rather to his relief, that little was expected of him here in the way of conversation and he was entertained for the next fifteen minutes by a discourse on the subject of "futures". He missed the significance of some of the earlier remarks owing to a mistaken belief that "futures" were commodities dealt with on the Stock Exchange. It was some time before he realised they were things which the sergeant grew in the garden of his house at Winchmore Hill.

As ten o'clock approached there was a tendency amongst the elder members of the party to think about the times of trains and the crowd began to thin out. Bohun drifted with the current, which had set towards the stairs leading down to the ground floor and the cloakrooms.

Immediately ahead of him he noticed Bob Horniman and the red-haired girl. As they reached the foot of the staircase he heard Bob say: "Would you like me to see if I can get you a taxi?"

"Thank you, Mr. Horniman. I can look after myself quite easily."

Now this was an answer which might have been made in any tone of voice and denoting any shade of feeling ranging from indifference to something fairly rude. The red-haired girl managed to invest it with a degree of venom which surprised Mr. Bohun considerably. He saw Bob Horniman flush, hesitate for a moment, and then dive down the stairs leading to the cloakroom.

The girl stood looking after him. There was a quarter of a smile on her lips but her light blue eyes said nothing but "Danger".

"It's far too early to go to bed," said John Cove. "Come and have a drink."

"All right," said Bohun. He wondered whether John had observed the curious little scene; and if so, what he had made of it.

"Who's the redhead?" he asked.

"That's Anne Mildmay," said John. "She works for Tubby Craine. Lecherous little beast. Craine, I mean," he added. "Come on, I know a place in Shaftesbury Avenue which stays open till midnight."

Over the bar of the Anchorage (which is "in" Shaftesbury Avenue in approximately the same sense that Boulestins is "in" the Strand) John Cove fixed Bohun with a gloomy stare and said: "Tell me. What brought you into the racket?"

"Which racket?" enquired Henry cautiously.

"The law."

"It's hard to say. I was a research statistician, you know."

"Well, I don't," said John, "but it sounds quite frightful. Who did you research into statistics for?"

"It wasn't a question of researching *into* statistics," said Henry patiently. "I collated statistics and other people used them for research. It was a nice job, too. All you needed was a fairly good memory and a head for figures."

"Decent hours?"

"First class. Come when you like, go when you like."

"Congenial company?"

"Very much so."

"Then I say again," said John, "why come into our racket at your age? No offence—I'm not a dewy-eyed youngster myself—two more, please, Ted. But at least I've got the excuse that I was in the game before the war. I would have finished my articles in 1941 had Hitler not willed otherwise."

"Well," said Henry slowly. "I couldn't go back to my old firm. It was an oil combine, and it went and got itself amalgamated whilst I was away, and although mine was a good sort of job they're pretty few and far between. So I thought I'd take up law as a soft option."

"You thought what?" John was so overcome that he spilt a good deal of his whisky, and quickly drank the rest of it before it could come to any harm.

"Why, certainly," said Henry. "What I really like about the law is that it's so restful. You never have to think. It's all in the books."

"Two more whiskies," said John to the barman. "Doubles."

"No fooling," said Henry. "I did two years as a medical student when I left school, and I can assure you there's absolutely no comparison. Think how easy it would be to perform a surgical operation, if you had Butterworth's *Forms and Precedents* ever at your elbow. One, take a scapula, size six, in the right hand. Two, grasp the appendix firmly round the broad end—"

"Bung-ho!" said John.

"Can't I buy you a drink for a change?"

"Not unless you're a member."

"Well, let's go somewhere where I can."

At Raguzzis, which is near the Berkeley Square end of Bruton Street, the conversation turned, not without a certain amount of wilful steering on Henry's part, on to the subject of the firm of Horniman, Birley and Craine.

John had, by now, reached that well-defined stage in intoxication when every topic becomes the subject of exposition and generalisation, when sequences of thought range themselves in the speaker's mind, strewn about with flowery metaphor and garlanded in chains of pellucid logic; airborne flights of oratory to which the only obstacle is a certain difficulty with the palatal consonants.

"Horniman, Birley and Craine," said John, "is not one firm but four firms. It is a quadernity. It is the Gordon Selfridge of solicitors, different departments to suit all tastes and purses. For the humble but well-meaning citizens of Streatham or Brixton Mr. Brown and Mr. Baxter labour unceasingly, resting not day nor night. For the hard-faced, stern-browed moguls of commerce and industry our City offices are ever open, and the warm hearts and subtle brains of Mr. Bourlass, Mr. Bridewell and Mr. Burt beat in a mighty diapason, and their cunning fingers are never still—here underwriting a charter party, there endorsing a Bill of Exchange *sans recours*; and if all else palls, why, bless me, they can always fill in the time between lunch and tea by forming a limited company. In Piccadilly, those gilded darlings of fortune, Osric Ramussen and Emmanuel Oakshott, pin carnations to the palpitating bosoms of a horde of comely divorcees and spend their time, or such time as they can spare from race meetings and first nights, in drawing fantastic leases of flats in Half Moon Street and shops in the Burlington Arcade—"

"Two more whiskies," said Henry. "What do *we* do in Lincoln's Inn?"

"I've never really found out," said John, "but it's all most terribly gentlemanly. Our books of reference are Burke and Debrett and we're almost the last firm in London that draws up strict marriage settlements and calls the heir up on his twenty-first birthday to execute a disentailing deed and drink a glass of pre-1914 sherry."

"I thought that the peerage were all broke these days."

"So they are," said John regretfully. "So they are. I expect that's why we bought up the other offices. All the real money's in Streatham."

At the Silver Slipper, which is between Regent Street and Glasshouse Street, and of which Mr. Bohun appeared to be a member, John found occasion, between glasses of champagne, to ask:

"You didn't seriously mean what you said, did you?"

"What are you talking about now?"

"About solicitoring being so easy."

"Certainly I did. If you want a really difficult job you ought to try actuarial work. I trained for eighteen months as an actuary in New York."

At the Lettre de Cachet, a small club off the west end of Old Compton Street, John swallowed his thimbleful of apricot brandy, started to say something, folded neatly forward over the table and fell into a dreamless sleep.

When he woke up the electric clock beside the band platform showed four, the band was packing up and the last of the clientele were leaving.

Henry Bohun finished his drink and rose to his feet.

"I think we ought to be getting along," he said regretfully. "It's been a splendid evening."

"Splendid," said John. Something odd about his companion struck him.

"Aren't you tired?" he asked.

"No," said Henry.

"Don't you ever get tired?"

"Not often," said Henry.

"Why not?" said John. For himself an overmastering desire to sleep was rolling round him, enveloping him, dimming his eyes and anæsthetising his brain.

"I've no idea," said Henry truthfully. "It's just one of those things."

CHAPTER TWO

—TUESDAY—

The Irritating Absence of a Trustee

The Law is utilitarian.

JAMES BARR AMES: *Law and Morals*

I

"ALL THAT MESSUAGE TENEMENT OR BUILDING," SAID JOHN Cove reluctantly, "together with the outbuildings farmbuildings cottages barns sheds closets and other buildings of a permanent or quasipermanent nature erected thereon or on some part thereof together also with the several pieces or parcels of land thereto belonging and the several brothels and—"

"I beg your pardon, Mr. Cove."

"I'm sorry, Miss Bellbas. The word was 'abuttals'. I'm afraid my eyesight isn't quite what it should be this morning."

"No, Mr. Cove?"

"In fact, if I may let you into a secret, I find some difficulty in opening both eyes at once."

"I expect it was all those drinks you drank last night, Mr. Cove."

"And when I do open them," said John, properly ignoring this interruption, "what do I see?"

"I—"

"I see a greyish-yellowish mist, Miss Bellbas, and floating round in it, like the corpses of men long drowned, are Things, frightful indescribable Things."

"I expect you need a cup of coffee, Mr. Cove."

"That's a very sensible idea, Florrie. See if you can get the sergeant to produce a cup—two cups. Mr. Bohun will have one as well."

When Miss Bellbas had departed Mr. Cove said petulantly: "I really don't know how you contrive to look so disgustingly fit. So far as I can recollect you drank exactly the same as I did."

"I'll let you into the secret some day," said Bohun. "It's a system you have to start young or not at all—like tight-rope walking and Yogi."

"Then it's altogether too late," said John, "for I am at death's door."

Nevertheless, after a cup of strong coffee, he found himself revived sufficiently to begin Mr. Bohun's education.

The latter was staring in a rather helpless way at a small mountain of filing cards.

"That is the Horniman Case Index Card. At the top you will see the name of the client. On the left, in purple ink, a series of letters; on the bottom, in pencil, a number. Now what's the first card you've got there? Dogberry and Usk... That's the ninth baron. 'Children's Settlement No. 5', well, that's plain enough. It's a tax-dodging stunt, of course. Now the letter 'C'. That tells you what stage the thing has got to. I forget just what 'C' stands for in Settlements—appointment of trustees, I think. You'll find all that explained in the Horniman Index. Then last of all the number—52. That means that letter No. 52 was the last one to go out from this office. When you write the next letter you rub that out and put 53. Simple."

"Do we have to number all our letters then?"

"Every letter written in this office," said John, "is numbered, top copy and carbon, press-copied for the letter book and stamped for outgoing mail. The carbon is then filed and indexed."

"Nothing else?" said Henry. "Surely you send a copy to *The Times* as well?"

"No. But you mustn't imagine that your labours are over when a letter has been dispatched or an answer received. In the inside of every cardboard file cover—specially designed, I may say, by Abel Horniman—is a pro-forma into which you fill the essential details of each transaction. This pro-forma is finally reproduced, in a slightly condensed form, on one of the cards you've got there. Once a file is closed, it may go into a number of different places. If the client is a grade three client—one whose affairs are of small importance or who himself possesses only minor status—"

"The younger sons of younger sons of dukes?"

"That's it. You're getting the hang of it nicely. Well, his files will go in the tea-room—that's the glory-hole next to Sergeant Cockerill's lair. A second-class client travels the same route, but ends up in a locker in the muniments room. But a first-class client—" John waved his hand round the room.

"Has a BOX!"

"Right. And no ordinary box."

John went over to the rack at the far end of the room and drew out a black tin receptacle labelled "The Venerable the Archdeacon of Melchester, D.D."

It was after the same style as, but larger than, the normal deed box found in a solicitor's office. Its most unusual feature was the closing device on the lid. This was a cantilever and clip, like the gadget which operates a simple trouser-press. Henry pulled the handle upwards and backwards and tugged at the lid. Nothing happened.

"You have to open it with a jerk," said John. "It's hermetically sealed."

When the lid came off, Henry saw what he meant. It was not, in point of scientific fact, hermetically sealed, but it was very tightly shut. Round the inside lip of the box ran a thick rubber lining into a groove in which the sharp edges of the lid fitted, pressed down by the leverage of the clamp.

"What a contraption. I've never seen anything like it. Surely the ordinary deed box is good enough."

"It was commonly believed in the office," said John, "that once, just before the turn of the present century, one of Abel Horniman's leases had the signature eaten off by a mouse, a mishap which gave rise to expensive litigation in the Chancery Division. Accordingly he sat down and devised the Horniman dust-proof, moisture-proof, air-proof and, indeed, mouse-proof deed box—"

"I see."

"With all due respect for the departed"—John placed both his feet tenderly on the desk—"it's typical of a lot that the old boy did. All his ideas were sound enough in themselves, you know, the indexes and the cross-checking and what not—it was just the *lengths* to which he carried everything—Hello, yes—"

"Mr. Craine wants you."

"Curse him. All right, Anne—"

"Miss Mildmay to you."

"I say, you haven't got a hangover too, have you?"

"Certainly not, Mr. Cove."

"Well, stop trying to put me in my place, Anne, and convey my respects to Tubby and tell him I'll be along in a minute."

"You convey your own respects," said Miss Mildmay. "And take the Batchelor file with you. I gather Mr. Craine wants to discuss the arithmetic in your completion statement."

"Does he though," said John uneasily.

He took his legs off the desk and departed.

"Have you got all you want, Mr. Bohun?"

"Thank you," said Henry. "John Cove has been initiating me gently into some of the mysteries of the Horniman office system."

"No doubt you were scared. I know I was at first. However, cheer up. It works quite well when you get used to it."

"I expect it does. Can you tell me who's going to do my work?"

"That'll be Mrs. Porter. By the way, she's new, too. She arrived at the end of last week. She doubles for you and Mr. Prince—he's our Common Law clerk. You'll find her in Miss Bellbas's room. Just inside the door on the right as you come in."

"Thank you," said Henry. "I'll go and have a word with her—as soon as I've got some ideas about what I want her to do."

However, when he did get there, the room just inside the door was empty. Judging from the sounds coming out of it the entire staff of Horniman, Birley and Craine was collected in the partners' secretaries' room, on the other side of the entrance hall. He guessed that this was the hour of morning coffee. After some hesitation he hardened his heart, opened the door and went in.

He might have spared himself any embarrassment. Nobody took the slightest notice of him.

"But, Florrie," Miss Chittering was saying, "when you'd made all your arrangements. It's *too* bad."

"You haven't changed your mind again, have you?" said Miss Cornel.

"You can't go altering your holiday"—Miss Mildmay sounded angry. "You'll put everyone else's out."

"You've bought your ticket and everything."

"Pull yourself together, Florrie."

"It's no good," said Miss Bellbas. "The stars are against it."

"Then defy the stars."

"It's no good, Miss Cornel."

"Or take a different newspaper."

"It isn't the paper, Anne, it's the stars."

"Nonsense," said Miss Mildmay. "How can you suppose that the stars can take any interest in your holiday. They *must* have more important things to think about."

This reasoning fell on deaf ears. Miss Bellbas was fumbling in her capacious handbag and eventually produced a folded newspaper. The others crowded round her.

"Last month it was all right," she said. "Look, there you are. 'Virgo, August 24th to September 23rd'—that's me—'You will find fortune and a good companion on the great waters. Proceed boldly and overcome your natural qualms'—that's right, too. Why, sometimes I'm sick before I even get on the boat. 'Lucky colour red.' Well, that was plain as plain. I went straight out and got a ticket for this cruise—"

"Why a Baltic cruise?"

"Well—lucky colour red—"

"Some might think it so, I suppose," said Miss Cornel. "What happened next?"

"What happened?" said Miss Bellbas, almost in tears. "Why, look at it now!" She pointed to another paper, and Miss Cornel read out "'Virgo, etc., etc. Avoid the sea at all costs. Your happiness lies in the hills. Turn your eyes to them. Things will open up surprisingly about the middle of the week. From a sum of money expended now you will reap a modest benefit in fourteen days' time. Lucky colour grey'."

"It's so *definite*," said Miss Bellbas. "I couldn't go on, not in the face of that. Luckily the company took back the cruise tickets. I shall just have to wait till the stars come round again."

"But, Florrie—"

"Now wait." Miss Cornel spoke in an authoritative voice. She picked up both newspapers and a deep silence fell on the secretaries' room, broken only by the plaintive ringing of the inter-office telephone, of which no one took the least notice. After close study of both papers she announced: "I have it. No—wait. Yes, of course."

"What, Miss Cornel?"

"Last month's paper doesn't actually mention the sea, does it? As I thought. It says 'the great waters'. Why, it's as clear as clear can be. You must take your holiday in the Lake District. Great Waters and High Hills. Red for the—let me see—for the ironstone crags and grey for the lakes."

"Yes, yes," said Miss Bellbas.

"And the last bit's quite clear, too. You must take a cheap fortnightly return ticket. That'll save you a modest sum in fourteen days' time."

This last stroke convinced everybody. Even Mrs. Porter, a quiet, middle-aged woman who had so far held herself aloof from the discussion, joined in to contribute an account of how her brother had avoided a train accident by intelligent reading of the tea leaves.

"I wonder if you'd mind coming in and taking a few letters," said Bohun timidly, and as it proved inaudibly, since no one looked in his direction.

"You must make it a walking tour," said Miss Chittering. "You can have that big walking-stick. You know—the one the Duke of Laxater left in the waiting-room—and Miss Cornel will lend you her big green rucksack."

"Well," said Miss Cornel, "since you're so kindly lending her every-body else's belongings, why not start with your own dressing-case?"

"Oh, no, really. I couldn't do that," said Miss Chittering, anxiously. "You wouldn't want a dressing-case, would you, Florrie? Not on a walking tour. Why, it's made of real crocodile skin. A rucksack would be much more suitable."

"I—" said Miss Bellbas.

"If your dressing-case is crocodile, my fur coat's polar bear," said Miss Cornel flatly.

"Mrs. Porter," said Bohun.

"I was assured when I bought it," said Miss Chittering, "that it was absolutely genuine Congo crocodile—"

"MRS. PORTER!"

"Oh, Mr. Bohun, I didn't see you come in."

"Would you mind coming in and taking some letters?"

At this moment John Cove appeared looking slightly flushed. Evidently he had got the worst of his arithmetical discussion with Mr. Craine.

"Heave ho, Miss Bellbas," he said. "We've got to do it all again." Miss Bellbas, however, seemed to have something on her mind.

"I should never have thought it," she said to Miss Cornel.

"Thought what?"

"That your fur coat was polar bear."

"That's just it," said Miss Cornel patiently. "It isn't."

"But I thought you said—"

"Florrie, my love," said John Cove. "You really are the most literal creature on earth. Does irony mean nothing to you? Has sarcasm no place in your life? Do the shafts of satire pass you by? Have you never even heard of the homely figure of speech?"

"Yes," said Miss Bellbas doubtfully.

"If I said to you, 'I'm dying of hunger' would you hurry out to summon the coroner and the undertaker? Would you search yourself anxiously for traces of strawberry jam if someone accused you of being a—"

"Really, Mr. Cove!"

II

"It would appear, Miss Chittering," said Mr. Birley smoothly, "that you must imagine me to be a highly moral man."

Miss Chittering looked blank but surmised it was something to do with the letter she had just typed and which Mr. Birley was now perusing.

"I take it as a compliment, of course."

"Yes, Mr. Birley."

"But I'm afraid it won't do." He scored the letter heavily through. "When I said, 'This is a matter which will have to be conducted entirely by principals,' I intended it to be understood that the work would be done by a partner in the firm concerned, not that it would be carried out according to ethical standards."

"I never really know the difference between principal and principle," said Miss Chittering apologetically. "It's often been explained to me, but I just never seem to pick on the right one."

"Oh, and another thing," said Mr. Birley. "You do *not* address a man as Thomas Smallhorn, O.B.E., Esquire."

"I'm sorry, Mr. Birley."

"It's not that I object myself, of course, Miss Chittering, but the recipient might imagine that I was unaware of the commoner usages of polite society, and the reputation of the firm would suffer accordingly."

Mr. Birley tore both pages of the letter slowly across and dropped them into the basket—which Miss Chittering felt to be rather mean, since the top page could quite easily have been salvaged, and attached to a new second page, which in any case only had three lines on it, besides the offending address.

"I sometimes wonder what we pay you such a princely salary for," went on Mr. Birley.

This might conceivably have been intended as a joke, and Miss Chittering rewarded it with a nervous titter.

"If you are uncertain about these things, ask Miss Cornel or someone who knows their job—"

This was definitely unkind, and Miss Chittering flushed, but was spared the responsibility of answering by the arrival of Mr. Craine with some papers.

She made her escape.

"I don't know if you've got a moment," said Mr. Craine.

"What is it?" said Mr. Birley, in a far from gracious tone.

Now the real trouble was—and it is pointless to pursue this narrative further without being quite honest about it—that the two partners disliked each other; and the reason for it was inherent in the characters of the men themselves, which were as immiscible as oil and water.

Mr. Craine had performed throughout the 1914 war with some credit in an infantry battalion. Mr. Birley had evaded most of the war with an allegedly weak heart. Mr. Craine was a cheerful little extrovert, and a heavily-married man. Mr. Birley was a confirmed bachelor, who had bullied his adoring mother into the grave and was now engaged in nagging his elderly sister in the same direction.

Even the type of work in which each specialised reflected their discrepant natures.

Mr. Craine was a devotee of a certain swashbuckling sort of litigation; with occasional forays in the direction of avoidance of death duties and evasion of income tax; twin subjects exceedingly dear to the hearts of the firm's exalted clients. One sub-section of the 1936 Finance Act, it may be mentioned in passing, was thought to have been drafted expressly to frustrate Mr. Craine's well-meant efforts.

Mr. Birley, on the other hand, was a conveyancer. A pedlar of words and a reduplicator of phrases. A master of the Whereas and Hereinbefore. He was reputed to tie a tighter settlement than any conveyancing counsel in Lincoln's Inn.

Both men were very competent lawyers.

"I've had a letter from Rew," said Mr. Craine. He referred to Mr. Rew, General Secretary of the Consequential Insurance Company, one of their biggest clients.

"What has he got to say for himself?"

"You know what Rew is. He never says very much. But what he seems to want to know is, can Bob Horniman look after their business as his father used to."

"I thought we'd argued all this out before."

"So we did," said Mr. Craine. "So we did. And in principle we all agreed that we'd keep the division of work exactly as it was—Bob taking on all his father's clients with Bohun to help him. But I must admit, I'd forgotten about the Consequential—"

"What about them?"

Mr. Craine nearly said: "You know as well as I do what about them." Instead he kept his temper and merely remarked: "Well, we aren't bound to them in any way, you know. Neither side is under any obligation to the other. They used to give us their business—a lot of business—because Abel did their work as well or better than anyone else could do it. I'd hate to lose them."

"Do you mean that Bob doesn't know his job?"

"No, I don't. I mean that he's young—and, well, Abel taught him a lot about filing systems and the Horniman method of office management, but I sometimes thought he kept him a bit in the dark about the clients themselves."

"Yes," said Mr. Birley. "Well, what do you suggest?"

"I don't suppose you could—"

"Certainly not. I've got more than enough work as it is. I think you're worrying unnecessarily. He'll pick it up as he goes along. By the way, how's Bohun shaping?"

"He could hardly be said to have shaped yet," said Mr. Craine, "since it's his first morning in the office. He's got a remarkable record."

"First-class honours in his Final, you mean."

"Not only that. It's the speed he did it all. He only took up law just over two years ago, you know. He got a special exemption to sit the exam early. He was a statistician before that, and a very brilliant one, I believe. And he holds actuarial qualifications."

"Well, then, he ought to be able to deal with insurance work."

"I expect he will, eventually," said Mr. Craine. "I'll try and make time to keep an eye on him and Bob—"

"Hrrmph!" said Mr. Birley. Having got his own way he became a shade more amiable and the conversation turned to other topics.

Meanwhile both subjects of this conversation were experiencing their own difficulties.

Henry Bohun, having dismissed Mrs. Porter, was once more staring thoughtfully at the little stack of cards on the desk in front of him, trying to relate them in some comprehensible manner to his allotted share of that morning's post. The more he read them the less they seemed to mean, but finding that there were fifty-two of them he dealt out four bridge hands and came to the conclusion that he could make three no trumps without difficulty on his holding, which included such obvious winners as "The Duchess of Ashby de la Zouche—(questions relating to her claim for Dower)", "Lieutenant-General Fireside's Marriage Settlement No. 3)" (his third marriage or his third settlement, Henry wondered), and most promising, "The Reverend the Metropolitan of Albania—Private Affairs." He reshuffled the cards and started a card house, which was destroyed at its fourth storey by the interruption of Miss Cornel in search of the Law List.

"Never mind," he said, "it couldn't have gone much higher. We shouldn't have got planning permission for more than six floors. Now that you are here perhaps you can help me to sort things out a bit. Only start from the beginning and go slowly."

Miss Cornel suspended her search in the Law List and said: "Well, it would take all morning to explain the office system in detail—"

"Horniman on Office Management I have already had from John Cove," said Bohun. "What I really want to know are the more practical points. Who works for who? Who am I under? Who signs my letters for instance—"

This simple question seemed to give Miss Cornel considerable food for thought. "I'm not sure," she said. "In the old days it was quite straightforward. Mr. Duxford—I don't think you've met him—works under Mr. Birley. John Cove with Mr. Craine. And young Mr. Horniman, of course, worked under his father. If they're going on with that, I suppose you will be working under Bob Horniman."

"You sound doubtful."

"You must forgive an old retainer's licence," said Miss Cornel. "I've known Bob since he was a prep-school boy in shorts when he used to come up here on the day he travelled back to school, and swing his legs in the waiting-room until his father was free to take him out to lunch—"

"Those awful last-day-of-holiday lunches," said Bohun. "Indigestion tempered by the hopes of an extra ten shillings pocket-money."

"Yes—well, he came in here as soon as he left his public school which, in my humble opinion, was a mistake. Then he'd only just qualified when the war broke out, and he went straight into the Navy. So what with one thing and another he doesn't know all he might about the practical side of a solicitor's work. He did very well in his exams, I believe—but that's not quite the same thing—"

"You're telling me."

"If it hadn't been for his father, I think he'd have stayed on in the Navy. He was doing very well—"

Miss Cornel broke off rather abruptly—possibly with the feeling that she had said more than she intended. ("He's got such a damned insinuating way of saying nothing," she confided afterwards to Anne Mildmay, "that you find yourself telling him the most surprising things.")

"I see," said Bohun. "But look here, if Bob's taking over his father's work, and I'm taking over Bob's work—what are all these cards? Are these the things Bob used to do himself, because if so—"

Miss Cornel picked up some of the cards and ran an expert eye over them. "Well," she said. "You've got some soft options to start with. There's nothing much here to worry about. 'Lady Buntingford—Affairs.' That practically only means we pay her laundry bills once a month. 'The Marquis of Bedlam, deceased.' That's a probate matter, but the accounts have all been settled. If you really want some stuff to get your teeth into, I'll slip you some of Bob's. He's got some matters there that—why, they even tied his old man up—"

Something in the tone of this last remark led Bohun to say: "You liked working for Abel Horniman, didn't you?"

"Well, yes, I did," said Miss Cornel. "He was a great man, he really was. And a good man to work for, too. I ought to know—I was his secretary for nineteen years."

"He certainly seems to have been a man of method."

"Now you're laughing at him," said Miss Cornel. "Perhaps he did overdo order and method a bit. Usually it made things easier. Of course, it didn't always work that way." She gave a particularly masculine chuckle. "I expect you've grasped that we've got rather a peculiar type of client here—upper five hundred and so forth. When Abel or his partners were dictating the letters themselves it was all right. They put in all the correct little twiddly bits and personal touches. Some of the assistants we had didn't quite get it—I mean, their law was sound enough, but you need something more than law when you're writing a personal letter to a duke. Of course, Abel tackled the problem in his own unique way. He sat down and made out a list of suitable sentences for ending *every* letter with—you know the sort of thing: 'I hope the pheasants are coming over strongly this year,' and 'Did you have any luck with your runner in the National?' and so on. Of course, the first thing John Cove did when he arrived in this office was to include the whole boiling lot in all the letters he wrote—and it just happened that Mr. Craine was away that day, so John signed his own letters and sent them off. When Abel saw the carbons next morning he nearly had a fit... Well, I mustn't stop to gossip. Ask me if you want anything."

"Right," said Henry. "Yes, I will." After she had gone he sat for some time, then resummoned Mrs. Porter from the typists' room and dictated a vigorous letter to Lady Buntingford's laundry.

III

Bob Horniman was reading slowly through a letter and frowning as he did so. When he had finished it, he pushed back his rather long black hair and read it through again. Then he placed it in the In-basket, regarded it with distaste, transferred it to the Out-basket, where it looked no better, and rang the bell for his secretary.

"This Anthrax-Plumper insurance, Miss Cornel," he said.

"I'll get you the file," said Miss Cornel, lifting down a fat-looking folder.

"I don't think I'll tackle the file yet," said Bob hastily. "It looks a very complicated business. I wondered—I mean, you used to look after these things for my father—"

"I just wrote down what I was told," said Miss Cornel dryly.

"Oh, quite. Yes, of course. I just thought that perhaps father might have said something—given some opinion—"

"The only thing I can remember him saying about Mrs. Anthrax-Plumper was that she was a woman who would mortgage her own virginity, if she could persuade anyone she still possessed it—"

"She certainly mortgaged everything else," said Bob, running a finger distastefully through the bloated file. "It's this reversionary business I can't quite get hold of. Perhaps I ought to go to Counsel—"

"You could do that, of course," said Miss Cornel. "But the Consequential are very sticky about paying Counsel's fees unless they have to."

"Oh, well," Bob sighed again. "I'll see what I can ferret out."

Miss Cornel turned to go, but relented at the last moment and said: "I seem to remember the same problem on double reversion cropping up—oh, about ten years ago. The client was Lady Bradbury. And that time, we *did* go to Counsel. There's a copy of his opinion in the 1937 file."

"I don't know what I should do without you," said Bob. He took a key-flap from his pocket. "What's the number of Lady Bradbury's box?"

"Seventeen."

Bob thumbed through the ring. "Why the deuce they all had to have different keys!" he said. "Here it is." He snapped the box open and picked out the file whilst Miss Cornel withdrew to the secretaries' room to try and make up on her morning's work. Five minutes later the bell went again. She suppressed an unladylike exclamation and picked up her shorthand book.

Bob had apparently abandoned Mrs. Anthrax-Plumper and was reading another letter.

"What do you think of this?" he asked.

Dismissing the temptation to say that she wasn't paid to think, Miss Cornel dutifully perused the letter which was from Messrs. Rumbold & Carter, solicitors, of Coleman Street, and was headed "Stokes Will Trust".

"According to your request," it said, after the usual preliminary flourishes, "we endeavoured to contact Mr. Smallbone to secure his signature to the proposed transfer of Stock. We wrote to him enclosing the transfer form (in duplicate) on the 23rd February and sent him a further communication on the 16th ultimo and the 8th inst., in all three cases without receiving any answer. If Mr. Smallbone is absent abroad or indisposed possibly you could so inform us—"

"Isn't that the funny little man whom father used to dislike so much?" said Bob.

"I don't think your father and Mr. Smallbone got on very well," agreed Miss Cornel. "Unfortunately they were co-trustees—"

"The Ichabod Stokes Trust?"

"Yes; otherwise I think he'd have refused to have anything to do with him. Seeing that he was a fellow trustee, though, I expect he felt he could hardly refuse to look after his private affairs too—"

"Did he have any private affairs? I mean—"

"He isn't a person of very great substance," said Miss Cornel, interpreting this remark accurately. "He was involved in some litigation just before the war, and we look after his annuity for him, and I think we made his will."

"I remember the fellow," said Bob. "A scrawny little brute with an eye like a rat. I could never understand how Dad put up with him."

"I think," said Miss Cornel, "that he found him very tiresome. If it hadn't been that the Stokes Trust was such a big thing—and of course it was tied up with the Didcots and Lord Hempstead—I think he might have refused the trusteeship, rather than be forced to work with Mr. Smallbone."

"As bad as that, is he," said Bob. "It must be a deuce of a trust. What does it figure out at?"

"We've sold the real property now," said Miss Cornel. "It's all securities. At the last account they were worth just under half a million pounds."

"I expect you can put up with quite a lot for half a million pounds. The point is, however, what's happened to the little blighter?"

"He really is a hopeless person," said Miss Cornel. "He never answers letters. Whenever we didn't particularly want to see him he'd be round here every day, and when we *did* want him, when we were selling the real estate, to sign the big conveyances and so on, as likely as not he'd disappear altogether and go on a walking tour in Italy."

"Italy?"

"Yes. He's a great collector of pottery, though your father used to say he's got as much knowledge of it as a market gardener. I believe that the two little rooms in the house in Belsize Park where he lives are full of urns and statuettes and heaven knows what."

"Well," said Bob. "I can only see one thing for it. If the mountain won't come to Mahomet—you know. You'd better slip over to Belsize Park and stir him up."

"What, now, Mr. Horniman?"

"Why not—go after lunch."

"I've got an awful lot to do—"

"Take a taxi," said Bob. "The firm will pay."

"Yes, Mr. Horniman."

IV

Accordingly, that afternoon, Miss Cornel made her way out to Belsize Park. She went by Underground. She was not by nature dishonest over small matters, but she reckoned that if she was prepared to put up with the discomfort and pocket the difference, that was her affair.

Wellingboro' Road was some distance from the Underground station, and her search for it was made no easier by the fact that the first two persons of whom she enquired appeared to speak only Czechoslovakian, the third, a large and helpful lady, chiefly Polish, and the fourth, a starved-looking Indian, seemed willing to commit himself only to the language of signs.

Eventually, more by good luck than judgment, she discovered herself outside No. 20 Wellingboro' Road.

A grey-haired lady opened the door, said, "No, Mr. Smallbone was not at home," and prepared to shut it again.

Twenty years of miscellaneous experience in a solicitor's office had hardened Miss Cornel to this sort of thing. She placed herself in such a position that the door could not be shut without actual violence, and said: "It's rather important. I come from his solicitors, you know, Messrs. Horniman, Birley and Craine, of Lincoln's Inn."

She produced from her handbag an impressive piece of the firm's best headed notepaper, addressed to the "Occupier, Head-Lessor or Sub-Lessor as the case might be of 20 Wellingboro' Road" and authorising him (or her) to permit the bearer to make all proper enquiries as to the whereabouts of one of the firm's clients, viz. M. Smallbone of the same address, etc. etc. Miss Cornel had actually typed it out and signed it herself with a thick nib in a flowing hand, and altogether it looked rather good.

It was good enough for Mrs. Tasker, anyway. And Miss Cornel was allowed to enter. It was not, she reflected, the type of tenement or dwelling-house usually associated with the clients of the firm. The front hall exuded that unforgettable miasma which clings to a certain type of north London residence which has been built too long and interiorly decorated too seldom: a smell altogether different from, and more repellent than the racy odours of the slums. The whiff of decayed gentility was almost physical. It was as if some very faded spinster had been allowed to fade away altogether and her body had been laid to rest beneath the floorboards.

"The first floor he has," said Mrs. Tasker. "Two rooms and the use of the gas-ring in the back room, which he shares with the second floor. This way, and mind the edge of the linoleum, some day 'twill be the death of us all."

Miss Cornel found herself on a narrow landing. Mrs. Tasker led the way to the front room. Looking over her shoulder Miss Cornel could see a visiting card pinned to the door—"Marcus Smallbone, B.A."—and, in smaller writing in the bottom left-hand corner, "and at Villa Carpeggio, Florence."

"Goodness," said Miss Cornel, "he's got an Italian residence as well."

"I expect he has," said Mrs. Tasker. "A remarkable man, Mr. Smallbone. The things he's got in that room of his, you'd be surprised. Valuable. But there, I have to get in to dust over them." With this remark, which seemed to be in part an excuse and in part an explanation, Mrs. Tasker drew a key from the mysteries of her upper garment and unlocked the door.

The contents of the room were certainly unexpected. Round three of the walls stood glass-fronted cases containing coins, medals, a few cameos and intaglios, and a number of objects which looked like large fishbones. On top of the cases, and on shelves which stood out from them were rows of statuettes, figurines and uninspiring clay pots of the dimmer shades of umber and burnt sienna.

"Where on earth does the man sit down?" asked Miss Cornel.

"He has his meals in his bedroom." Mrs. Tasker sounded quite unsurprised. She was indeed hardened to the vagaries of her lodgers. One of them kept parrots and another belonged to the Brotherhood of Welsh Buddhists.

"When'll he be back?"

"I couldn't say," said Mrs. Tasker.

"Well, when did he go away?" asked Miss Cornel patiently.

"About two months ago."

"What? I mean, didn't he—doesn't he tell you when he's going away? What about his rent?"

"Oh, if it's his rent you're worrying about," said Mrs. Tasker complacently, "you needn't. Six months in advance he pays. Has his own meters, too. I don't care where he goes or when he goes. It's all the same to me. Why, last year he was away for three months—"

Miss Cornel nodded. She remembered it well. Mr. Horniman had been moving heaven and earth to get his signature to a Trust document.

Another thought struck her.

"What about his letters?"

Mrs. Tasker pointed to a little heap on the sideboard.

"There's a few come for him," she said. "Mostly bills."

Miss Cornel looked through them quickly. Three of the cleaner envelopes were, she guessed, Messrs. Rumbold & Carter's communications of the 23rd February, the 16th ultimo and the 8th instant. The rest were, in fact, circulars and bills.

"Well," she said rather hopelessly. "You might ask him to telephone us as soon as he turns up. It's rather important."

"I'll tell him," said Mrs. Tasker.

CHAPTER THREE

—WEDNESDAY MORNING—

A Capital Asset Comes to Light

The body (or corpus) of the trust estate will normally be invested in approved and easily realisable securities.

I

APART FROM THE ROMAN CHURCH, WHO ARE ACKNOWLEDGED experts in human behaviour, there is nobody quicker than a solicitor at detecting the first faint stirrings of a scandal: that distinctive, that elusive odour of Something which is not Quite as it Should Be.

Mr. Birley was only voicing the uneasiness of all his colleagues when he said to Mr. Craine next morning:

"The fellow can't have disappeared. He'll have to be found."

"It's awkward," said Mr. Craine. "By the way, who are the other trustees?"

"As a matter of fact," said Bob apologetically, "there isn't another. Father was one trustee, you know, Mr. Smallbone was the other."

"Wasn't another trustee appointed when Abel died?"

"Well, no. That is, not yet."

"Who has the power to appoint?"

"I think the surviving trustee—"

"So it amounts to this—that unless we can induce Smallbone to come back to England we shall probably have the expense of going to the court—"

"I don't *know* that Mr. Smallbone's gone abroad," said Bob. "His landlady only said that he'd gone away. She said he went to Italy last year—"

"It's perfectly absurd. He must have left an address. People don't walk out into the blue. Not if they're trustees."

"Well, that's what he seems to have done," said Bob. He always found Mr. Birley alarming; and the fact that they were now, in theory, equal members of the partnership had not gone very far towards alleviating that feeling. "Perhaps if we wait for a few weeks—"

"With half a million pounds' worth of securities," said Mr. Birley. "This isn't a post office savings account. There must be questions of reinvestment cropping up every day. I wonder you've managed to get by for as long as you have—"

Bob flushed at the obvious implication of this remark. Mr. Craine came to his rescue.

"Wouldn't it be a good thing," he said, "to take this opportunity of going through the securities. We'll have to appoint a new trustee and that will mean an assignment. We'll get a broker's opinion on any necessary reinvestments at the same time."

"I'll do that," said Bob gratefully.

"Where *are* the securities?" asked Mr. Birley.

"They're in the muniments room. I'll get Sergeant Cockerill to bring them up."

"You might get the trust accounts out of the box, too, and run through them," suggested Mr. Craine.

"All right," said Bob. "But—I'm sure there's nothing wrong."

"Why should there be anything wrong?" said Mr. Birley, looking up sharply.

"About Mr. Smallbone, I mean. He often used to disappear like this. Miss Cornel was telling me about him. He's a bit of a crank."

"Fact is, the fellow ought never to have been appointed a trustee," said Mr. Birley. "But Stokes was mad for years before he died. None of his relations had the guts to say so. Served them all right when he left his money on charitable trusts—"

"Only he might have chosen his trustees a bit better," agreed Mr. Craine. "Now then, about this death duty scheme of Lord Haltwhistle…"

Bob stole gratefully away.

About half an hour later when Lord Haltwhistle's death duties had been partially mitigated, Mr. Birley broke off what he was saying to come round suddenly on a fresh tack.

"You remember," he said, "we were talking yesterday about this new fellow Bohun—"

"Yes."

"I thought you'd be interested in something I heard at the club yesterday—from Colonel Bristow. He got slung out of the army."

"Good heavens!" said Mr. Craine. "I thought they retired the old boy on half-pay."

"Not Colonel Bristow. Bohun."

"Oh." Mr. Craine sounded only mildly interested. "What for?"

"Bristow didn't know. Bohun was attached to his staff in the Middle East and the War Office removed him. Medical reasons, they said."

"Perhaps that was what it was," suggested Mr. Craine.

"Chap looks fit enough to me." Mr. Birley stopped and lifted his head. "What the devil are they making all that noise about out there?" he said. "Is that someone screaming?"

II

At about eleven o'clock that morning Henry Bohun sat back in his swivel-chair, said "Ouch!" and sat forward again quickly.

"Don't say I didn't warn you," said John Cove, looking up from the study of a crossword puzzle. "When I shared this room with Eric Duxford it was *my* lot, as the junior, to sit in that chair."

"What's wrong with it?" said Henry, massaging his back.

"It is possessed," said John, "by an active and malignant spirit, a sort of legal gremlin which leans out and pinches you when you are least expecting it."

Henry upended the chair on his desk. "It's the join in the back piece," he announced. "The support's worked loose. If I had a screwdriver I could fix it—"

"Sergeant Cockerill will have a screwdriver. He keeps things like that. Can you think of a town in Bessarabia in ten letters?"

"Not at the moment."

When Henry came back he brought Sergeant Cockerill with him. The sergeant assessed the damage with an expert eye, grasped the back of the chair firmly in his right hand, picked up a screwdriver and gave some exploratory twists.

"Screw's worked right loose. I'll have to plug it first."

"Azerbaijan," said John.

"Take the chair away with you if you like," said Henry. "I can use this spare one."

"Where's Mrs. Porter going to sit," said John, "on your knee?"

"I'll fix you up, sir. There's a spare in the tea-room." The sergeant picked up the swivel chair in one surprisingly muscular hand and departed.

"I'm afraid it can't be Azerbaijan," said John, "or we shall have to find a word beginning JV—"

"Anyway, I don't believe Azerbaijan is in Bessarabia."

"*Delendum est.* By the way, what's wrong with the Chittering this morning?"

"I don't know," said Henry. "Now that you mention it, she did look a bit cool when I said good morning to her."

"Cool! That's an understatement. She's behaving like the young lady in Handel's aria. You know: where'er she walks cool gales shall fan the glade—"

"I believe she's annoyed about something La Cornel said. She cast aspersions on the parentage of her dressing-case. Said that it wasn't crocodile, or alternatively, if crocodile not Congo crocodile."

"Girls, girls."

"Upon which Miss Chittering cast counter-aspersions upon Miss Cornel's fur coat—"

"What an awful thing it must be," said John complacently, "to have a quarrelsome nature. I have always managed to look on the lighter side of these unfortunate differences which, we must face it, do crop up from time to time. I remember when I was expelled from Rugby at the age of seventeen… However, I won't distract you, for I see you want to work."

"I am getting things a bit more sorted out." Henry picked up a letter. "I still can't quite see what the Duke of Hampshire actually wants us to do."

"Doesn't he say? They do sometimes, if you read the letters right through. The gist of it's usually in the ducal postscript."

"It's plain enough. He wants us to realise the securities in his marriage settlement and reinvest them in the construction of a

Channel tunnel. We seem to have written a number of letters to him pointing out—"

"Oh, he's quite mad," said John. "I believe his grandfather got a red-hot tip from Disraeli and cleared a packet on the Suez Canal. Gave the family rather a *fixe* about short cuts and transportation stock."

"Yes," said Henry, "but what do I say to him?"

"Say you're consulting the brokers and what are the prospects for the salmon fishing this summer."

"All right," said Henry doubtfully.

At least ten minutes were devoted to work before the door opened again. Henry saw that it was the man whom he had noticed sitting next to Anne Mildmay at the staff dinner.

"What do you want?" said John. "If you've come to borrow the Law List it's not here. If you want your copy of Tristram and Coote, I've lent it to Bob."

"Thought I'd drop in and say hello," said the newcomer, ignoring this. "If John won't introduce me, old fellow, I'd better do it myself. I'm Eric Duxford." He clicked on a smile.

"Rise," said John to Bohun, "fall forward on both knees, and knock your forehead seven times on the floor."

"Very good of you to bother," said Henry. "I gather that you used to share this room with John."

"Yes," said Duxford. "Yes, I did." It did not need much discernment to see that Eric Duxford disliked John Cove perhaps even a shade more than John disliked him.

"We were a famous pair," said John. "'Blest pair of sirens, pledges of Heaven's joy. Sphere-born harmonious brothers.' Debenham and Freebody, Fortnum and Mason, Duxford and Cove... Inseparable—"

"Yes. Well, you must come and have lunch with me, Bohun; we'll run up to my club."

"It's not an easy club to run up to," said John, "since it occupies a basement in Fleet Street. The United Philatelists and Numismatists. It shares the premises with the P.P.P. or Pornographic Photographic Publications, and the S.S.S. or—"

"You mustn't pay too much attention to Cove," said Duxford coldly. "He suffers from a suppressed inferiority complex. That's why he talks so much. Actually I belong to the Public Schools—"

"I'd love to have lunch with you some day," said Henry hastily, forestalling a perfectly outrageous remark by John.

"Very good of you to bother."

"Not at all," said Duxford. "We must all muck in and help one another, eh? That's what makes the world go round."

"Well," said John, when the door had closed on their visitor. "Now you've plumbed the depths. If you want to get out, the emergency hatch is under the pilot's seat—"

"Oh, come on," said Henry, "he isn't as bad as that. A bit hearty."

"You haven't had to live with him yet," said John. "If you had you wouldn't be so tolerant. To start with, as you have appreciated, he is a line-shooter. There are line-shooters and line-shooters. Eric is *the* line-shooter. He is the man about whom the phrase was invented. He literally never stops shooting lines. Of course," John grinned, "it's a profession which is not devoid of danger. Sometimes it plunges him into deep waters. There was the time when he took the Town and Country Planning Act under his wing—you remember that it was rather the fashion in early '48. He read a couple of very simple articles about it, and of course took the next opportunity of cornering an inoffensive stranger at lunch and giving him a dissertation on some of the finer points of the Act. Sheer bad luck that he should have happened to have picked on Megarry."

"Oh, no!"

"Even funnier, in a quiet way, was the time when he took up golf—a chap must take exercise, you know, keeps a fellow fit, you know. One meets a lot of interesting chaps at the club too, doesn't one? I think his handicap at this time was about thirty-six with the wind behind him... Well, who should he pick on to give a little lecture to on the mysteries of the game but La Cornel. Thanks to Providence I was in here when he started. I wouldn't have missed it for the world. She took it without batting an eyelid. 'Yes, Mr. Duxford. No, Mr. Duxford. How *interesting*, Mr. Duxford. Now what was it you said you called that club with the curly end, Mr. Duxford?' It was terrific... When she'd gone out I told him the joke."

Seeing Henry looking a bit blank he added: "Didn't you know? She's terrifically hot. She reached the last four in the Women's Open. She'd have gone to America with the British Women's Team before the war if Abel hadn't been stingy about letting her have the time off—"

"That's it," said Henry. "I thought her face was familiar. I must have seen it in one of the illustrated papers... What on earth was that?"

"It sounded," said John, "like a scream, didn't it?"

III

It is undeniable that the morning had not started well in the partners' secretaries room.

Though it would have been difficult to have selected three more diverse types than Miss Cornel, Miss Mildmay and Miss Chittering, they usually managed to get along in an easy enough way on a basis of working-day tolerance helped out by the fact that they were all really kept rather busy. It must be remembered that in addition to the normal duties of taking down letters, typing them, engrossing, fair copying, taking telephone calls, heading off awkward clients and trying to arrange definite appointments with the less clear-headed members of the aristocracy, they had also (that nothing might be wanting) to cope with the Horniman cross-filing system.

However, that particular morning was an unhappy one. Anne Mildmay had arrived late. She was flying storm signals and had a look in her eye which would have been recognised at once by anyone who had served in a ship under her father, the celebrated "Conk" Mildmay (the only man who ever told Beatty what he thought of him and got away with both ears).

"Good morning," said Miss Chittering brightly. "You'll be qualifying for the D.C.M. if you arrive at this hour."

"The what?"

"The Don't Come Monday."

"Oh."

Miss Mildmay ripped off the cover of her typewriter, sorted out a sheet of demi, a carbon and a flimsy, stuffed them together and banged them into her machine.

"Well, anyway," she said. "Old Birley doesn't chase *me* round telling me I don't know my job, and suggesting I find out how to do it from Miss Cornel." In an incautious moment Miss Chittering had repeated Mr. Birley's strictures of the day before.

"Well, I'm sure," she said. "There's no need to be unpleasant. I was only having a joke."

"So was I," said Miss Mildmay.

There was silence for some time after this, broken only by the flagellation of three typewriters.

Miss Chittering, however, was not a person who was able to keep silent for very long. It was perhaps unfortunate that she had to address all her remarks to Anne, since she was still not on speaking terms with Miss Cornel owing to certain heresies on the subject of genuine crocodile dressing-cases.

"Poor Mr. Horniman," she said. "I think he's getting thinner every day. Worry, that's what it is."

"What's he got to worry about?" said Anne.

"Well, I expect it's all the new work—and the responsibility."

"He gets paid for it."

"And the hours he works. He's always here last thing at night."

"It won't kill him." Anne sounded so unnecessarily bitter that Miss Cornel looked up curiously.

"He says the strangest things, too."

"Like 'O.B.E., Esquire'," suggested Miss Cornel unkindly from her corner. Fortunately, before any further hostilities could be provoked, the signal bell gave a buzz. Miss Cornel collected her shorthand notebook and went out.

"Some people," announced Miss Chittering to no one in particular, "think that because they've been here a long time they can say anything they like."

"Oh, I don't know," said Anne. "How many r's in referred?"

The typewriters resumed their clatter.

Meanwhile in Bob Horniman's room he and Miss Cornel were looking rather hopelessly at a large black deed box labelled Ichabod Stokes.

"He can't have *lost* the key," said Miss Cornel. "He kept them all together on one ring. Let me have another look. Consequential, Marquis of Curragh, Lady Burberry, General Pugh—he always kept twelve boxes on this rack and six more under the bookshelf. That's eighteen." She counted the keys again. "You're quite right," she said. "There are only seventeen keys here. Stokes is missing—"

"First the trustee, then the key," groaned Bob. "I knew it. I knew it. The next thing we shall find is that half the securities are gone."

Miss Cornel looked at him sharply. "The securities aren't kept in here," she said. "They're with Sergeant Cockerill in the strong-room. There's nothing in this box but old files and papers and trust accounts."

"I know," said Bob, "but how am I to start checking up the securities unless I can get hold of the last set of trust accounts. Hasn't Cockerill got a key?"

Miss Cornel thought for a moment. "There *was* a master-key with each set," she said. "When your father had these new deed boxes put in, they came in sets. There was a master-key with each one, and it was a good thing there was—they were always losing single keys—not your father, he was very careful, but the others—"

"As a matter of fact, I don't think Mr. Craine ever keeps his boxes locked at all," said Bob. "Do you think his master-key would fit this lock?"

"I know it wouldn't," said Miss Cornel, "because about five years ago your father lost *his* master-key, and I remember we had to have another one made. It took months."

"Well, we don't want to go through all that if we can help it," said Bob. "Ask Sergeant Cockerill to come up here for a minute."

Sergeant Cockerill, summoned from the basement, denied any knowledge of master-keys.

"All the other keys I've got," he said. "Strong-room, lockers, doors. Inside doors and outside doors. But not boxes. The partners look after them." He spoke rather resentfully.

"I suppose we shall have to get through to the firm that made the boxes," said Bob. "But, heavens, that'll take weeks, and goodness knows where Mr. Smallbone will have got to by then."

"I might be able to get a copy of the trust accounts from the auditors," suggested Miss Cornel. "We could at least start to check the securities. After all," she added, with considerable logic but a curious lack of conviction, "what's all the fuss about, we don't *know* that there's anything wrong with this trust."

"Excusing me," said Sergeant Cockerill suddenly. "But do I understand that all you're wanting is to open this box?"

"That's right."

"And it's important?"

"Well," said Bob, rather helplessly. "We don't really know. Until we open the box we can't tell whether it's important to open it or not—if you see what I mean."

"Well, if that's all," said the sergeant, "I'll have her open in half of no time."

"Don't tell me," said Miss Cornel in a thrilled tone of voice, "that you're a retired burglar. One of those people who open locks with a little bent bit of wire."

"Never you believe it," said Sergeant Cockerill. "There's no lock with a spring inside it worth the name was ever opened with bent wire. That's a thing you see on the films—it's not real..." He went away and came back with an ordinary heavy ball and plane hammer.

"Put her up on the window-seat where I can get at her," he said.

"Let me give you a hand," said Bob. "It's mighty heavy—up she comes... Yes, what is it, Miss Bellbas?"

"Could you sign this receipt for Mr. Duxford, sir?"

"In a minute," said Bob. "Hold her steady."

Sergeant Cockerill took a careful sight down his hammer, swung it up, and brought it down fair and square on the circular brass lock.

IV

The senses sometimes record events in an illogical order. The first thing that Henry Bohun noticed as he came out of his room was that someone had been sick.

Then he saw Sergeant Cockerill, who said in his curiously gentle voice: "Look out you don't tread in it, sir—it's Miss Bellbas. I'm fetching something to clear it up."

Then his ears insisted that someone was screaming; had been screaming for some seconds.

He pushed past the sergeant and through the door of Bob Horniman's room. Here his nose took charge. Three years of active service had taught him the sweet, throat-catching smell of corrupted flesh.

He saw Bob, white to the lips, standing beside his desk, and Miss Cornel, the corners of her mouth drawn into a pucker.

"What's happened?" he said sharply.

"It's in that box." It was Bob who spoke. "We've just found him. For God's sake, someone, stop that girl screaming."

Henry went quickly out of the slaughter-house stench, and found Miss Bellbas sitting on a chair inside the secretaries' office.

Most of the other members of the staff seemed to be crowding round her.

"Give her room," he said with unconscious authority. "Stand back."

He placed himself in front of her and gave her a swinging smack on the face with his open palm.

Miss Bellbas stopped screaming.

Then she opened her mouth and observed conversationally: "It's the voice of the stars. You remember what they said. 'Things will open up surprisingly about the middle of the week.'"

CHAPTER FOUR

—WEDNESDAY EVENING—

A Contract Is Entered Into

A contract is sometimes described as being *uberrimae fidei*. This is not a term which has ever received exclusive definition but it signifies that the contract is one of those—a contract of insurance is the commonest example—in which both parties are under an obligation to make the fullest disclosure of a relevant circumstance.

I

"BLAST!" SAID THE ASSISTANT COMMISSIONER.

"Yes, sir," said Chief Inspector Hazlerigg.

"It's damned inconvenient."

"Yes, sir."

"I particularly don't want to take you off your regular work"—he meant Inspector Hazlerigg's permanent Black Market assignment—"but I don't see what I can do. With Aspinall and Hervey in Lancashire looking for that damned maniac and Cass in Paris; and now Pannel has to go and crock himself."

"I expect I can manage it, sir. Pickup can do my job here…" But there was more to be said, and both men knew it.

"Look here," said the Assistant Commissioner. "I think I'd better give you a quick outline, and then you'll see how—well, never mind that. I won't start by prejudicing you. Now. At eleven o'clock this morning a partner in this firm of solicitors—what's their name?—Horniman, Birley and Craine, opened one of their deed boxes. The box was supposed to contain papers relating to a trust. What they found in it was one of the trustees. Name of Smallbone—Marcus Smallbone—very dead."

He paused: then added inconsequentially: "The late senior partner in that firm was Abel Horniman. Friend of the Commissioner."

"Wasn't he the chairman of a committee on Criminal Law Revision?"

"That's the man. Quite a leading light in the Law Society, and between you and me pretty widely tipped for the next Honours List. His name was a big one in legal circles and he was beginning"—the Assistant Commissioner, though he didn't know it, was here paraphrasing Mr. Birley—"he was beginning to be a bit of a public figure, too."

"But if he's dead, sir," said Hazlerigg cautiously, "I can't quite see how—"

"He died about four weeks ago," said the Assistant Commissioner, "of angina. He'd been ill for some time. I think it would be fair to say that he knew he was booked. His doctor had told him as much."

"I see, sir."

"Our pathologist's first opinion," went on the Assistant Commissioner, with elaborate casualness, "is that Smallbone had been dead for at least six weeks—possibly eight—maybe ten."

"Yes," said Hazlerigg. "Yes, I see."

"Abel Horniman and Marcus Smallbone were fellow trustees—the only trustees—of a very big affair—the Ichabod Stokes Trust. That's an obvious line on the thing, of course. It's almost the only direct connection between the two men."

"And is this trust—I don't know the proper legal word—is it in order?"

"That's one of the things you'll have to find out. Colley—he's the D.D.I.—I'll give you his full report in a minute—asked them about it. Apparently it isn't just as easy as all that. One of the difficulties is that all the papers which might have helped should have been in that deed box—"

"And they were all gone?"

"Every one of them. Good Lord, as it was, there was hardly an inch of room to spare. If Smallbone hadn't been quite unusually small and slight his body would never have gone in at all."

"Ten weeks," said Hazlerigg. "I should have thought they'd have begun to notice him by that time."

"In the ordinary way, yes," agreed the Assistant Commissioner. "But these were special boxes, as you'll see. A rubber sealing-band round the edge and a compressor lid."

"Rather unusual, sir," said Hazlerigg. "Whose idea were they?"

"Abel Horniman's."

"Yes," said Hazlerigg again. He was already beginning to see the outlines of a simple but unsatisfactory affair with a lot of work and not much kudos. He also realised why the case had been handed to him. The implied compliment added only a little to its attractions.

Another thought struck him.

"What room was this in?"

"Young Horniman's—that's the son. He's taken his father's place in the firm."

"And his father's room, I suppose."

"Yes. I've got the first pictures here." He opened a folder. "The deed box was kept on a shelf under the window—there—you can see the space it came out of."

"I take it it was locked."

"Yes—that was one of the things. They couldn't find the key. The box was actually opened in the end by their commissionaire. He 'sprung' the lock with a hammer, and the lid flew open. Must have been quite a moment."

Hazlerigg was studying one or two of the reports. Something seemed to have puzzled him. He looked through the photographs again and selected one gruesome close-up which showed the body of Marcus Smallbone as it had lain packed in its metal coffin.

Then he looked again at the statement.

"I can't quite make out from this," he said, "who actually identified the body first?"

"I thought it was young Horniman."

"Not from what it says here. Horniman says that the first time Smallbone's name was actually mentioned was when Miss Bellbas— she's one of the typists, I gather—ran out of the room screaming 'It's Mr. Smallbone' and something about the stars foretelling it. Miss Bellbas denies it. She says she had never seen Mr. Smallbone when he was alive so how could she have recognised him when he was dead. Miss Cornel, one of the secretaries, says that she thought Bob Horniman mentioned the name first. Sergeant Cockerill says, No. He doesn't think anyone actually mentioned the name, but there had been so much speculation about Smallbone's disappearance that he, for his part, assumed at once that the body must be his."

"Sounds plausible," said the Assistant Commissioner. "Why are you making a special point of it…?"

"Well, sir"—Hazlerigg pointed to the photograph—"you see how the body was lying. The face was pushed right down on to the chest. Then again, after eight or ten weeks, I shouldn't have imagined that anyone could say with certainty—"

"Yes. There may be something there. Bland did the autopsy. Have a word with him and see what he says. Incidentally, I can set your mind at rest on one point. There's no doubt it *was* Smallbone. We've got very good prints which match up a dozen test samples from his lodgings. The man was a sort of pottery collector, bless him, and has left hundreds of beautiful prints. Colley will tell you about that."

"Right," said Hazlerigg. He replaced the photographs and gathered the typewritten sheets of Divisional Detective-Inspector Colley's report, patting them into a neat bundle, then rose to go.

"There *is* one thing," said the Assistant Commissioner. "You may need a bit of expert help. It doesn't need me to point out to you that there is an obvious line here, and the obvious line is often the right line. On the face of it, there's only one man who could have done this job. And his motive, when you get to it, is almost certain to be tied up in some legal jiggery-pokery. That's the logical supposition, anyway. Now would you like me to lend you one of our legal fellows to help you. Just say the word..."

Hazlerigg hesitated. The offer, he knew, was helpfully meant: and yet it had a faint suggestion of dual control which was hateful. However, it was no doubt the sensible course and he had actually opened his mouth to say "Yes" when his eye caught a name on the top of the typescript report.

"May I take it that the offer will be kept open," he said. "I'd like to start this in the ordinary routine way. I may find myself out of my depth. Quite likely I shall. If so—"

"Certainly," said the Assistant Commissioner. "Just say the word. By the way," he added shrewdly, "what was it on that paper that made you change your mind?"

Hazlerigg smiled.

"I saw a name I recognised," he said. "Here—in the list of recent arrivals at the office."

"Henry Winegarden Bohun," said the Assistant Commissioner. "Never heard of him. What is he?"

"Presumably he is a solicitor. He was a statistician. Before that, I believe, an actuary. And at one time almost a doctor."

"I don't believe," said the Assistant Commissioner, "that any normal man could find the time to train for all those professions."

"Quite so, sir," said the chief inspector. "No normal man could. Bohun's not normal. I'll tell you how I know about him. He happened to be in the same battalion as Sergeant Pollock—you may remember him—"

"The man the Garret crowd killed. He worked with you, didn't he?"

"Yes. Well, he was a friend of Bohun's. They were in the same company in North Africa. He told me about Bohun's peculiarity. If this is the same chap—and heaven knows it's not a common name—then he might be useful. Particularly if we can be certain that he wasn't involved—I'll check on that first, of course."

"A friend in the enemy's camp," said the Assistant Commissioner. "It's quite a good idea. Only for heaven's sake don't be like that mug in the detective story who confides all his best ideas to a friendly sort of character who turns out to be the murderer in Chapter Sixteen."

II

Bohun was one of the first to leave the office that evening. In view of the fact that he had only joined the firm two days before, and had had no previous ascertainable connection with any member of it, if we except a very distant schoolboy acquaintanceship with Bob Horniman, he had occupied only a few minutes of Inspector Colley's time.

In common with all the other members of the staff he had had his finger-prints taken.

This was typical of Inspector Colley who was elderly, soured by lack of promotion, and extremely methodical. He knew the necessary moves to a hair, and made them all. His reports were models of conciseness and monuments to a staggering lack of imagination.

However, he was a worker.

In the short time at his disposal he had taken statements from everyone in the office, set his photographers in motion, commissioned a detailed drawing of Bob Horniman's room and an outline sketch of the whole office,* set his finger-print men to work on the room, its walls, its door, its fittings, its approaches and its very varied contents; had taken check sets of prints from all other members of the staff; had dispatched a man to Smallbone's lodging to obtain prints from there, together with a check set from his landlady; had, in due course, sanctioned the removal of the body for pathological examination and on the strength of the doctor's preliminary report had divided the personnel into two lists. List One, those who had been with the firm less than a month: Mr. Bohun, Mr. Prince, Mr. Waugh (the cashier), Mrs. Porter and Mr. Flower. Mr. Flower, it might be explained, was none other than Charlie the office-boy. He kept his surname a secret in the office, having suffered from it at school. List Two, the remainder.

He had also contrived to make everyone on both lists feel thoroughly uncomfortable.

*　See plan on page 12.

"It's not what he says or does," as Miss Cornel observed to Anne Mildmay; "it's his general frightful air of 'You're all presumed guilty until you're proved innocent'."

Bohun walked quietly home in the dusk, across New Square.

He was thinking of the extraordinary events of the day. He was thinking that shock revealed the oddest traits and flaws in the human character. He was thinking that he was glad he was on List One.

He stepped into Malvern Rents, which is a passage off a turning off Chancery Lane, and turned in at the Rising Sun Restaurant, which, in spite of its pretentious name, was a tiny eating-house, the total furnishing of which consisted of four small tables, a few chairs and a wooden counter with an urn on it. The room, as was usual at this hour of the day, was empty. Bohun paused for a moment at the half-open door behind the counter to shout: "I'm back."

A muffled echo from the depths seemed to amount to some sort of acknowledgment.

He then pushed on through the second doorway, covered by an army blanket, up two flights of the narrow stairs, and through a second door. He was home.

It was an unexpected room to find in such a house. Originally, no doubt, it had been a large loft or storeroom, belonging perhaps to some scrivener at a time when the focus of the legal world had centred on the east rather than the west of Chancery Lane. It was a big room—quite thirty feet long and about half as wide, and looking surprisingly attractive with its grey fitted carpet, its stripped wooden walls and its carefully arranged lighting. The wall on the right as you came in from the landing, the inner of the long walls, was all books, covered with books, from floor to ceiling and from end to end. There was nothing esoteric about them, no tall folios, no first editions swathed in wash-leather—rather the well-handled tools of a reading man's trade. Poets, essayists, historians, sets of novels, textbooks, even school books; there must have been more than a thousand of them.

Two formal steel engravings of battle scenes filled the space between the tiny uncurtained windows of the long outer wall. At the far end of the room stood a large electric log fire (there was, of course, no fireplace). Over it hung a portrait in oils of a severe-looking lady. In front of it stood a single leather arm-chair.

Bohun whistled softly to himself as he walked through the room and disappeared into the small annexe which opened off it and which was his sleeping quarters.

When he reappeared he was dressed in corduroy trousers and a khaki shirt, and had a white muffler round his neck. With his plain, serious, rather white face, he looked like some mechanic with a bent for self-improvement, a student of Kant and Schopenhauer, who tended his lathe by day and sharpened his wits of an evening on dead dialecticians.

"Well, Mr. Bohun," said Mrs. Magoli, descendant of Florentines, owner of the Rising Sun Restaurant, and Bohun's landlady. "And how are you finding your new office?"

"Thank you," said Bohun. "I'm liking it very much."

"Dry as dust, I expect."

"Oh, I don't know," said Bohun. "We found a trustee in one of the deed boxes today."

"Lor!" said Mrs. Magoli, who clearly had no idea what a trustee was. "What will you lawyers get up to next? Now what could you fancy for your afters?"

Bohun inspected the table in the middle of the room which Mrs. Magoli had spread with a fair cloth and covered with a number of dishes, backed by a promising looking wicker-covered flask.

"Ham," he said. "How on earth do you get ham? I didn't think there was that much ham in London. Pasta schuta. Bread. Butter. Green olives. To add anything else would be sacrilege and profanation—unless you've got a little bit of Carmagnola cheese…"

"I thought that's what you'd be after," said Mrs. Magoli. "Got some this morning. Shocking price, I don't like to tell you what it cost."

"Then don't," said Bohun.

"You'll be the ruin of me," said Mrs. Magoli complacently.

"Then we will go down together into bankruptcy," said Bohun, "fortified by the blamelessness of our lives and strengthened by the inspiration of your cooking."

When Mrs. Magoli had cleared away the last of the dinner, Bohun took a book from the shelves and started to read. He read steadily, reeling in the lines of print with a nice unfettered action. Page after page was turned, until the little clock on the mantelpiece tinkled out eleven: whereupon Bohun closed the book, marking the place with a slip of white paper on which he scribbled a note. Then he got to his feet and looked out of the window, stooping his height a little to get a view of the skyline over the gable opposite.

The sky was clear, and the night warm for mid-April.

Bohun went back into his bedroom and returned carrying an old raincoat, turned out the fire and the light and went quietly downstairs. A few minutes later he was in Holborn, boarding a late bus, going east.

It was half a dozen fare-stages beyond Aldgate Pump before he alighted. Thereafter he turned south, towards the river, following his nose.

The public houses were long since closed and the only lights which showed were from one or two little all-night cafés. Bohun seemed to know where he was going. He left even these rare lights behind him as he turned down a side street. He was in the factory and warehouse area now, and the street along which he was walking was lined with heavy double doors, steel-roller covered vanways alternating with hoardings.

After a hundred yards he turned down an alleyway which came to a dead end in an ugly square yellow-brick building. Lights were showing in one or two of the windows and Bohun knocked. The front door was unlocked and he went in without waiting for an answer.

The room into which he turned was some sort of office. A gas-fire burned in the grate, and at a table a small bald middle-aged man was seated drinking cocoa out of a large mug.

"Good evening, 'Enery," said the bald man. His voice declared that he had been born and bred within striking distance of Bow bells. "I thought I reckernised your fairy plates. 'Elp yerself to a cupper."

"Thanks," said Henry. "Anything doing tonight?"

"Not tonight, son. You mighter used the blower and saved yerself a journey."

"That's all right," said Henry. "I like the exercise. When's the next job coming along?"

"I can fitcher in next week, most probable. Peters need a pair for their new place."

"Peters—isn't that whisky?"

"Wines and sperrits."

"That's apt to be a bit rough, isn't it?" said Bohun. "I'm not *looking* for trouble, you know. A quiet life is all I want."

"Quiet," said the little man. "It'll be quiet as a fevver bed. Peters are all right. Very scientific. All the fixings."

"All right," said Bohun. "I'll try anything once. Give me a ring nearer the time. How have you been keeping? How are the pigeons?…"

"Pigeons... There's no money left in our fevvered friends—take pigs..."

It was an hour and more before Bohun finally set out again into the night. The last bus had long gone to its garage and the streets were empty. He faced the prospect of the walk with equanimity. Walking in the country bored him, but London he loved, and most of all he loved it at night. The shuttered warehouses, the silent streets of offices. The grave, cloaked policemen, the occasional hunting cat. The death of one day's life.

His long legs carried him steadily westward.

Three o'clock was striking from Lincoln's Inn Chapel when he turned once more into Malvern Rents.

As he turned his key in the door he stopped in some surprise. Ten yards down, opposite the entrance of the narrow passage, he noticed the rear light of a car. This in itself was unusual at that time of night, but it was not all. Looking up from where he stood he saw that there was a light in his room.

"Curiouser and curiouser," said Bohun. He shut the shop door quietly and went upstairs.

The thickset man who got up as he came in, said: "I'm sorry to disturb you at such an unorthodox hour, Mr. Bohun. Your land-lady gave me permission to make myself at home till you came back."

He might have been a farmer, with his red face, his heavy build and his hardworn tweed suit. He might have been a soldier in mufti. The hand which he held out to Bohun had the plumping muscles behind the fingers which meant that the owner used his hands as well as his head. The only remarkable thing about this generally unremarkable person was his eyes, which were grey, with the cold grey of the North Sea.

"My name's Hazlerigg," went on the newcomer. "I'm from Scotland Yard."

Bohun had recognised the police car and managed not to look too shaken. The next remark, however, did surprise him.

"I believe you knew Bobby Pollock," said Hazlerigg.

"Lord, yes," said Bohun. "Won't you sit down. Bobby and I were second loots in the Rum Runners. We were in Africa and Italy together. I heard—didn't he get killed?"

"Yes," said Hazlerigg. "I had the pleasure of hanging both the responsible parties," he added.

"I'm glad," said Bohun. "Bobby was a first-rater. I believe he broke every regulation known to officialdom to get into the army."

"Yes," said Hazlerigg. "He told me a lot about you too."

"Well, I expect you know the worst. About my disability, you mean."

"I should hesitate to describe para-insomnia as a disability," said Hazlerigg, "although I know the army regarded it as such."

"I don't think that anyone really knows very much about it," said Bohun, "or that's the impression I've got from talking to a number of different doctors."

"It's true, then, that you never sleep more than two hours a night."

"Two hours is a good night," said Bohun. "Ninety minutes is about the average."

"And you don't suffer any ill effects—excuse me. It's bad taste, I know, asking questions like that, only I was interested when Pollock told me."

"It doesn't make me feel tired, if that's what you mean," said Bohun. "It isn't straightforward insomnia, you know—not as the term is usually understood. The only detail on which the medical profession are at all agreed is that some day I may drop down dead in the street. But what day—or what street—they can't say."

"I can't do better," said Hazlerigg, "than quote Sergeant Pollock. He said some nice things about you as an infantry officer, then he added, 'Of course, he was God's gift to the staff. Imagine a G.S.O. who could work indefinitely for twenty-two hours a day!' I gather that an officious M.O. tumbled to it in the end and the net result was that you were boarded out."

"Once they knew about the para-insomnia I don't think they had any option."

"I should have thought the most difficult thing was filling in the spare time."

"Oh, I do a good deal of reading," said Bohun. "It's useful, too, when I'm taking an exam. And I do a good deal of walking about the streets. And sometimes I get a job."

"A job?"

"As night watchman. I combined most of my reading for my Law Finals with a night watchman's job for the Apex Shipping Company. Believe it or not, I was actually reading the sections in Kenny on 'Robbery with Violence' when I was knocked out by Syd Seligman, the strong-arm man for one of the—"

"I know Syd," said Inspector Hazlerigg. "I helped to send him down for a seven last month. Well, now…"

"The preliminaries are now concluded," thought Bohun. "Seconds out of the ring. Time!"

"I've got a proposal to put to you. I don't know if you'll think it's a good one or not…" Shortly he laid before Bohun the idea which he had already put to the Assistant Commissioner and the facts on which it was based.

"We might as well face it at once," he went on. "Almost the only person who could and would have killed Smallbone is your late senior partner, Abel Horniman. If you're inclined to look anywhere else for a likely candidate just ask yourself how anyone else could have got the body into the room unobserved, and opened the box—of which only Abel had the key. For Abel himself, the box was the obvious place to put a body. He knew he was dying. He only needed a few weeks' grace—a few months at the most. But for anyone else, the idea was madness."

"Yes," said Bohun. "Of course. When you put it like that it seems obvious enough... But why?"

"That's where *you* come in," said Hazlerigg. "Again, we'll start with the obvious solution. You'd be surprised how often it's the right one. Abel Horniman and Marcus Smallbone were fellow trustees. I don't understand all the ins and outs of it, but I realise this much. They had joint control of a very large sum of money. It might be more accurate to say that Horniman had control of it. He was the professional. One would expect Smallbone to do what he was told—sign on the dotted line and so on."

"I don't think," said Bohun slowly, "that Smallbone was quite that sort of man."

"I don't expect he was," said Hazlerigg. "That's why he's dead, you know. It's so obvious that it must be so. Some swindle was going on. I don't mean that it was an easy swindle or an obvious swindle. Nothing that an outsider could spot. But Smallbone wasn't an outsider. The thing had to be put up to him—to a limited extent. And he just happened to spot the rabbit in the conjurer's hat."

"So the conjurer popped him into his disappearing cabinet."

"Yes. Think of Horniman's position. Think of the temptation. On the one hand, disgrace, the breaking down of a life's work—probably jail. On the other hand—he could 'die respectit', as the Scots say. Once he was dead it wouldn't matter. It was so easy. Into the box with the body, lose the key, sit tight. Even if it went wrong, what matter. The hangman would have to get the deuce of a move on if he wanted to race the angina. How many people, I wonder, would commit murder if they knew they were going to die anyway. And Smallbone was such an unimportant, such an insignificant creature. How dared he imperil the great Horniman tradition, cast doubts on the Horniman legend, besmear the great Horniman name. No, no. Into the box with him."

"I see," said Bohun. "How are you going to prove all this?"

"That's it," said Hazlerigg. "We shall have to find out what's wrong with this trust."

"Well," said Bohun, "I expect I could help you if you're keen on the idea. But surely an accountant or an auditor could do it better than me. It'll just be routine."

"I wonder." Hazlerigg suddenly got up. He strolled across to the window. The first light of dawn was coming up. The roofs opposite showed blacker against the faintest greying of the dark.

"It may not be as simple as all that," he said. "Anyway, I'd like your help if I may have it."

"Of course," said Bohun.

"And then again, we've always got to face the possibility that it may not have been Abel Horniman. That is going to open up quite a wide field of speculation."

"List Two," said Bohun.

"Ah! You've seen the testament according to Colley. I'm afraid his classification may not be as exhaustive as it seems—"

"You mean, someone who came after?…"

"On the contrary—someone who was there, but has now left."

"Oh, yes. Yes, I suppose that's possible," said Bohun slowly. "I hadn't thought of it. I had no predecessor. My typist, Mrs. Porter, came when I did; I mean, she didn't replace anyone. The Common Law clerk, Mr. Prince, took the place of another old boy who'd been umpteen years with the firm. But he—the other one, I mean—left months ago. Just after Christmas. I believe they had some trouble over finding a replacement. You don't get Common Law clerks easily. Then there's the cashier—we had a cashier, before, a Mr. Clark—he's well in the running, I suppose. He only left three weeks ago."

"Colley mentions him in his report," said Hazlerigg. "But he's out for another reason. He couldn't have done it, he was a last war casualty. He only had one hand."

"And why does that mean he couldn't have killed Smallbone?" said Bohun quietly.

"I quite forgot," said Hazlerigg. "You don't know how he was killed."

"I don't," said Bohun steadily, "and I suggest," he added, "that if you're going to trust me you don't set traps for me."

Hazlerigg had the grace to blush. "Just second nature," he said, and added: "No. It would have been quite impossible. Smallbone was strangled with picture wire. Definitely a two-handed job."

CHAPTER FIVE

—THURSDAY—

Time Is of the Essence

How matter presses on me!
What stubborn things are facts
HAZLITT: *Table Talk*

I

HAZLERIGG FOUND GISSEL, THE POLICE PHOTOGRAPHER AND finger-print man at work in Bob Horniman's office.

"I've done jobs in junk-shops, in Lost Property offices, in warehouses and in the mistresses' common-room at a girls' public school," said Gissel, "but never before in my life have I see one room with quite so much *stuff* in it."

"Then thank your lucky stars that you're in a Horniman office," said Hazlerigg, looking round at the rows of black boxes, the neat files and the orderly assemblage of folders. "This is child's play to what you'd find in the office of an ordinary uninhibited solicitor, really it is."

"It's all these books," said Gissel. "In open shelves, too. Anyone might have touched them or brushed against them. They don't look as if they've ever been read." He picked one down and blew a cloud of black dust off the top. "*Queen's Bench*, 1860. Who in Hades would be interested where the Queen put her bottom in 1860?"

Hazlerigg said thoughtfully: "We shan't be able to let young Horniman come back here until we've finished, and that looks as if it may take a bit of time. I think I'd better use this room myself for working in. You've done the desk, I take it?"

First came the senior partner, Mr. Birley. In an interview of limited usefulness the most that could be said was that both sides managed to keep their tempers.

It irritated Mr. Birley to see a stranger behind one of his partners' desks: it irritated him to have to sit himself in the client's chair: it irritated him unspeakably to have to answer questions instead of asking them.

After fifteen unhelpful minutes Hazlerigg dismissed him and asked for a word with the second partner.

The tubby Mr. Craine was more obliging.

"Ichabod Stokes," he said, "was a Presbyterian fishmonger. He was one of Abel's oldest clients." Seeing a slight look of surprise on the inspector's face, he added: "I don't say that he was the sort of client we should have taken on nowadays, but when Abel was starting, way back before the turn of the century, well, he was like every other young solicitor—to him a client was a client. And I don't think either of them regretted their association. Ichabod, you know, was one of those men who really understand money. He started with one fish-shop in Commercial Road, and when he died he owned almost a quarter of the East Coast fishing fleet."

"When was that?" Hazlerigg was making an occasional note in his amateur shorthand: notes which would later be expanded into the journal of the case.

"Ichabod died—now let me see—at Munich time, Autumn, 1938. He left a will appointing Abel Horniman and Marcus Smallbone executors and trustees. Why Smallbone? God knows. He and

Smallbone had a common passion for collecting pottery, and had met at one or two sales, and struck up some sort of acquaintanceship. And I believe they used to write long letters to each other about ceramics and what-have-you, though between you and me," said Mr. Craine, with that cheerful vulgarity which is often a characteristic of tubby extroverts, "I don't think Stokes really knew the difference between the Portland Vase and a pisspot—or that was the impression I got when I had to put his collection on the market after his death. However, that's by the way. The whole estate, as I said, was left to his trustees on trust for a dozen charities. There was no disputing the will—they were very sound and sensible charities; mostly to do with fish. The Herring-fleet Homes and the Destitute Drifters and so on. He nominated them himself, got us to make certain that they *were* charities, and had 'em listed, by name, in his will—and if every testator took those simple precautions," concluded Mr. Craine with feeling—for he, like others of his profession, had suffered from the decision in *re* Diplock—"the lawyer's lot would be a very much happier and a very much easier one."

"So now," said Hazlerigg, "all you have to do is to divide the income among these charities?"

"In theory, that is so. In fact, there's more to it than that. Of course, when Ichabod died his estate consisted of a lot of different things. There was real property—he bought a number of farms cheap at the time of the 1931 slump—and there were the assets and the goodwill of his various businesses, which had to be valued and paid out. However, you can take it that by now everything has been realised and invested in securities. In round figures, Ichabod added up to nearly a million pounds. When the death duties had been paid we salvaged just over half a million—and we worked like

Trojans to keep that much." Mr. Craine spoke with genuine feeling. This was one aspect of his work which genuinely appealed to him. Sometimes, indeed, he went so far as to visualise himself as an archangel, a rotund St. Michael, armed with the sword of Dymond and defended by the shield of Green, protecting the helpless from the assault of the massed powers of Darkness, those arch-fiends, the Commissioners of Inland Revenue.

"Half a million," said Hazlerigg. "And all invested. It will just be a matter of checking the stocks and shares, I take it."

"There again," said Mr. Craine, "in theory, yes. In fact, no. I don't know how much you understand about these things, but a lot depends in any particular trust on the investment clause. It's much easier, in a way, if you are limited to trustee securities. That's dull, but fairly straightforward. In this case, we had wider powers. Not absolutely discretionary, but almost so. That meant that we had to keep the fund in the best possible state of investment compatible with security—stop me if I'm confusing you."

"You are being very clear," said Hazlerigg. "Please go on."

"Well, that was Abel's job—and, if I may say so, he earned his professional retainer a dozen times over. He knew the stock market as well as any broker, and he bought and sold to meet the demands of the day. That's why it isn't possible, without looking through all the recent files and folders, to say exactly what the trust fund *ought* to consist of. I can tell you what it *does* consist of. I'm having Sergeant Cockerill make a list of the securities at this moment. But most of the accounts which would have told me what it ought to have been—the history of the various investments, as it were—they were in that box."

"I see," said Hazlerigg. "Does that mean that you'll never know—?"

"Oh, no. We'll find out," said Mr. Craine. "It'll just take a little time, that's all."

"I see. Let me know what the answer is, please, as soon as you get it." Hazlerigg thought for a minute and then said: "If Abel Horniman had been embezzling funds, do you think he would have taken them from this trust, or some other one?"

He was watching Mr. Craine as he said this, and found more interest in his reactions than in the actual words of his reply.

One thing was quite evident. Mr. Craine was neither surprised nor shocked at the suggestion. On the contrary, he was plainly very interested in it.

"Yes," he said at last. "Yes. *If* he had embezzled money I think this was the trust he would have gone to."

"Why do you say that?"

"Tell me first." Mr. Craine looked the chief inspector shrewdly in the eye. "Have you any reason for your question—any grounds for your supposition?"

"None at all," said Hazlerigg. "The case was purely hypothetical."

"On those grounds, then," said Mr. Craine, "I'll answer it. As a hypothesis only. The Stokes Trust would have been a suitable vehicle for fraud for several reasons. First, because the only other trustee was a layman. Secondly, because the funds were all here, and under our effective control. They had to be. As I explained, Abel was constantly buying and selling; so no question would be asked. Thirdly, the beneficiaries were all charities. The secretary of a charity is, on the whole, so glad to see his annual cheque that he doesn't usually question its amount very closely. If he was told that all the investments in the trust were showing lower yields, or that some income was being put back for administrative reasons, he would probably accept the explanation without further question—far more readily, anyway, than a private beneficiary whose own pocket was being touched."

"Yes," said Hazlerigg. "I see. Thank you. You've been very frank. You'll tell me at once if anything *is* wrong with the trust fund. In the meantime, perhaps you would ask Mr. Bohun to step along."

II

Meanwhile, Detective-Sergeant Plumptree had made his way out to Belsize Park and was interrogating Mrs. Tasker.

Sergeant Plumptree was a pink-and-white young man, with the well-scoured look of one who has but recently emerged from his mother's wash-tub. His methods were unorthodox and some of the results which he achieved surprised even himself.

"Young man," said Mrs. Tasker, "pour yourself out a second cup of tea, do, and be guided by me. Never take in lodgers. Go to the poorhouse, go to prison, commit arson, larceny and what you like, but never take in lodgers."

"What—" began Sergeant Plumptree.

"Take this Mr. Smallbone. A quiet man. An inoffensive man. A good payer. Never should I have thought that by his deeds he would have brought anxiety to my bosom and police into my house—the sugar's behind the clock. Five years ago he came here to lodge. Put down six months' rent on the table, the one we're sitting at at this moment, and said to me, 'Mrs. Tasker, I'm a rolling stone. I gather no moss. But somewhere I must have to lay my head.' 'The first floor front pair's vacant,' I said, 'and use of the ring at the back for cooking.' That's all that passed between us, if I go to my Maker tonight."

"Which—" said Sergeant Plumptree.

"It wasn't as if he didn't warn me straight out. 'I'm a collector, Mrs. Tasker,' he said. 'Pots and pans there'll be in my room a-plenty. And if it's extra trouble for you to dust we'll come to an understanding.' And another thing he said: 'I'll come and go as I like.' And so he did. 'Expect me when you see me.' That was the rule. Last year he was in Italy, at his house in Florence. The address is on his card. You can see it for yourself. Three months he was away, and one morning back he came, without a word, with a carpet-bag full of flower-pots."

"How—" persevered Sergeant Plumptree.

"And then this February he goes away again. The twelfth of February. I've marked it in the rent-book—see, Friday the twelfth of February. I'm going down to Kent, he said. I didn't catch the name. Stanton, I thought he said. It may have been Stancomb."

"I thought—" said Sergeant Plumptree.

"I know what you're going to say," said Mrs. Tasker. "But wait. He went away on the Friday. I'm going down to Kent, he said. And if I find what I'm looking for, that'll be the beginning of great things, Mrs. Tasker. Great things. I'll be back tonight, he said."

"And he never came back?"

"Certainly he did. That night, as he said. Then the next day he went out again. No luggage. Nothing. That was always his way. 'Ah,' I thought. 'He'll be off to Italy. He's found what he's looking for.' And when one week went by and then another, I knew I was right."

"You knew he—?"

"I knew he was in Italy, where he is now," concluded Mrs. Tasker triumphantly. "Enjoying the hot weather."

With a discretion beyond his years Sergeant Plumptree refrained from any comment on this interesting speculation.

III

"It's the question of access which is worrying me," said Hazlerigg, "and that's the sort of thing where you can help."

"Access to what?" asked Bohun.

"Access to that deed box in which we found the body," said Hazlerigg. He added as an afterthought: "Access to this room, access to the office building, access to Lincoln's Inn."

"Well," said Bohun. "Anyone can get into any of the public parts of Lincoln's Inn at any time by day. If you came in very late or very early—or on Saturday afternoon or Sunday—then you'd probably be noticed."

"Particularly if you were a prominent resident like Abel Horniman."

"Yes. The porters certainly knew him by sight. At any time during office hours you can get into the Inn by at least six routes and there's no check of any sort."

"Right," said Hazlerigg. "Now the office."

"That's more difficult," said Bohun. "I haven't been here long, and perhaps this week hasn't been exactly a typical one, but I really have been surprised at the number of people who wander through these offices without question. Not only the staff, but outsiders, too. On our side of the office we've got the reception-room—where the junior typists sit. All visitors to the office are supposed to look in there first—clients, messengers, clerks from other offices, people examining deeds, people selling office accessories, and even the friends and relatives of the staff. The other side is a bit more select. There are only these three partners' offices and the partners' secretaries' room. But even so, a lot of people who know the ropes short-circuit the system by going straight in to see the secretary of the partner they're interested in—or to bring messages—or collect mail—or wind up the clocks, or spray the telephones or clean the typewriters."

"In short," said Hazlerigg, "anyone who looked as if they had some business to transact could walk into either side of the office during business hours whenever they liked without anyone stopping them, and probably without anyone noticing them. After business hours no one could get into the Inn without a strong probability of being noticed—or into the offices?"

"Certainly not into the offices," said Bohun. "Sergeant Cockerill locks the two doors at night. He leaves about seven. He's the last to go."

"Who has keys?"

"No one has keys except him, I understand. If he's away he hands them over to someone else. He's the locker-upper in chief. He looks after the strong-room as well."

"Supposing one of the partners wanted to get in after hours?"

"I'm not sure," said Bohun. "I asked John Cove and he said that no partner in a fashionable firm of solicitors ever did work after hours—that sort of thing being left, one gathers, to the shirt-sleeves brigade in the City. If a partner wanted to work late I suppose he would get the door keys from Sergeant Cockerill and do the locking up himself."

"Even Abel Horniman didn't have the keys?"

"Not of the outer doors."

"I see," said Hazlerigg. "Well, that would seem to dispose of that. Not forgetting that any key can be copied—these big heavy door-keys easier than most. Now what about Horniman's room."

"In office hours," said Bohun slowly, "there is one very serious obstacle. If you look at the lay-out you'll see that the partners' secretaries' room is really designed to control the entrance to all three of the partners' rooms. And at least one of the three secretaries—Miss Cornel, Miss Chittering or Miss Mildmay—had always to be in it."

"You say they *have* to be in it," said the inspector doubtfully. "How well was the rule observed?"

"Pretty well, I imagine," said Bohun. "First of all, this was a Horniman office and system's the watchword. But apart from that, the partners' telephone exchange was in the secretaries' room. It was all part of the system for keeping irritating or unwanted clients at arm's length—which is a fairly important thing in any solicitor's office. The actual telephone exchange—the one that connects up with the outside world—is in the basement and is looked after by Sergeant Cockerill or his young stand-in, Charlie. When a call comes for one of the partners it is plugged through first to the partners' secretaries' room and vetted there before being put through to the partner concerned. It really does mean that one of the secretaries *has* to be there the whole time."

"I see," said the inspector. "And they'd have noticed at once if Mr. Smallbone had gone into Mr. Horniman's office?…"

"Not only would they have noticed it," said Bohun, with a smile, "but they'd have made a note of it in the journal, and, when Smallbone finally left, the secretary concerned—Miss Cornel in this case—would have noted the length of time he'd been there—with a view to typing out an 'attendance' on the subject later. How do you think we poor solicitors live?"

Hazlerigg thought about all this for some time, but made no comment. Finally, he said: "Well, then—that box."

"That's more difficult still," said Bohun. "You can see that it's a good lock—a five-lever—more like a strong box than a deed box. It can be forced, as Sergeant Cockerill demonstrated—but it wouldn't be easy to pick, I should think—not without leaving traces."

"Right," said Hazlerigg. "And the keys."

"The boxes were in sets. Each partner's room had a set. There was a master-key for each set, with a 'single variant' key for each box in the set. But no key of one set would fit another set. The partner concerned kept the ring of keys for his boxes, and the master-key, in case he lost an individual key."

"Wasn't that rather over-elaborate?"

"You just didn't know Abel Horniman," said Bohun.

"It was right up his street. One key—one box—one client. I don't think the other partners enjoyed the system quite so much. Birley lost all his keys in the course of time and had to have a new set made. Craine, I know, keeps his boxes permanently unlocked. But that doesn't affect the point at issue, since none of their keys would fit the Ichabod Stokes box, anyway. Only Abel Horniman had that key—and apparently he didn't have it either. I don't know what Bob Horniman's story is—but Miss Cornel says that he couldn't find either the key for this particular box, or the master. The other seventeen were there all right."

"Thank you," said Hazlerigg. "I think I'd better have a word with Bob Horniman."

Bob could tell him very little about the keys.

"I was father's sole executor," he explained. "And I took every-thing over. There *were* a lot of keys. House keys as well as office keys. I knew that this bunch belonged to the office, so I brought them here and kept them in my desk drawer. I never realised that one of them was missing. I used the others from time to time to open various boxes—"

"But, of course, you'd never had occasion to go to this particular box until this morning."

"Well, no, I hadn't," said Bob. "As a matter of fact I hadn't really done much about the Ichabod Stokes Trust at all. It had been on my conscience a bit—but a trust isn't like a conveyancing or litigation matter that has to be kept marching strictly along—and you know how it is. I was a bit rushed and the least urgent job went to the wall."

"I quite understand," said Hazlerigg. "Now, about your father. Can you give me some idea of his routine? When he arrived at the office, and so on. Particularly in the last months of his life."

Bob looked faintly surprised, but said: "He had to take it quite easily. He was under doctor's orders for the last six months. I think they'd have been happier if he hadn't come to office at all, but that was out of the question with Dad. The office *was* his life, you know. He used to get here at about half-past ten and leave at about half-past four."

"I suppose that the rest of you arrived earlier than that."

"Good Lord, yes," said Bob. "Nine-thirty sharp. Even Mr. Craine was usually behind his desk before ten o'clock."

"I see. Were you and your father living together?"

"No," said Bob shortly. "I've got a flat."

"I suppose that your father's house comes to you under the will. Are you going to live there now?"

Bob looked for a moment as if he was searching for some cause of offence in this question. In the end he said: "No. Certainly not. I couldn't possibly keep it up. It's a great barracks of a place in Kensington."

IV

Sergeant Plumptree would have assented to this description. It wasn't an attractive house. In colour it was greyish-yellow. In size it was enormous. It was designed on the sound Victorian principle which kept the kitchen in the basement, the family on the ground and the first floor, the guests on the second floor, the servants on the third floor and the children in the attic.

A bearded lady with one stationary and one roving eye opened the door and showed Sergeant Plumptree into a morning-room heavy with black satinwood and maroon chenille. She motioned him to a penitential chair, folded her plump white hands, and awaited in silence whatever indignities her interrogator might see fit to heap upon her.

"Well, ma'am," said Sergeant Plumptree pleasantly. "It's a question of times—"

Without too much prompting he obtained the following information. It would have seemed that Abel Horniman was as much a creature of habit in his home as in his office, particularly during the last six months of his life. Everything had been done to render his course smooth. A nurse had always been in attendance. Sergeant Plumptree noted her name and address, feeling glad of a chance of corroborative evidence. Abel Horniman had got up at eight-thirty and had his breakfast at nine-fifteen and had read his *Times* and his *Financial Times* until the car came to fetch him at five past ten. In the evenings he had always been home by five o'clock for tea, and had then liked to sit and listen to the wireless before changing into a dinner jacket for his evening meal.

"Did he ever go out at that time?"

The housekeeper looked faintly surprised. "Certainly not," she said.

"Never," persisted the sergeant. "I'm sorry. It's just that we must be certain—"

"Mr. Horniman"—the housekeeper pursed her lips—"was a dying man. He *never* went out in the evenings."

"Thank you. And then..."

"After that," said the housekeeper, "at ten o'clock he retired to bed. The nurse had the bedroom across the passage and I had the room next to her. Between us we were certain to hear if he cried out. His attacks, you know—very sudden."

"Thank you, ma'am," said Sergeant Plumptree.

It seemed to him to be pretty conclusive. There would be just time, he thought, to call on the nurse, before reporting back to Inspector Hazlerigg.

V

Dr. Bland, the pathologist, was a dry man but an enthusiast.

The photograph which he exhibited for Hazlerigg's attention looked, at first blink, like an aerial view of the Grand Canyon of Arizona. There were the innumerable fissile crevices running in from either side towards the centre, the gulfs and gullies, the pot-holes and pockmarks of the surrounding terrain; and there down the middle, as if ruled off by a draughtsman, was the deep, steep-sided indenture of the canyon itself, and far down at the bottom the dark line of the stream.

"Effect of picture-wire on the human neck," said Dr. Bland. "Two hundred magnifications."

"Extraordinary," said Hazlerigg with distaste. "I suppose that dark line at the bottom is the—just so. You needn't explain. What does it all prove?"

"Quite a lot," said the doctor. "Would you like a picture of the weapon. Subject to very slight possible errors, here it is. Take a short piece of ordinary seven-strand brass picture-wire. Drive a small hole between the strands, about two-thirds of the way along—you could do that with a nail, or a sharp gimlet. Then thread one end of your wire through the hole. That gives you a nice smoothly-running noose, or slip-knot. I suggest that you then fasten toggles of wood—anything to afford you a good grip—one at either end of your wire. There's an inexpensive, neat, household model of the garrotter's loop—"

"Inexpensive," said Hazlerigg. "Neat, and untraceable."

"Oh, quite," said the pathologist. "It's a household weapon. Anybody could make one."

"Thank you."

"I haven't done yet," said Dr. Bland. "That's a picture of the weapon. Would you like a picture of your murderer?"

"If it's not asking too much of you," said Hazlerigg politely.

"Well, to a certain extent the weapon implies the user. He must be methodical, neat with his hands, with enough imagination to devise such a weapon, and enough ruthlessness to use it."

"You surprise me," said Hazlerigg.

"He is also, most probably, left-handed."

"What!"

"Ah—I thought that might stir you out of your confounded dismal professional indifference," said the pathologist. "That's a clue, isn't it? That's something to go on. Not just one of Jimmy Bland's pawky generalisations. I repeat, he was left-handed. I mean it in this sense—not that he was a man who only used his left hand, but he was a man whose left hand—or, at all events, his left wrist was better developed and stronger than his right."

"Where did you get all this from?"

"From the wire. From the enlarged photograph of the neck, which you so rudely threw back at me a moment ago." Dr. Bland laid the photograph on the table again and ran the tip of his finger along some of the north-bank tributaries of the Colorado. "Observe," he said, "how all the creases on the right are drawn backwards—that is, towards the spine. That means that when the murderer started to pull, he held the *right* handle of his machine steady, and excited the actual pressure with his left hand. No other explanation will fit. Now for an ordinary, right-handed man, the tendency would have been just the opposite. He would have held steady with the left hand and done the pulling with the right. Cast your mind back to the last time you pulled a tight cork out of a bottle of old port—"

"Yes, I think I see what you mean."

Hazlerigg went through the motions of garrotting an imaginary victim, whilst the pathologist watched and nodded his approval.

"One other thing, doctor. You say 'he' and 'him' and 'the man'. Is that certain? Could it have been a woman?"

"Certainly. A man or a woman. Using this little weapon all you need is the initial surprise, and a certain amount of luck. Consider now. I am going to strangle you." He pushed the inspector into the late Abel Horniman's office chair. "You have no cause to suspect me. Right? I am standing quietly behind you. I put my hands round your throat. What do you do? Ah—as I thought. You put your own hands up and try to tear away my fingers. You find it difficult because, strong as you are, you're sitting down, your knees are under the desk, and you can't use your weight. But not impossibly difficult. You catch one of my little fingers and bend—all right—all right—you needn't be too realistic. You manage to break my grip. If you are a man and I am a woman you'd probably break out quite easily. But consider the murderer who is using a wire loop. It's strong, and it's as sharp as a cheese-cutter, and it's an inch into your neck before you know what's happening. You can't shout. You're half paralysed with the shock of the attack and *there's nothing to catch hold of.* That's the crux of it. You can't get so much as the tip of a finger between the wire and your neck. Yes, yes. I think a woman could kill a man with a weapon like that."

VI

Hazlerigg had a word with Bohun before he left the office that evening.

He summed things up, principally for his own comfort and edification.

"Abel Horniman is out," he said. "That's a pity, because he was our number one candidate. He was the man who *ought* to have committed this murder. He was the man who might have had every reason for removing Smallbone. But he didn't do it."

He paused for a moment; then went on: "I don't say that we could get up in court and prove that it was impossible for him to have done it. It's difficult to prove a negative. I suppose he *might* have crept out of bed in the middle of the night and made his way to Lincoln's Inn. He might have got in without attracting attention, let himself into the office and killed Smallbone, though I can't imagine how he'd have got him there unnoticed. It's theoretically possible. But so improbable that I intend to disregard it. It's my experience that in real life criminals tend to do their jobs the easiest way. Not the most difficult or the most picturesque. They don't haul the corpses to the top of Nelson's Column or exhibit them in the Chamber of Horrors at Madame Tussaud's. Not unless they are mad."

As Hazlerigg said this he contemplated for a moment the uncomfortable spectre which must haunt all policemen. He thought of Chief Inspector Aspinall and Inspector Hervey scouring the Midlands for a man who specialised in the murder of six-year-old girls. A man who might be a clerk or a labourer. A lay preacher or a lawyer or a Lord Mayor. A kindly father, an indulgent elder brother, a rational man for twenty-nine days out of thirty. And on the thirtieth—a creature, in the hunting of whom there was no logic and in the hanging of whom no satisfaction.

He shook his head angrily. "I'll believe in a madman if I have to," he said. "Not till then. Good night."

"Good night," said Bohun.

He walked home across the darkening square, his mind astir with alarming fancies.

CHAPTER SIX

—FRIDAY—

Preliminary Enquiries

But above all, those judicious Collectors of bright parts and flowers and observanda's are to be nicely dwelt on; by some called the sieves and boulters of learning; tho' it is left undetermined, whether they dealt in pearls or Meal; and consequently whether they are more value to that which passed thro' or what staid behind.

SWIFT: *Tale of a Tub*

I

"BOHUN SEEMS TO SPEND A LOT OF HIS TIME CHATTERING to that policeman," said Mr. Birley.

"Which policeman?" It seemed to Mr. Craine that the office was full of policemen. Already he had been forced to postpone visits from one ducal and two lesser clients.

"The one who asks all the questions."

"Oh, yes. The chief inspector."

"Chief inspector? I don't think the fellow's even a gentleman." Mr. Birley himself had been to Sherborne.

"Oh, well," said Mr. Craine, tolerantly, "I expect the fact is that he—er—rose from the ranks: or whatever they do in the police force. We mustn't mind his questions. He's got his job to do."

"I don't mind *him* doing *his* job," said Mr. Birley. "It's Bohun spending all day chattering to him. If he wants advice why doesn't he come to me? Bohun can't know much about things. He only joined us this week."

"No, I suppose not."

"We don't pay him a large salary for him to spend all his time chattering with policemen."

"Of course not," said Mr. Craine. "I'll have a word with him about it. By the way, let me see, what do we pay him?"

"Four hundred and fifty a year," said Mr. Birley without a blush.

II

"The trouble with you," said Inspector Hazlerigg, "is that you read too many detective stories."

He pivoted slowly round in the Horniman swivel-chair.

"How do you make that out?" said Bohun.

"Admit," said Hazlerigg, "that you expect me to spend my time sitting here asking a million questions. Occasionally moving round the office in a catlike manner, popping up unexpectedly when people are talking to each other, stooping to pick up minute scraps of paper and invisible threads of wool; all the time smoking a foul pipe or playing on a mouth organ or quoting Thucydides in order to establish a character for originality with the book reviewers—"

"Well—"

"Then, at the end of about seventy-five thousand words I shall collect you all into this room, and inaugurate a sort of verbal game of grandmother's steps, creeping up behind each of the suspects in turn and saying Boo! to them in order to make them jump. At the end of which, when everybody is exhausted, including the reader,

I shall produce a revolver, confess that I committed the crime, and shoot myself in front of you all."

"Well," said Bohun, "omitting the melodramatic conclusion, isn't that just about how it's done?"

"As a practical method of detection," said Hazlerigg, "it would be about as much use as leaving an open creel beside a trout stream and expecting the fish to jump into it." He scratched his nose thoughtfully, watched a small girl teasing a cat on the other side of New Square, and went on: "So far as I've found out, there are only two ways of fishing for men. One is to drop a grenade into the water: you might call that fishery by shock. The drawback is that you haven't always a grenade of the appropriate size and power ready to your hand. The other method is more laborious but just as certain. You weave a net. And you drag it across the pool, backwards and forwards. You won't get everything at first, but if your mesh is fine enough and you drag deeply enough, everything must come up in the end."

"Well," said Bohun. "I can quite understand why the detective story writers don't set about it in your way. They'd never get any readers."

"You're right," said Hazlerigg. "It's a damned dull process."

III

But even as he spoke the process was beginning.

Hazlerigg's orders to his assistants, given the night before, had been explicit.

To Mr. Hoffman he had said: "I want you to go through the accounts and the papers of the firm. First I want to find out if they are solvent. They look solvent, I agree, but you never know. And even if they're solvent I want to know how their profits at the present day compare with their profits—let's say, ten years ago. I don't want you to confine yourself strictly or solely to the money side of it. It's wider than that. I want a note of any bit of business which is reflected in their papers and records which seems in any way out of the ordinary; any references which aren't self-explanatory; anything which doesn't quite fit in."

Mr. Hoffman nodded. He was a qualified accountant attached to the Fraud Squad. A man who hunted down facts with the passionless pleasure of a butterfly collector and pinned them to his board with the same cold precision. His last six months had been spent investigating the affairs of two Poles who specialised in treading that narrow path which runs between bankruptcy and favourable compositions with creditors. Mr. Hoffman had dropped both these over-ingenious gentlemen into his killing-jar the week before, and was therefore luckily available to help Hazlerigg.

"I've given instructions," went on the chief inspector, "that you're to be treated as one of the firm's auditors. Any books or papers you want will be shown to you. Of course, if you find that anything is being kept from you—that'll be helpful, too."

Mr. Hoffman nodded again.

To other gentlemen Hazlerigg entrusted the detailed investigation into the lives and habits, the pasts and the presents of all the members of the firm who figured on Colley's List Two.

Into the life's history of William Hatchard Birley, a Bachelor of Laws of Oxford University, who lived in a large sunless house in St. George's Square, Pimlico, and spent a surprising proportion of his income on patent medicines.

Into the daily round of Tristram Craine, possessor of the Military Cross, father of two children and the owner of a house at Epsom.

Into the doings of Robert Andrew Horniman of Harrow School and the Royal Naval Volunteer Reserve, the passion of whose otherwise dull life was the sailing of small boats in dangerous waters.

Down into the questionable genesis of Eric Duxford, the colours of whose old school tie proved puzzling to the pundits of the Burlington Arcade, and whose expenditure seemed, contrary to Mr. Micawber's well-known dictum, to exceed his income without diminishing his bank balance.

Into the vivid past of John Ambrey Cove, whose public school had grown reluctantly but definitely tired of him in 1935, and who had spent the succeeding three years, before he became articled to Horniman, Birley and Craine, in a series of half-hearted jobs in the United States of America, Canada and Japan; who had had a markedly successful war, moving from staff to staff, keeping a step ahead of Providence and the Postings Branch of the War Office.

Into the career of Eustace Cockerill, late a sergeant in the Royal Artillery, a member of the Corps of Commissionaires, who expended such tender care over the fuchsias in the garden of his house in Muswell Hill, and had, as appeared later, another and more surprising hobby.

Nor were the ladies forgotten. From Elizabeth Cornel, of Sevenoaks, that participator in women's golf championships, via Anne Mildmay, daughter of a celebrated father, to Cissie Chittering who lived in Dulwich and spent her evenings in country dancing and decorative poker-work, and Florence Bellbas, who lived in Golder's Green but apparently had no other hobbies.

To Sergeant Plumptree, in whose unspectacular methods he had great confidence, Hazlerigg allotted an important part of the routine.

"I want to find out more about Smallbone," he said. "I want to know what sort of man he was. We've had one picture from the people who did his business for him in this office, and quite a different one from his landlady. I expect you noticed that. Which one was the truth? I want you to find out. Talk to his friends and family—"

"I don't think he's got any family, sir."

"If you go back as far as the twelfth century," said Hazlerigg gravely, "you will find that everyone in England is related to everybody else in England in at least one hundred and thirty-five different ways."

"Indeed, sir," said Sergeant Plumptree insubordinately.

He started his investigation by revisiting Wellingboro' Road; but beyond another cup of strong tea he got little that was new from Mrs. Tasker. She suggested that Sergeant Plumptree might try at some of the museums. Mr. Smallbone had been quite an enthusiast for museums. Apparently, he'd often spend his whole day there.

This did not seem to be an outstandingly hopeful idea, but for want of anything better the sergeant started on a tour of the many large museums which lie in a compact belt along the southern edge of Hyde Park and Kensington Gardens. He paid particular attention to the china and pottery sections. None of their custodians could give him any help. It appeared that all museums are full of small, earnest, elderly men who spend timeless days drifting from exhibit to exhibit, along the marble aisles.

It was late in the afternoon, and Sergeant Plumptree was very tired indeed when he arrived, on his pilgrimage from west to east, at the last and greatest of all the museums: and here he had both an inspiration and a piece of luck. At the reading-room he exhibited his card and was soon in conversation with the senior librarian. Indexes and files were produced, and with a speed which any Horniman disciple might have envied, the name of Marcus Smallbone was unearthed.

"We make them register," said the librarian, "when they first come here; a matter of routine. We can't have just anyone at all wandering in and out. And we take a reference, one reference, at least. Some of the books are valuable, you know. Can't be too careful."

In the section of the card devoted to Mr. Smallbone's references Sergeant Plumptree noted with quickening interest the names of Abel Horniman and the Reverend Eustace Evander, Vicar of St. Cuthbert's-Within-the-Minories, E.C. The librarian obligingly departed in search of an up-to-date Crockford. Sergeant Plumptree had a momentary presentiment that the Reverend Eustace might have died or been promoted Bishop of Hawaii. However, all was well. He was apparently still at his post. Plumptree took a bus for the City.

Evensong at St. Cuthbert's takes place early, to suit the convenience of the few City workers who can be induced to attend, and it was just finishing as the sergeant arrived.

The Reverend Eustace, a vast red man who had taken his college eight to the head of the river in '08, sinking outright two of the four boats which stood in his way, and had been treating the powers of darkness in the same summary manner ever since, welcomed Sergeant Plumptree with a paralysing handshake and invited him round to a cup of cocoa.

Ten minutes later they were seated in his snuggery, which was liberally adorned with school and college groups, cross-laced with oars and topped with the head of a water buffalo which had been rash enough to cross the Reverend Eustace's path on a holiday in South Africa. Sergeant Plumptree sipped at his mug of scalding cocoa and manœuvred his notebook on to his knee so that he could write unobtrusively.

"First of all," said the priest, "what is it all about?"

There seemed to be no object in suppressing the facts, so Sergeant Plumptree related the essentials of the case to his host and summarised the information that Hazlerigg had asked him to obtain.

"Well," said the clergyman, "I haven't seen Smallbone for more than a year. Tell you why in a minute. But if you want to know what sort of man he was, then I can probably give you as much help as anyone alive. I've known Marcus Smallbone for more than thirty years. We first met at the university—we were both up together at Angelus. Our tastes were rather different, but we happened to live on the same staircase, and on one occasion"—the Reverend Eustace smiled reminiscently—"I saved him from being immersed in an ornamental fountain. Six against one seemed to me heavy odds so I weighed in and—er—lent him a hand. Dear me, yes. That was a long time ago. After we had both come down we still corresponded occasionally. When I had my first London living I looked him up, and we met once or twice for a meal." He got to his feet, kicked a bull-terrier off the sofa and resumed. "The chief thing wrong with Marcus was a small settled income. Big enough to save him the trouble of earning his living, but not big enough to keep him busy looking after it. He had too much time. He used to spend a good deal of it over his collections. One year it was first editions, then it was Toby jugs. Lately, I believe, it's been pottery. He never stayed in any one branch long enough to acquire any real knowledge of it. Well, that's a harmless enough pursuit. But there was a worse side to it, I'm afraid—there's nothing to be gained by not being absolutely frank—he had rather a small and uncomfortable mind. Possibly, again, this was due to having too much time on his hands. He loved writing to the papers, you know, to expose the errors of authors, or to call rather malicious attention to discrepancies in the statements of public men. These people were fair enough game, I suppose, but it didn't stop there. I can only give you one example of this, because it's the only one that came personally to my knowledge, but about two years ago a fellow parson of mine got into bad trouble with the bishop. He was lucky to keep his cloth. I won't tell you the details—but the information on which the bishop acted came from Smallbone—"

Sergeant Plumptree nodded. He didn't need to be told that this information was important. It opened, in fact, a startling vista. But there was a question which had to be asked and he found it difficult to frame it. The Reverend Evander saved him the trouble.

"I know what you're thinking," he said, "and you can put it right out of your mind. Smallbone was *not* a blackmailer. That wasn't the way his mind worked at all. He'd ferret around unearthing these awkward and unsavoury facts, but he didn't expose them for gain. I don't know why he did it. It's a question that won't be answered now, this side of Judgment. Get off that sofa, Bungy, or I'll brain you. Partly, as I said, it was not having enough to occupy himself with. It's a terribly true tag about Satan and idle hands. Partly, I think, it was because that sort of business gratifies an overdeveloped sense of self-importance. Have another mug of cocoa, sergeant? That's right. I can't think why people should glorify beer at the expense of cocoa. It was that hearty vulgarian, Chesterton, who started it…"

IV

A thousand miles to the south.

Although it was only mid-March the sun of Central Italy already had power in it. Il Sergente Rosso, of the Carabinieri Reali, district of Florence, sub-station of Arrugia, sweated and grumbled as he wheeled his black-painted bicycle up the steep hill from the Arno Valley to the upland village of La Chioccola.

It was a Sunday and it was a fiesta: one of the many fiestas which bestar the Italian Catholic year. At lunch in the sub-station there had been consumed, besides the inevitable pasta schuta, lamb, a rare delicacy, and great square wedges of Monte Nero cheese. Wine had been drunk. Sergeant Rosso sweated.

Nevertheless, he persevered. There was a certain measure of pride in the perseverance. It was not every day that appeals for help came from England to the police of the sub-station of Arrugia. Prestige was involved. And beside and above all this, Sergeant Rosso was a friend of the English. Had he not fought, in the black days of 1944, as a member of *the partigiani*? Had he not shared in the triumphs of 1945? Had not the very bicycle which he was wheeling been stolen from the Royal Corps of Signals?

Sergeant Rosso sweated but persevered.

Presently he reached the iron gate and white walls of the Villa Carpeggio, and five minutes later he was in official converse with Signora Bonaventura. He produced for her inspection a photograph and a card. Signora Bonaventura laughed over the one and clucked over the other. Certainly she recognised the photograph. It was Signor Smolbon, who stood apart from all other Englishmen in her memory, in that he was of a reasonable size. Not two metres high and one metre broad, like most Englishmen. But of reasonable stature: smaller, almost, than an Italian. But to say that he owned *her* house! She examined the card and clucked again. Certainly, he had stayed there for some weeks—two months, perhaps, in the previous summer. He had visited the galleries of Florence, and had purchased a number of earthenware cooking utensils of doubtful value. She had not seen him since, nor heard of him. What was it that brought the sergeant on his mission? So! Signor Smolbon was dead. *Santa Maria!* All must come to it.

A thousand miles to the north.

Sergeant Plumptree called on the secretary to the Bishop of London. He referred briefly to the circumstances outlined to him by the Reverend Eustace Evander. The secretary was able to reassure him. The clergyman concerned in the incident was now on missionary work in China; he had been out of England for more than a year. Sergeant Plumptree thanked the secretary. It had not seemed to him a very hopeful line, but all lines had to be hunted out.

Meanwhile, Sergeant Plumptree's colleague, Sergeant Elvers, had visited Charing Cross and spent a tiresome hour in the stationmaster's office. All the booking-office clerks who had been on duty on the morning of Friday, February 12th, inspected a photograph of Marcus Smallbone and they all said that he looked very like a lot of people they had seen but they certainly couldn't swear that he had taken a ticket to anywhere in Kent on that particular morning. Sergeant Elvers thereupon departed to repeat the process at London Bridge, Waterloo and Victoria. One of his difficulties was that there was no station in Kent called Stanton or Stancomb.

At Maidstone, a member of the Kent Constabulary, equipped with a gazetteer, a large map, a county history and other useful books of reference, was compiling a list. Stancomb Peveril, Stancombe Basset, Stancombe Earls, Stancombe House, the Stancombe Arms, Stanton-le-Marsh, Stanton Heath, Staunton, Staunston-cum-Cliffe...

So the little wheels clicked and the spindles bobbed and curtsied, and the mesh was woven.

V

"The monetary position would seem, at first sight, to be fairly straightforward," reported Mr. Hoffman that evening. "Under the Articles of Partnership the total net profits of the firm—and by that I mean, of all the allied firms—are to be divided into ten equal shares. Of these shares Abel Horniman took four, Mr. Birley three, and Mr. Craine three. The whole of Abel Horniman's share has now passed to his son, who is, I understand, his sole executor and beneficiary."

"What about the other partners—Ramussen and Oakshott and those people?"

"They are salaried partners only."

"I see. Yes. What did the total profits amount to last year?"

"After everything had been paid"—Mr. Hoffman consulted his notes—"a little short of ten thousand pounds."

"That's not an awful lot, is it," said Hazlerigg. "That would mean that Abel netted—let me see—a little under four thousand. He had that big house in Kensington to keep up—and I understand, a country house."

"A large farm-house," said Mr. Hoffman. "Almost, as you say, a small country house, with about two hundred acres of land, in Kent."

"Yes. I thought he was making rather more. How do the figures compare with ten years ago?"

"A gradual but marked decline. In 1938 the net profits were in the neighbourhood of fifteen thousand."

"But he was solvent. I take it—"

"That's not a question I can answer at once," said Hoffman cautiously. "There may be undisclosed debts. But I think that the probability is that he was solvent."

"Is there any real doubt about it?"

"Both the house in Kensington and the farm in Kent were subject to very full mortgages. No doubt, with house and farming property at their present levels, they could afford to carry them. But there was no margin in them."

"What about other assets?"

"There's just his current account at the bank. As I say, it's difficult to be precise about it at this stage. There is about four thousand pounds in it at the moment."

"I see." It didn't accord very well with Hazlerigg's notion of the senior partner of a well-known firm of solicitors. "It's a bit hand-to-mouth, isn't it? Are you sure there were no securities—no investments?"

"None that I can trace," said Mr. Hoffman. "Most of the entries in his account are self-explanatory. There is his share of the firm's profits coming in, and regular payments out for housekeeping, tradesmen, club subscriptions and so forth. It's all done very methodically. There is a quarterly payment out of £48 2s. 6d, for which I can see no immediate explanation. It may have been an insurance premium."

It was not for him to comment or speculate. He was interested only in facts. Figures were facts. And facts, if handled aright, could be considered as so many figures. They could be grouped and set in proportion; they could be added together or subtracted from each other. And someone would doubtless say what the result signified. But not Mr. Hoffman.

"I'll be quite blunt with you," said Hazlerigg. "I want to know if Abel Horniman had been embezzling money from clients. Our first idea, as you know, was that he might have been embezzling from a certain trust—the Ichabod Stokes Trust. If that trust proves to be all right, then I want equally to know about all the others. All the trusts of which Abel was trustee and the estates of which he was executor. Any place where he may have dipped his fingers into money which did not belong to him."

"The present system of solicitors' accounting," said Mr. Hoffman, "was designed to prevent that sort of fraud, or if it could not prevent it, then to bring it easily to light. I can assure you that if any such irregularity exists I shall very shortly know about it."

"I'm sure you will," said Hazlerigg. "But don't forget—Abel Horniman was a very good lawyer. He was also a methodical and painstaking man."

Mr. Hoffman said nothing. He himself was exceedingly methodical and infinitely painstaking. It was not his place to say so.

As he was going a thought occurred to the chief inspector. "That farm that Abel had. You said it was in Kent. It hadn't got a name like Stanston or Stancomb?"

"Not that I know of," said Mr. Hoffman. "As I recollect the name, it was something like Crookham—Crookham Court Farm, I think. I'll check it up for you."

"Don't trouble," said Hazlerigg. "It was just a passing thought."

VI

"I couldn't help noticing," said Eric Duxford to Bohun, "that the chief inspector confides a good deal in you. I understand that you knew him previously."

"He is the friend of a friend," said Bohun cautiously.

"Ah, yes." Eric on-offed his smile briefly. "It must be very nice to have a friend at court."

Bohun was not unduly upset by this innuendo. He was too busy speculating on what might lie behind the approach. Nor was he kept long in doubt.

"If I was the inspector," said Eric, "there's one person I should keep a very careful eye on, and that's John Cove." He leaned a bit closer and added: "I suppose you know that he was expelled from his public school for dishonesty."

"As a matter of fact, I believe he did mention it," said Bohun. "I didn't take him very seriously though. Even if it is true," he added mildly, "I can't think that it forms a very firm ground for suspecting him of murder."

"Once a bounder, always a bounder," said Eric.

"Well, I'll pass it on to the inspector."

"I thought you'd like to know."

VII

"Are you off?" said John Cove.

"I think so," said Bohun. "It's been quite a week, hasn't it?"

"Never a dull moment," said John. "I say—you seem very pally with that copper."

"Er—yes. Yes. He's a friend of a friend of mine."

"Good," said John. "Well, you can pass this on from me. If he really wants to lay his hands on the murderer, he can't do better than watch our Eric."

"Eric Duxford?"

"That's the chap. Oleaginous Eric, the only man who has been to more public schools than the Western Brothers."

"What makes you say that—not about the public schools, I mean about the murder?"

"Well," said John. "I admit it's not much to go on, but you can take it from me that he's a slippery customer. When he used to share this room with me he was always sliding out somewhere, and saying to me, 'If anyone asks where I am, tell them I'm at the Law Society,' or 'Tell them I'm examining deeds in the City.' He'd always have the excuse cut and dried. Well, that's fair enough in a way, and I expect I shall ask you to alibi me if I want to get off early or push out and have some coffee or something. But Eric was *always* doing it. I got quite browned off telling lies for him. And another thing, I believe he fiddled the petty cash—"

"Even so," said Bohun, "that's a long way from murder."

"Once a cad, always a cad," said John.

"Well," said Bohun, "I'll pass it along to Inspector Hazlerigg."

"That's the stuff," said John. "After all, even if we don't get him for murder, we may catch him for embezzlement. Well, if you're coming my way, I'll walk across with you."

They were putting on their coats when John said: "Just a second, whilst I warn Mrs. Porter. She's on with me tomorrow."

"What do you mean, 'on'?" said Bohun. "Tomorrow's Saturday."

"Of course, you only arrived on Monday, so you wouldn't know. We always keep a skeleton staff here on Saturday mornings. You know—to attend to telephone calls and deal with any important letters."

For a moment the full import of this did not strike Bohun. "Who has to do it?" he asked.

"We do it in pairs, in turn. I expect you'll be next on the list, being the new boy."

"You mean," said Henry slowly, "that on Saturday mornings there are just *two* of you in the office—one qualified man and one secretary?"

"That's the style," said John. "What's so madly exciting about it? If you're looking forward to a long Saturday morning alone with Anne Mildmay, take my tip and lay off. That girl's ginger."

"No. It wasn't that. Tell me, who opens up the office on these occasions?"

"Sergeant Cockerill. He gets here at nine, and opens everything up. Then he comes back after everyone's gone and locks up again. That's about twelve-thirty, after the mid-morning post has come in."

"Excuse me a moment," said Henry, and fled.

He found Hazlerigg on the point of departure.

"Yes," said Hazlerigg, when he had told him. "Yes. That certainly does sound promising. I'm afraid we've been wasting our time a bit. Thank you very much. Oh, and by the way, you might get me a list showing who was on duty on different weekends for the last three months."

He took up the phone and dialled a code number, asked for an extension, and found Dr. Bland in his laboratory. "Hazlerigg here. That Smallbone job. Yes. I want a re-autopsy."

The telephone said something grudging.

"Certainly it's important," said Hazlerigg. "I want to know exactly when he died. Anyway, to within a week."

This time the telephone sounded distinctly rude.

CHAPTER SEVEN

—SATURDAY AND SUNDAY—

Local Searches

I have often been told—I do not know whether it is true—that, in country cases particularly, local searches are often not made (laughter). Well, if that is so, I dare say it is all right, but it will not do in future.

A. F. TOPHAM, K.C.,

to the Solicitors' Managing Clerks' Association (1925)

I

SATURDAY MORNING IN LINCOLN'S INN WAS GENERALLY A REST-ful time. Most of the firms observed the Saturday truce, and such members as turned up were apt to appear, briefly, in loose and disreputable clothes. Contrary to the general rule, however, a good deal of quiet activity seemed to be taking place in the offices of Horniman, Birley and Craine.

True, none of the partners put in an appearance, and the only official representatives of the firm were John Cove and Mrs. Porter. But in other rooms Mr. Hoffman and his industrious assistants were poring over books and papers, only too glad of a free hand for forty-eight hours. In Bob Horniman's office Mr. Gissel pursued his patient study of the bound volumes of Law Reports. He had disposed of the courts of Queen's and King's Bench and was working his way, via Admiralty and Probate, to Divorce.

John Cove was looking unenthusiastically at the morning mail when he was surprised by a visit from Bohun.

"What on earth are you doing here?" he asked. "You needn't imagine," he went on uncharitably, "that you'll get any credit for attention to duty. None of the partners are here."

"It isn't that," said Bohun. "I want your help. You know you were talking about this weekend roster business. Can you tell me who was on duty and when—in the last few months, I mean?"

"It's all on the notice board," said John.

"Yes, I know. I've got the list here. But did it actually happen as it says or was it fiddled about?"

"The Horniman system is not susceptible to fiddling. Let me look—yes. That's about right. I was 'on' last on March 15th, and it was Tubby the week before, I remember, and Bob before him: then Eric. That would have been February 20th, and that's right, too, because he wanted me to stand in for him and I couldn't, because I had a heavy date—not that I would have done it anyway. The week before was Bill Birley, and before that, me again. You could check it with Sergeant Cockerill, of course."

"Abel Horniman didn't take a turn with the rest of you?"

"Good heavens, no. Not in my time, anyway. He may have done it in the old days."

"What about the girls—are they as stated?"

"I'm not sure," said John. "I think so. I say, what's it all about? Are we supposed to have murdered the old boy on a Saturday morning?"

"Well—I—"

"Not a bad idea at that," said John. "The office would be nice and quiet. Supplies a motive too. I mean, any client who comes to see you on a Saturday morning is really asking for trouble, isn't he?"

II

Sat., Feb. 13th	Mr. Birley and Miss Chittering
Sat., Feb. 20th	Mr. Duxford and Miss Cornel
Sat., Feb. 27th	Mr. R. Horniman and Miss Mildmay
Sat., March 6th	Mr. Craine and Miss Bellbas

"That's far enough," said Hazlerigg. "Until we get a re-autopsy. Bland said that Smallbone had been dead at least six weeks and he always errs on the side of caution. It gives quite enough scope as it is. In fact, unless Bland can be more definite it doesn't take us much further than List Two."

"It lets out John Cove."

"It would seem to do so," agreed Hazlerigg cautiously. "Has the list been checked?"

"Not exactly. Cove says the male side of it is right."

"Does he now?" The inspector regarded the eight names thoughtfully, clothing each set of symbols with its living flesh.

"If you accept this idea," said Bohun diffidently, "about the murder being committed on a Saturday morning, does it mean that it must have been a joint effort by two people?"

"Not necessarily. It depends a little on the Saturday routine. Let's get in young thingummy and ask him about it."

"John Cove?"

"Yes. He ought to be able to help us."

"You're accepting his innocence as proved?"

"Not a bit of it," said the inspector cheerfully. "I'm only going to ask him some questions. If he tells us the truth then we know what we want. If he doesn't, then that's interesting, too, isn't it?"

John Cove was apparently a candid witness. He said: "I'm not sure how other people manage it. When I'm on duty I turn up about half-past ten. Sergeant Cockerill gets here first and opens the offices, and takes in the post and sorts it out and so on. When I arrive, or the girl, whichever turns up first, that's the signal for the sergeant to push off. I don't know what time he gets back to lock up, because, speaking personally, I'm always gone by then. About half-past twelve, I think, or perhaps one o'clock."

"And when do you leave?"

"That all depends what my programme is," said John frankly. "I have been away as early as half-past eleven. But it's usually a bit later than that. Say midday."

"And does the typist get away at the same time, or later?"

"Usually about the same time. Earlier if anything. There's not much for her to do really. She takes a note of any telephone calls, and she might have to type a couple of letters. The man who's on duty on Saturday is supposed to read everything that comes in, and deal with anything absolutely urgent. So far as I'm concerned I usually decide it can wait over till Monday."

"Well, now, what do we get out of all that?" said Hazlerigg, when the door had shut behind John Cove.

"It looks," said Bohun diffidently, "as if the scheme would work out quite well for a man, but it would be very risky for a woman. I mean, for instance, Mr. Birley could easily have arranged an appointment with Smallbone for midday. At a quarter to twelve he would tell the typist that there was nothing more to be done, and that she could depart—a hint she would be happy enough to take, I expect. This would give him an absolutely safe forty-five minutes, or perhaps an hour, before Sergeant Cockerill came back to lock up."

"Yes, I think that's fair enough. Or if he wanted to avoid suspicion altogether he could leave the office at the same time as the girl—he could easily slip back again as soon as the coast was clear."

"But if one of the girls was planning the job"—Bohun considered the idea—"it wouldn't be impossible, but the risks would be bigger. She'd have to take a chance on the man leaving early, and then come back herself. Besides, could she get Smallbone to the office at the time she wanted him—?"

"There's nothing much in that," said Hazlerigg. "She'd only have to telephone him and pretend to be speaking on behalf of one of the partners. 'Mr. Birley wants to see you at the office. Would twelve o'clock on Saturday be possible?' That sort of thing. She'd have to accept the risk that he might check back on the appointment."

Hazlerigg leaned back again, and treated himself to another bout of swivelling. It was a lovely chair.

"There's one thing we get out of this weekend business," he said at last. "I don't know whether you've spotted it, but I think it explains the rather curious method of concealing the body. What puzzled me before about this choice of hiding-place was this—that the body was certain to be discovered in the end. It was a fair chance that it might be several weeks before anyone opened any individual deed box. From that point of view the particular box was rather well chosen, for as I understand it, the Ichabod Stokes Trust was a matter in which Abel Horniman did most of the work himself and, as he was ill, it was the least likely to be disturbed. We can see now that all the murderer was concerned with was that the body should not come to light *too soon*. It had to stay hidden just long enough to make it uncertain which weekend was the fatal one."

III

"Excuse me, Inspector."

"Of course. Come in."

"You wanted to know at once if I found anything at all…"

"Certainly."

"It's only a small thing."

Mr. Hoffman held in his hand two receipts.

"I found them among some miscellaneous papers belonging to Abel Horniman."

Hazlerigg read the first. "Dear Mr. Horniman, I write to thank you for your cheque £15 0s. 0d. which arrived safely today and very welcome. Thanking you once again for your great kindness and hoping you are keeping well. Ada Groot (Mrs.)." The second was in similar terms and was signed by Clarissa Holding.

"What about them?"

"Three things," said Mr. Hoffman primly. "First, I can't find any record of any client of the name of Groot or Holding. And it ought to be easy to locate any client, with the system they've got here. Secondly, I can't find any record in the books of these particular payments having been made. Thirdly—well, look at the date. March 29th. The receipt says: 'Your cheque which arrived today.' So it must have been posted on March 28th."

"You mean—?"

"I mean," said Mr. Hoffman slowly, "that Abel Horniman died on March 15th."

"Yes," said Hazlerigg. "That's quite a point. What's your idea? Do you think they are faked receipts? Cover for some payment that was never made?"

"I should require more positive evidence before committing myself to a definite assertion—"

"And a very proper Civil Service reply," said Hazlerigg. "However, there's one place we might look for corroboration, if you haven't done so already." He led the way out into the secretaries' office. "All these secretaries keep address books. Try Miss Cornel's."

One theory fell to the ground at once. Both Mrs. Groot and Miss Holding were in the book.

"They both live at Sevenoaks. The same street, too," said Hazlerigg thoughtfully. "Sevenoaks. Now isn't that where—yes, of course it is. Miss Cornel herself has a habitation at Sevenoaks. Is that only the arm of coincidence or is it something more sinister? We will send Sergeant Plumptree down there. Get hold of Mr. Cove, Hoffman, and find out Miss Cornel's address."

Mr. Cove, who was busy in his office, managed to disengage his attention from his six-away forecasts long enough to oblige with Miss Cornel's address.

Inspector Hazlerigg telephoned Sergeant Plumptree with a fresh set of instructions, and went back to Scotland Yard in the hope of securing a few moments' conversation with Dr. Bland. In one of the basement rooms—the one used by Mr. Prince, the litigation clerk, Mr. Hoffman made a final note in his meticulous handwriting, cast a couple of columns of figures and then re-cast them absent-mindedly, closed the books and went home to a vegetarian lunch.

Mr. Gissel finished with the last volume of the reported cases from the Judicial Committee of the Privy Council and straightened

his aching back. He thought that it was all very probably a waste of time, but it didn't do to leave anything undone. He had once hanged a man by finding a single strand of wool caught in the join of a lavatory seat.

In his room John Cove listened to these sounds of diminishing activity. Twelve had struck some time ago from the Temple Church and Mrs. Porter had long been dismissed to her flat and her husband at Bow. At last he got to his feet and set out on a careful tour of the offices. It was as he had thought. They were empty.

John consulted his watch again.

Sergeant Cockerill, he knew, would be back at any time between half-past twelve and a quarter to one. He had, therefore, twenty minutes.

With rather a malicious smile on his face he made his way into the room next to his own—the one normally occupied by Eric Duxford.

Once inside he slipped the catch and started to search. In deference to what he had observed of Mr. Gissel's methods he took the trouble to put on a pair of wash-leather gloves and wore them throughout the proceedings.

A knowledge of Horniman routine saved him a certain amount of trouble, and he paid only nominal attention to the card index, the neat rows of folders and the stack of black deed boxes.

"It's the desk or nothing," said John to himself, and without more ado he sat himself down in Eric's chair and started to pull open the drawers. The bottom ones on either side of the knee-hole contained the usual jetsam of a lawyer's office—old appointment diaries, prints of the National Conditions of Sale, apportionment tables, a paper-knife (put out as an advertisement by an enterprising Law stationer), a carton of saccharine tablets, several sets of

auction particulars, a small box of legal seals, a number of rubber bands and the endless lengths of red tape which coil, Laocoön-like, through the pigeon-holes of any solicitor's desk.

Only one drawer was locked: the one in the top left-hand corner: and finding this circumstance suspicious, John immediately devoted his whole attention to it. Like Sergeant Cockerill, he was of the opinion that opening locks with bent pieces of wire was an operation confined almost entirely to fiction. First, therefore, he tried all his own keys in the lock, only stopping when he had nearly jammed one of them on the pivot. "And it wouldn't look too good if I had to leave half a key broken off in the lock," he reflected. "I think perhaps the time has come for some brute force and bloody ignorance." He examined the office fire-irons with an eye to their felonious possibilities, but finally left the room and went downstairs, bringing back with him a strong, stubby spade used by Sergeant Cockerill for shovelling coke.

He inserted the steel end, which fortunately had worn both flat and thin, into the space between the top of the desk and the drawer, and leaned downwards on the handle. The result was excellent. There was a sharp crack and the whole of the top of the desk came up three inches. Keeping his weight on the spade John used one hand to slip the drawer open under its now ineffective lock.

The only thing in the drawer was a book, which he saw, when he'd taken it out, was an appointment diary for that year. This didn't seem very promising and John was on the point of putting it back when a further idea occurred to him. He searched round among the papers on Eric Duxford's desk and presently unearthed another similar diary. This second one was clearly used for ordinary office appointments. John looked through it quickly, recognising the names of several clients.

"Then what the hell's the other one?" said John. He picked it up carefully and walked over to the window. At first sight it seemed very similar. Times were noted on various days in the weeks just gone by, only here, instead of names, were sets of initials. H.V.S. cropped up in most of the entries. Against February 20th was "H.V.S. and self to see C.P.G.", and later, "H.V.S. to see M.L. I am to see him next Tuesday if possible." John turned the page to next Tuesday which was, in fact, the Tuesday of the previous week. Sure enough, against 3 p.m. was the entry, "M.L. re 20 H.G." The only other notable point about the entries was that a lot of them seemed to be rather late at night; 8 p.m. and 9 p.m. were favourite times.

"Damned suspicious," said John. "Obviously comes back here after everyone else has gone." He slipped the book into the drawer and withdrew the spade. The top settled back quite comfortably. John cleaned off the marks as well as he could.

"I wonder," he said to himself, "if I ought to tell the inspector about this. Rather a pity to spoil the fun. I can always tell him later if it turns out to be serious. Better put this spade away before Cockerill comes back."

As he left the office he noticed that the time was a quarter to one.

IV

Scotland Yard, like the British Army, is fond of its weekends. But once war has been declared even Sundays are apt to go by the board. Sergeant Plumptree caught the two o'clock train from Charing Cross and, after a leisurely progress, arrived at Tubs Hill, Sevenoaks, shortly before three. It was a warm afternoon, with April beginning to relent towards May, and enthusiasts were already out for a net on the Vine cricket ground.

A lot of Sergeant Plumptree's troubles would never have occurred if he had managed to secure the proper address of either of the ladies he was visiting. The receipts unearthed by Mr. Hoffman had both said "Styleman Road, Sevenoaks". No number in either case. Sergeant Plumptree debated for a moment the advisability of going to the police station and looking at the householders' list, but then thought better of it. After all, he reflected, Groot and Holding weren't terribly common names. Also he was in plain clothes, and if he went to the police station it would mean presenting his credentials and giving a long account of what he was up to: also, whilst Styleman Road was conveniently close to the railway the police station was uphill and at the other end of the town; also it was a hot day.

Fortunately, Styleman Road was not a very long thoroughfare— one large house at the near end, and about fifteen small houses on either side. Sergeant Plumptree selected one of these at random and knocked. The door was flung open at once by a lady of inde-terminate age. Her light yellow hair was cut in a page-boy bob, and she was wearing a smock.

"Oh, I beg your pardon," said Sergeant Plumptree, with well-simulated surprise. "My fault entirely. I thought this was Mrs. Groot's house."

"That's right," said the lady.

"Oh, I see. What a bit of luck." Sergeant Plumptree wished that thirty-to-one chances came off as frequently on the race course.

"Are you Mrs. Groot?"

"That's right."

"I wonder if I might have a word with you."

"Yes."

"Shall we go inside. It's rather a confidential matter."

"Very well," said the lady. "Come into the parlour and be confidential in there."

She led the way into the front room, folded up on to the edge of a chair, and planted her hands, in a masculine manner, on her knees. Since she had not invited him to sit, Sergeant Plumptree, who was punctilious in these matters, remained standing.

"I wonder," he began, "if you could help us. We are enquiring about a Mr. Smallbone—"

"Oh, yes." Either she had never heard the name or was a fine natural poker player.

"I don't suppose you've heard of him?"

"Oh yes, I have," said the lady. "Often."

"You have! I wonder if you could tell me when you saw him last?"

The lady pursed her lips and opened them slightly, closed both eyes and then said faintly:

"The day before yesterday."

Fortunately, at this point, Sergeant Plumptree's system was spared further shocks by the arrival of a nurse, who led him out into the hall.

"Is she—er—?"

"Yes," said the nurse. "She is. Sometimes it's worse than other times."

"I'm very sorry to hear it." Some explanation, he felt, was necessary. "A friend asked me to look Mrs. Groot up—"

"Her name isn't Groot."

"She said—"

"She'd say anything. That's the form it takes. She told the postman yesterday that she was Mrs. Roosevelt."

"I see."

"As a matter of fact her name is Lemon."

Sergeant Plumptree found himself outside.

The next house he tried was either empty, or its inhabitants were all asleep. He crossed the road, walked along a few yards, and tried again.

This time a small shrewd, grey-haired woman answered the door and denied any knowledge of Mrs. Groot or Miss Holding. What number did they live at? Sergeant Plumptree was afraid he didn't know. What did they look like then? Sergeant Plumptree didn't know that either. The grey-haired woman said it was a pity he hadn't obtained a little more information before he had started. Sergeant Plumptree agreed and took himself out into the street once again. The grey-haired lady looked thoughtfully after him and then picked up the telephone.

Accordingly, when Sergeant Plumptree came out of the next house but two, and was beginning to doubt the existence of Mrs. Groot and Miss Holding, he found himself face to face with a member of the Kent Constabulary, who opened the conversation with a request for a sight of his identity card.

So he had to walk up the hill to the police station after all.

When they discovered who he was, the Sevenoaks police were, of course, helpful. They were also amused, and made little attempt to disguise their amusement. "'Suspicious character', according to our Miss Parkins," said the station inspector, "'snooping round the houses, with a very unlikely story about some ladies who lived there.' What were the names? Groot and Holding. Just take a look in the householders' register. No, no one of that name. That's an up-to-date list, too. You're sure you weren't mistaken in the name of the road?"

"No. It was Styleman Road right enough," said Sergeant Plumptree absently. His thoughts were elsewhere. *If* there was no Groot and no Holding in Styleman Road was that not in itself significant? Might the fiasco not have served a useful purpose? It certainly looks as if those two receipts—but wait a bit, the addresses *had* been in Miss Cornel's book. That fact began to assume an interest of its own.

"I think I'll make another call," he said. "Miss Cornel—Red Roofs—I understand that it's a bungalow out on the Wrotham Road."

"That's the one," said the inspector. "Would you like me to send a man with you?"

"Thank you very much," said Sergeant Plumptree with dignity, "but I think I can manage this by myself."

He found Red Roofs without difficulty and Miss Cornel driving a mower across a well-disciplined lawn. A few words with her cleared up quite a number of misconceptions.

"Mrs. Groot and Miss Holding? Yes, of course I know them. They both live in that corner house in Styleman Road—the large one. You probably noticed it. It calls itself the Rochester Homes. It's an almshouse, really, only they're both a bit shy about admitting it. I expect that's why they just put Styleman Road on their letters."

"I see," said Sergeant Plumptree. "Could you explain what these payments were?"

"Why on earth do you want to know?"

"The inspector asked me to check up," murmured Sergeant Plumptree. "Apparently he found the receipts and wondered—"

"What snoops you are," said Miss Cornel. It was difficult to tell whether she was annoyed or amused. "Well, if you'd looked far enough you'd have found three or four others—there's a Mr. Abetts, of Northampton, a Miss Mutch and a Mrs. Hopper, of Melset, and—let me see—yes, a Miss Percy, of Potters Bar."

"And who are these persons, miss?"

"They're a private charity. Abel Horniman had certain sums of money left him, from time to time, which he could spend at his absolute discretion. It wasn't very much—the income amounted to three or four hundred pounds a year. That was how he spent it. All those people have been servants or governesses in big families, and they're all in what is commonly called reduced circumstances. Mr. Horniman used to divide the money among them—it amounted to about sixty pounds a year each. I acted as unofficial almoner. I used to send them their money each quarter, and I'd visit them when I could. Particularly Mrs. Groot and Miss Holding, being almost on my doorstep."

"I see, miss."

"I observe in your eye a barely-suppressed desire to check all this up," said Miss Cornel. "I'll give you the addresses of the other four to write down in your notebook. And you might call on Mrs. Groot and Miss Holding on your way to the station. Ask for the matron and mention my name."

"Thank you," said Sergeant Plumptree. "I'll do that."

It was late when he got back to London, but he found Inspector Hazlerigg at his desk. When Plumptree had finished his account the inspector took out a sheet of paper headed "Ideas". It contained a list of numbered items. The inspector crossed one of them out.

CHAPTER EIGHT

—MONDAY—

Discovery of a Document

Women never reason, and therefore they are (comparatively) seldom wrong. They judge instinctively of what falls under their immediate observation or experience, and do not trouble themselves about remote or doubtful consequences. If they make no profound discoveries, they do not involve themselves in gross absurdities.

HAZLITT: *Characteristics*

I

MR. BIRLEY STARTED THE DAY IN A BAD TEMPER. He was never at his best on Monday mornings. He regarded the presence of the police in the office as a personal affront; and his outlook had not been improved by a masochistic weekend among the newspapers.

Accounts of the Lincoln's Inn murder were, in fact, less numerous and circumstantial than they might have been; this was partly due to shortage of space and partly to the climax of the Association Football season.

However, one paper had rubbed salt into his wounds by speaking of "the firm of Horniman, Barley and Craine", and the *Sunday Scribe*, which ought to have known better, had referred to them as "the well-known firm of divorce lawyers". (It was true that Horniman's had recently abandoned their pre-war niceness in this matter—as had most of their professional brethren—and the firm now clutched out occasionally at the lucrative hem of the goddess of matrimonial discord; but well-known divorce lawyers! Good God, people would be coupling their names with —— and —— next.)

And then, no sooner had he reached the office, than Inspector Hazlerigg had come asking for him, with impertinent questions about a Mrs. Groot, and a Miss Holding, and a Miss Someone-or-other else. Questions, too, which Mr. Birley found himself annoyingly unable to answer.

"Now look here, Inspector," he said, in his most intimidating voice, "I can understand that you have to ask questions about this—er—death, and about Smallbone, and his affairs and so on. But questions about the private workings of my firm, I cannot and will not tolerate. If you persist in wasting my time and my staff's time in investigating matters which have no possible connection with this—er—death, then I shall have no alternative but to speak to the Commissioner—close personal friend of mine."

"I am here," said Inspector Hazlerigg without heat and without rancour, "to investigate a murder. I shall question whom I like when I like and about what I like. If you inconvenience me in any way I shall apply for an order to close this building, and no business will be able to be transacted until I have finished my investigation. And if you would like a word with the Commissioner, ring Whitehall 1212 and ask for extension nine. I will see that you get put through."

"Oh, well—ah—hum—really," said Mr. Birley. "I don't want to be obstructive."

When Hazlerigg had gone he sent for Bob.

"Who are these Groots and Holdings?"

"I've just been asking Miss Cornel," said Bob. "It's quite all right. They're beneficiaries under Colonel Lincoln's discretionary will trusts. You know he left Dad about five thousand to use the income as he thought fit—"

"Whether or not it is quite all right," said Mr. Birley heavily, "I cannot say, since I have never been favoured with a sight of the will in question…"

"I'll get Miss Cornel to look you out a copy."

"If you please. I was about to add that as head of the firm I might perhaps expect to have been informed—"

"Well, I—"

"Your father saw fit to make you his sole beneficiary. That, of course, was entirely his affair. He also handed over to you, as he had power to do under our Articles of Partnership, his full share in this firm. In my opinion, and if you will excuse my saying so, that was a mistake. But it does not alter the fact that I have certain rights as the senior partner."

"Of course," said Bob.

"And another thing. I notice you lean a great deal on Miss Cornel. She is an admirable person in her way, but when all is said and done, she is only an employee—"

"Miss Cornel," said Bob, flushing a little, "was very attached to my father. She is also extremely useful to me. Neither fact seems to constitute any very good reason for wanting to get rid of her."

"I wasn't suggesting that we got rid of her," said Mr. Birley coldly. "But it is not a good thing for anyone to get too fixed in their routine. Supposing we made a change. Miss Cornel might work for Mr. Craine and you could have Miss Mildmay."

The blood rushed to Bob's face, and departed again as suddenly, leaving him white.

Fortunately Mr. Birley, who was in the full tide of oratory, noticed nothing.

"You know what we used to say in the army," he went on. "It's a bad officer who allows himself to be run by his N.C.O.s."

Mr. Birley's experience of the army was, in fact, confined to one year in the R.A.S.C., which he had joined in 1917 when it became clear that it was either that or conscription into the infantry, and Bob toyed for a moment with the unkind idea of reminding him of it.

Seeing no point in provoking hostilities, he said something non-committal and got out of the room.

Mr. Birley then rang for Miss Chittering, and as soon as she got inside the room started to dictate a lengthy lease at high speed. Miss Chittering was a competent shorthand-typist, but no one other than a contortionist could have taken down dictation at the speed at which Mr. Birley was speaking. As soon as she was forced to ask for a repetition Mr. Birley snapped at her and increased his speed.

Five minutes of this treatment was sufficient to reduce Miss Chittering to tears and to restore a certain amount of Mr. Birley's *amour-propre*.

II

In the secretaries' room Anne Mildmay and Miss Cornel, faintly assisted by Miss Bellbas, were trying to sort out the weekend roster for Bohun's benefit.

"I'm sure," said Anne, consulting a small diary, "that I came in on February 27th, because that was the day after my admiral took me out to the Criterion and tried to get me tight on gin."

"Who's your admiral?" said Miss Bellbas.

"A friend of father's," said Anne. "He's over ninety. He

commanded a gunboat in the Crimea. He's been trying to rape me ever since I left school."

"My goodness," said Miss Bellbas. "What a persistent man."

"So I remember perfectly well, I had a hangover like nobody's business. Every time the telephone went I felt like screaming."

"It was me the Saturday before. That's right, anyway," said Miss Cornel. "It shouldn't have been my turn at all, you remember, but Cissie asked me to take it for her. I can't think why—"

"Possibly she had a date," suggested Henry.

This suggestion was greeted with a certain amount of levity, but Miss Bellbas said: "Do you know, I believe Miss Chittering has got a boy-friend."

"Nonsense," said Miss Cornel. "She doesn't know one end of a man from the other."

"Then why does she come up to town on Saturday mornings? She lives right out at Dulwich."

"Shopping," suggested Henry.

"Don't be so Victorian," said Miss Mildmay. "Girls don't spend their Saturday mornings shopping in the West End. They do all that during their lunches."

"Where did you see her?" asked Miss Cornel.

"In the Strand, about twelve o'clock. I believe he works in a shop opposite Charing Cross, and she comes up and meets him when he gets off at midday on Saturdays."

"Oh! A counter-jumper. She's welcome to him."

"Anne. You're a snob."

"Certainly," said Miss Mildmay with composure.

"Be that as it may," said Henry. "Can anyone tell me about the other Saturdays."

"What do you want to know all this for?" asked Miss Cornel.

"Don't be silly," said Miss Mildmay. "It's Hawkeye the Inspector. He thinks we murdered the little man on a Saturday morning."

She said this lightly enough, but Bohun thought he detected a very slight edge of strain in her voice, an artificial lightness which was not so very far from the fringe of hysteria.

The others evidently noticed something as well, and there was an awkward silence, broken as usual by Miss Bellbas, who said with alarming frankness:

"I didn't murder him."

"Of course you didn't, Florrie," said Miss Cornel. "If you had you'd have told us all about it, immediately afterwards. What are the other weekends you've got on your little list? Saturday 13th—well, that was Cissie, of course. She did mine, in return for me doing hers. March 6th, that would have been you, Florrie."

"Oh, dear. I expect so," said Miss Bellbas. "If the list says me, then that's right. All I know is, I did my own turn."

"Who was it with?"

"Mr. Craine."

"That's right, according to the list," said Miss Cornel.

"I don't expect you'd forget a long morning spent alone with Tubby," said Anne. "It's a thing that lingers in a girl's memory. Did he make you sit very close on his left-hand side so that every time he opened his desk drawer he practically undressed you?"

"Good gracious, no," said Miss Bellbas. "Is that what he does to you?"

"Of course," said Miss Cornel. "It's all right, though, isn't it—he went to Marlborough."

"Well," said Anne. "What about that time he took you to the station in a taxi after the staff dinner?"

Henry withdrew.

III

"My husband's a jockey, a jockey, a jockey, my husband a jockey is he,"
sang Mr. Cove. "All day he rides horses, rides horses, rides horses—"

"Mr. Cove."

"Yes, my love."

"There's a man to see you," said Miss Bellbas.

"What sort of man, heart of my heart?"

"A little man, with grey hair."

"Indeed?"

"Mr. Cove."

"Yes, my sweet."

"You oughtn't to say things like that."

"Good God!" said John. "I only said 'Indeed'."

"You said 'my love' and 'my sweet', and something about your
heart. You oughtn't to say that to me unless you're in love with me."

"But I am," said John. "Madly."

Miss Bellbas considered this.

"Then why don't you ask me to marry you?"

"I would," said John, "but—please don't tell anyone, it's not a
thing I want generally known—I'm married already."

"Who to?" said Miss Bellbas.

"A female taxing master in Chancery," said John. "Show the gentleman in, there's a dear. You mustn't keep the aristocracy waiting."

"He said his name was Mr. Brown."

"That's just his incognito," explained John. "It's the Earl of
Bishopsgate."

The gentleman whom Miss Bellbas brought in certainly didn't
look like an earl. His salient features were, as she had said, smallness
and greyness. He looked not unlike a little beaver. John addressed

him as Brown and gave him a number of instructions which were accepted with servility. At the end of the interview a couple of pound notes were pushed across the table and the stranger departed, almost colliding, on his way out, with Mr. Bohun.

Henry, however, was too occupied with his own troubles to ask any questions.

"What unsatisfactory witnesses girls are," he said. "I've spent about half an hour with them and I'm still not absolutely certain who came in on what day."

"If it's your precious list you're worrying about," said John, "you needn't. It's all right. I've asked Sergeant Cockerill."

"Good," said Henry absently. He was still thinking about that curious little incident in the secretaries' room.

"Do you know Anne Mildmay well?" he asked abruptly.

"No," said John. "But it's not for want of trying. I rather went for her at one time, you know."

He sounded serious. Henry looked at him for a moment and then said: "Yes, a very nice girl."

"There's a certain lack of conviction in your tone," said John. "But don't apologise. Anne is that type. Either she gets you completely, or she leaves you cold. Cove on Love.

"Anyway," he went on, "I left *her* cold. She didn't allow me any doubts about that. If she didn't actually throw a lump of mud in my eye, that's only because it wasn't a muddy day. I then behaved in the most traditional manner, and went out and got roaring tight, and finished up in the fountain in Trafalgar Square and spent the night at Bow Street. Since then we've been fairly good friends."

"I see," said Henry. He hadn't invited the confidence, and he felt no scruple in docketing it for future reference. There was a point of chronology which it might be useful to confirm.

Later that morning the opportunity presented itself. John had gone out to examine deeds and Bob Horniman, dropping in to borrow a volume of Prideaux, stopped to chat.

"You were in School House, too, weren't you?" he said.

"Years ago," said Bohun. "I'd be lying if I said I remembered you."

"Well, that's a good thing, anyway," said Bob. "I remember you very well. You were aloof, thin, scholarly and mysterious."

"Good God!" said Bohun. "I expect I was covered with spots as well, but you're too kind to say so."

"How are you finding it here?"

"Splendid, thank you," said Bohun. "Never a dull moment, really."

"We can't guarantee a corpse a week. How's the work? I expect it's all quite easy. With your Final only just over you've probably got everything in your head."

There was a note of envy in his voice, and Bohun guessed that the responsibilities of partnership might be sitting shakily on an almost complete lack of technical knowledge.

"Here a bit and there a bit," said Bohun. "I'd hate to have to go through with my articles again. That really was uncomfortably like hard work. John Cove seems to bear up all right, though."

"John's a good chap," said Bob. "And not nearly such a fool as he makes out. If only he found things a bit more difficult he might have to work a bit harder—which wouldn't do him any harm. It's that fatal charm of his—"

"A charm," said Bohun, "which Miss Mildmay appears to have been the only person in the office capable of resisting."

He perpetrated this thundering indiscretion deliberately, turning his back on Bob as he did so. The glass front of the bookcase made a convenient reflector.

The shot went home with surprising effect. On Bob's face, in the fleeting, reflected glimpse which he allowed himself, Bohun saw a look which he had no difficulty in recognising. Half of it was made up of possession and the other half of apprehension.

A small section of the puzzle fell neatly into its place.

"Why do you say that?" Bob made a perfunctory effort to sound casual.

"Really," said Bohun. "I'm afraid that was very indiscreet of me. I imagined that it was public knowledge—from the way he discussed it with me."

"John and Anne—Miss Mildmay."

"Yes. Apparently she turned him down. It was unforgivable of me. If I hadn't thought that you knew, I should never have mentioned it."

"No, I didn't know."

"You'll oblige me very much, then," said Bohun, "by forgetting all about it."

"Of course," said Bob. "Naturally."

"Liar," said Henry. But this was to himself, after Bob had left the room.

IV

Mr. Birley, having disposed of Miss Chittering, looked round for fresh conquests. After a moment's thought he rang the bell and summoned Mr. Prince to his presence.

Mr. Prince, who has already flitted vaguely on the outskirts of the story, was an elderly Common Law clerk. He had spent his professional life with the firm of Cockroft, Chasemore and Butt, whom he had served efficiently, and on the whole happily, for forty years. Unfortunately the firm had failed to survive the war and Mr. Prince had found himself thrown on the labour market. Bill Birley had snapped him up gratefully, made full use of him and paid him a good deal less than he was worth. Since Mr. Prince stood in considerable awe of Mr. Birley, and in even greater fear of losing his job, he was a very convenient whipping-block. Mr. Birley reduced him to a state of quivering impotence in something less than five minutes, and then clumped downstairs to plague Mr. Waugh, the cashier.

Mr. Waugh had heavier reserves than Mr. Prince, but was at the disadvantage of only having been a fortnight in the firm. It was not long before Mr. Birley had cornered him into admitting several small breaches of the Horniman routine. Using these as his text he proceeded to preach Mr. Waugh a pungent sermon on the virtues of Order and Method.

Mr. Hoffman, who was working at a table in the cashier's room, was a silent spectator. When Mr. Birley had taken himself off he added at the foot of the account he was casting, a note in his meticulous handwriting. It seemed to cause him some amusement.

V

"You seem to be a bit off colour, Miss Mildmay."

"Yes, Mr. Craine."

"Not sickening for anything, I hope."

"I hope not, Mr. Craine."

"I expect you've been put out by all these unpleasant goings-on in the office. You mustn't let it get you down, you know."

"No, Mr. Craine."

"Anyhow. It's obviously nothing to do with you. We shan't begin to suspect a little girl like you of running round committing murders. Ha, ha."

"I feel like it sometimes," said Miss Mildmay, moving her chair two foot further to the left.

"Dear me, I expect we all do sometimes. But, seriously, my dear, the thing is not to *worry*."

"I'm not worrying, Mr. Craine."

"That's right, then."

"And, Mr. Craine."

"Yes."

"I only mention it in case it has escaped your attention, but that's my hand you've got hold of."

"Goodness gracious, so it is. Well, now. Dear Sir, We thank you for yours of the fourteenth ultimo enclosing the draft Conveyance as amended and approved, and we are now proceeding to have the same engrossed for execution by his Lordship."

VI

Mr. Birley felt as Napoleon might have felt after the destruction of a couple of minor European monarchies and a German bishopric. His appetite was sharpened by his victories, and he was contemplating with some pleasure the approach of lunch-time. It occurred to him that there was one more recalcitrant subject to reduce to submission.

He rang the bell and sent for Bohun.

Henry was on the point of going home to his own lunch at Mrs. Magoli's, but good-naturedly took off his coat again and followed Miss Chittering.

"You want to look out," she said. "He's in an awful temper."

"Indeed," said Henry.

Mr. Birley opened fire as soon as the enemy was inside the door.

"Now, look here, Bohun," he said. "There's something I've been meaning to say to you. We pay you to attend to our business. I've no doubt you do very good work—at all events I've no information to the contrary—but I can't have you spending so much of your time talking to that policeman. Anything that must be said, go along after office hours to Scotland Yard, or wherever it may be, and say it there. You understand."

"Perfectly."

"Well, then—"

"I mean that I *understand* perfectly," explained Henry. "Whether I shall take any notice of your advice is, of course, a separate question."

For a moment Mr. Birley was almost bereft of the power of speech. Then he recovered sufficiently to say: "If I understood that as insolent I should have no alternative but to have you dismissed."

"I have no doubt you would," said Henry pleasantly. "Only I doubt if you have the power. I understand that you need the consent of both your other partners before employing or dismissing anybody. It says so in your partnership articles, so I expect it's correct. If you think that you can persuade Mr. Craine and Mr. Horniman to support you, then no doubt it would be worth trying."

"I—"

"But there's one thing I must warn you about. If you did succeed in dismissing me frivolously—out of mere temper, I mean, and not for professional incompetence or inattention to duty—then I should put the whole case in writing before the Law Society."

This time Mr. Birley really was speechless. Henry resumed, even more pleasantly: "In any case, since you pay me the lowest possible salary for a qualified man, I can't see that I should be much worse off if I did have to go. Mind you, I don't want to leave. I like it here.

It isn't every solicitor's office which has an undetected murderer working in it. Why, it's even possible that he may repeat his performance." Pausing at the door he added thoughtfully: "He might even pick a more suitable victim this time."

VII

And so, after a thoroughly unsatisfactory and irritating morning, the various components of the firm departed for their lunches: Mr. Birley and Mr. Craine to their clubs, Bob Horniman and Eric Duxford to the dining-room of the Law Society. John Cove to the less exclusive canteen of the same. Henry Bohun to his home. Mr. Prince and Mr. Waugh to a subterranean and cavernous restaurant attached to the Law Courts. Miss Cornel and Miss Mildmay to an A.B.C., and Miss Bellbas and Mrs. Porter to a Lyons. Sergeant Cockerill and Charlie ate sandwiches in the basement and Miss Chittering, who was on duty at the partners' telephone, stifled the pangs of hunger with a bag of macaroons.

Comparative silence descended on the offices of Horniman, Birley and Craine.

It was later that afternoon, in the secretaries' room, that a scene took place which was not without importance in the scheme of things. And it is sobering to reflect that the fact that it took place, and the far-reaching results which sprang from it, were directly attributable to feminine vanity.

Miss Chittering decided that the small wooden mirror screwed to the back of the door, was badly placed to fulfil the functions for which it was designed.

"It's absurd," she said, "to put a mirror where no light falls on it at all."

"I suppose it is," said Miss Cornel. "It's always been there, though," she added, as if this was a conclusive argument in a legal office.

"Anyway," said Anne, "it isn't as if any of us were such ravishing beauties that we always wanted to be looking at our faces."

The use of the first person plural did little to soften the aspersion. Miss Chittering flushed slightly and said: "If we've got a mirror we might as well put it somewhere where it's going to be some use."

"Why not put it up beside the window," said Miss Bellbas, who usually dropped in about that time for her afternoon cup of tea.

"Well, it's all the same to me," said Miss Cornel. "Only someone will have to unscrew it first. If you're so keen on the idea nip down and get hold of Sergeant Cockerill."

"Why bother the sergeant," said Miss Chittering. "It's only two tiny little screws. Look, I've got a pair of nail scissors. I'll use the tip of the—oh!"

"Bang goes one pair of nail scissors," said Miss Cornel complacently. "You know, you might just as well fetch the sergeant."

"Is there anything I can do?" said Bohun, poking his head giraffe-like over the partition.

"Cissie's broken her scissors trying to undo those screws," said Miss Mildmay. "The general idea is to move the looking-glass from behind the door to over there, beside the window."

"The task," said Bohun, "should not be beyond our combined resources. Has anyone got a large nail-file?"

"So long as you don't break it," said Miss Mildmay.

"I promise to temper vigour with discretion," said Henry. Using the butt-end he soon had the screws undone. "Now, if I may use your scissors, for a moment, Miss Chittering."

"Well, you can't make them much worse."

"Thank you." Bohun soon had two small holes bored in the woodwork beside the window, and he was on the point of inserting the screws when one of the inner doors opened and Mr. Craine poked his head out. "Oh, Bohun. I rang on the office phone for you, but I thought you must be out. I just wanted to check that address."

"So sorry," said Bohun. He deposited everything into the hands of Miss Cornel and followed Mr. Craine into his office.

"Just like men," said Miss Cornel. "Begin a job and leave it in the middle." She steadied the glass against the wall with one hand, grasped the nail-file in the other, put the screws in her mouth, and hooked a deed box into position with one foot. Having made these necessary preparations, she climbed on to the deed box, spat out one screw into her hand, placed it in the hole Bohun had made, and proceeded to line it up with as much concentration as if it had been a putt on the eighteenth green.

At this exceedingly critical moment the bell just above her head rang loudly twice, with the natural result that she dropped everything.

"Heavens, that's me," said Miss Chittering.

"Thank goodness the glass hasn't broken," said Miss Bellbas.

"What *are* you up to now," said Bohun, reappearing.

"Devil take those screws," said Miss Cornel. She was grovelling on her knees behind the deed box. "I've got one of them. The other seems to have rolled…" She scanned the wainscoting for some yards and finally gave a cry of triumph. "Yes, there it is, it's got under my desk." She poked with the nail-file. "It's no good. I can't quite get at it. It's lucky you're back, Mr. Bohun. Could you just lift the corner of the desk—"

"I suppose, sometime, I shall be allowed to do some of my own…" began Bohun. The words died.

He found himself staring, and Miss Cornel, Miss Mildmay and Miss Bellbas stared with him.

There was a very uncomfortable silence, which Bohun broke by saying:

"If I lift a little higher, could one of you pull it out carefully."

Miss Cornel bent forward, and edged out, very gingerly, the whole of a sheet of notepaper. The only part which had been visible before had been the cramped, characteristic signature: "Marcus Smallbone."

"The dead," said Miss Bellbas, with compelling simplicity, "have spoken."

"Nonsense," said Miss Cornel angrily. "It may have been written months ago—years even."

"It doesn't look very old," said Miss Mildmay.

"Well, there's one thing about it," said Miss Cornel, with the assurance of a Horniman expert. "It never came to this office—not in the ordinary way. Look—it hasn't been numbered or stamped—it hasn't even been punched for filing."

The letter was on a single sheet of cream bond notepaper, with the address, 20 Wellingboro' Road, embossed in heavy black letter printing. It was typewritten and undated. It said:

"Dear Mr. Horniman. I just write to confirm our arrangement. I will be at the office at 12.15 on Saturday. I hope that what you will have to tell me will be satisfactory."

It was signed, without any suffix: "Marcus Smallbone."

"I think this ought to go straight in to the inspector," said Henry. "Perhaps one of you would like to come along with me and explain about how it was found."

Inspector Hazlerigg read the letter without comment.

Then he handed it over to Gissel. "Let's have two or three handsome life-size portraits," he said, "and dust it over, of course, just in case. Then let Brinkman have it for the signature. I'll give him some cancelled cheques to compare it against. Oh, and you might send Plumptree out to Belsize Park to get hold of a few sheets of Smallbone's notepaper."

He then listened to Miss Bellbas's account of the discovery, and disappointed that lady bitterly by asking her no questions at all.

However, he said "Thank you" politely when she had finished and held the door open for her in, Miss Bellbas considered, a very gentlemanly way indeed.

It was later that evening, when the staff had all gone, that Hazlerigg took Bohun with him to inspect the scene of the discovery.

"First," he said, "just explain the lay-out once again. Who sits where? This desk, by the door, I suppose is Miss Mildmay's?"

"A fair deduction," said Bohun. "Being the last-comer she gets the draughtiest place for her desk. Under the window—that's Miss Chittering's. A good seat in summer but a bit draughty now. The big desk in the middle is Miss Cornel's."

The inspector made some quick measurements with a spring tape and jotted the figures down. His grey eyes passed coldly from point to point and finally came to rest on the long shelf which ran along the full length of the back of the room. There was an inch of space between the back of the shelf and the wall.

"Any paper," said the inspector, "which slipped off the back of that shelf, ought to finish up in the right place. Let's try it." He stood on a chair, and Bohun handed him three sheets of the firm's notepaper. "They're not quite as stiff as Smallbone's stuff," he said. "But here goes." Two of the pieces fluttered down on to Miss Cornel's desk. The third stayed close to the wall and planed away out of sight behind the desk. It came to rest, half upright, against the wainscoting.

"Not too good," said Bohun. "The one we found was lying flat, and almost under the front of the desk."

"Supposing it had blown off Miss Chittering's desk," said the inspector. "It was on that side, wasn't it?"

"It might," said Bohun. "It's an awfully long glide, though, isn't it? More than ten feet. It would have had to be a deuce of a wind to blow it that distance."

"I agree," said the inspector. He sat on the edge of the desk, swinging his leg and thinking.

"Did you notice anything odd about the letter?" he said at last.

"No," said Bohun, "except, as Miss Cornel noticed, that it hadn't been filed or marked. Was there anything?"

"Didn't you think," said the inspector, "that the signature was a bit high up the paper? It had the effect of cramping the rest of the letter."

"The spacing of the lines of type did look a bit amateur," agreed Bohun. "But then, I don't suppose Smallbone was much of a typist."

"No. I don't suppose he was. There was another thing, though. Did you look at the top left-hand corner of the paper?"

"No," said Bohun. "Not particularly. What should I have seen?"

"Two pin-holes," said the inspector. "A very important clue. I'm surprised you overlooked it."

Bohun would have been hard put to it to say whether the inspector was serious or not.

CHAPTER NINE

—TUESDAY—

A Matter of Execution

It often happens that Servants sent on messages are apt to stay out somewhat longer than the message requires—When you return, the Master storms, the Lady scolds; stripping, cudgelling and turning off is the Word. But here you ought to be provided with a set of excuses, enough to serve on all occasions. For Instance,—a Brother-Servant that borrowed money of you when he was out of place, was running away to Ireland: You were taking leave of an old fellow servant, who was shipping for Barbados: You were taking leave of a dear cousin, who is to be hanged next Saturday.

SWIFT: *Directions to Servants*

I

TUESDAY MORNING PASSED OFF QUIETLY.

There was prolonged debate in the secretaries' room covering the following subjects: When did the mysterious letter arrive in the office? Who could have received it? Why had no one seen it before? And lastly, and most intriguing, how had it come to be under Miss Cornel's desk?

None of these questions received any very conclusive answer.

Hazlerigg, who had learned by experience that it was better to take things in their proper order, had suspended all consideration of the letter until he should have received the reports of his hand-writing and finger-print experts.

Instead, he was sitting in his own office at Scotland Yard, considering the weekend roster. He had in front of him eight statements. He read them through once, and then again.

Pulling the telephone towards him with a sort of gesture of despair, he dialled a number and spoke to Dr. Bland. The pathologist proved so rude that Hazlerigg knew he was working unusually hard on the case: He rang off and returned to a third reading of the papers.

"On Saturday, February 13th," he said to Inspector Pickup, who happened to wander into his room at that moment, "Mr. Birley and Miss Chittering were at the office. Mr. Birley says that Miss Chittering left at about twelve o'clock, and that he left a few minutes afterwards. Miss Chittering, interrogated separately, says that she left at about ten minutes to twelve. She does not know when Mr. Birley left. On Saturday, February 20th, Mr. Duxford was on duty with Miss Cornel. Mr. Duxford thinks that he left at about eleven-thirty or a quarter to twelve. He says Miss Cornel left a few minutes before him. Miss Cornel says that she does not know what time she left, but she caught the eleven-fifty for Sevenoaks. On Saturday, February 27th, Mr. Horniman (junior) and Miss Mildmay were on duty. They state that they left at the same time—about ten past twelve—and walked together as far as Holborn Circus, a matter of about ten minutes, whence they took their respective ways home. Finally, we have Saturday, March 6th, when Mr. Craine and Miss Bellbas spent the morning together. Mr. Craine says that he thinks they finished work at about a quarter to twelve. He cannot remember which of them left first. Miss Bellbas cannot remember either. Mr. Craine says that on thinking it over, he is of the opinion that Miss Bellbas left before he did. Miss Bellbas says yes, she thinks so, too. Mr. Craine says that on thinking it over again, he recollects that Miss Bellbas was still in the office when he went and must therefore have left *after* him. Miss Bellbas, re-questioned, says yes, she thinks that's right."

"I should think they're all lying," said Inspector Pickup.

II

Bohun spent a quiet morning catching up with some of his arrears of work. He was rather assisted in this by the continued absence of John Cove, who had disappeared at about half-past ten without explanation.

At midday, however, John reappeared. He was plainly bursting with news and after some minutes spent scribbling on his blotting-pad, he could keep it to himself no longer.

"Look here," he said. "I think the time has come for me to let you in on something—"

Bohun made a non-committal sound.

"It's Eric Duxford," said John. "You know what I told you—that he was up to no good—and you said that I hadn't got any proof—well, I have."

"You mean," said Bohun slowly, "that you've got proof that he was the murderer of Smallbone?"

"Don't be so meticulous," said John. "No. Not exactly. Not in so many words. But I know that he's up to some sort of dirty work. I know that he comes back to this office, at night, after everyone else has gone."

"You know what?" said Bohun, considerably startled. "Where did you get this from?"

"I don't know who he meets," said John, evading the last part of the question. "But I shall know pretty soon. You see, he's got a meeting tonight. And I intend to be present at it."

"Good work," said Bohun. "But how—oh, yes, Mrs. Porter, what is it?"

"It's this letter, sir, about the insurance. I'm afraid I can't quite read my own shorthand note."

Bohun settled Mrs. Porter's difficulties, and when she had left the room John said:

"It's like this. Last Saturday I committed a little burglary."

"You committed—dash it, there goes the telephone. I won't be a minute."

In fact it took several minutes to dispose of a querulous person from the Public Trustee's Office who was worrying himself into a decline over the absence of one and ninepence from a trust account.

At the end of it, John said: "Look here, if I'm going to do justice to this dramatic revelation I insist on going somewhere where we won't be constantly interrupted. Come and have lunch."

"All right," said Bohun. "Where?"

"Let's go to the Law Society," said John. "There's always such a row in the canteen that no one can hear what anyone else says. We shall be safer there than in a restaurant."

"By the way," said Bohun, as they crossed Carey Street and turned into Bell Yard. "Are you a member of the Society?"

"In fact, no," said John. "But I expect you are, aren't you? That's all right, then. I'll go as your guest."

The canteen of the Law Society is not, as John Cove had indicated, a quiet place. At one o'clock it was full of food, light, steam, crosstalk and solicitors. However, it possessed the advantage of having a number of small tables, set in nooks and corners, and to one of these John led the way. Their nearest neighbours were two middle-aged solicitors, one of whom was eating spaghetti and reading a law journal, whilst the other appeared to be amending a draft contract on a diet of fish cakes.

"This is all right," said John Cove. "Now, as I was saying—"

When he had finished, Bohun said: "It certainly does seem odd. You say there was a second appointment diary for this year kept locked up in that drawer, and all the appointments in it were in code."

"It wasn't exactly a code. Everything was in initials."

"Is there any reason," said Bohun, "why they shouldn't have been social engagements. After all, he might easily keep two diaries, one for business and one for pleasure. He probably would keep the social one under lock and key."

"It didn't look like a social diary. Most of the engagements were in the evening but quite a lot of them were eleven in the morning and three-thirty in the afternoon, and that sort of time. You can't be social at three-thirty in the afternoon—not in a Horniman office."

"Then how does he get away with it?"

"As I told you—by getting us to alibi him," said John. "Of course, we all do it, to a certain extent. The only difference with Eric is that he makes a business of it. I'll give you an example. This morning he wasn't in his room at half-past ten. I asked Florrie Bellbas where he was. She said he had gone across to Turberville and Trout to examine deeds."

"So he may have," said Henry. "Aren't Turberville's acting for the vendor in the Rookery sales?"

"He *might* have," said John. "That's the point. But he ruddy well hadn't. I took the trouble to phone Turberville's and check up. Not only had he not gone over to inspect the deeds, but he couldn't have done so. They don't hold the deeds, they're in the hands of a mortgagee Bank."

"I see," said Bohun. "Yes. That certainly was a bit of a slip-up. What are you going to do about all this?"

"Well," said John. "My first idea was to follow Eric up when he went on one of these mysterious trips. However, I couldn't really see myself chasing round London after him in a false nose. So after a bit of thought I hired an assassin—I beg your pardon, sir. By all means borrow the mustard..." This was to a very old gentleman, bearing a striking resemblance to Tenniel's White Knight, who had drifted across and was bending vaguely over the table. "I'm afraid your sleeve is in my pudding. No, no, sir. Don't apologise. It couldn't affect the texture of the pudding. It's your sleeve I was thinking of."

"You were saying," said Bohun.

"Yes—I hired a detective. Rather fun, don't you think. This one is called Mr. Brown. He will follow Eric this afternoon. I noticed from Eric's diary that there were two appointments down for today—one at four o'clock and one at seven. So he ought to get something out of it."

"Personally I think you ought to tell Hazlerigg," said Bohun. "I won't if you don't want me to, but I think it would be the wise thing."

"What a damn dull life it would be," said John, "if we always did the wise thing. Come and have some coffee upstairs."

III

That afternoon Bohun divided his time between drawing up a trust deed for the Countess of Chiswick—a lady who appeared to have an almost Elizabethan ardour for the founding of strange settlements—and a steady consideration of Eric Duxford as Murderer.

Quite frankly he found this latter proposition hard to swallow. Eric as a swindler, yes. Eric as an embezzler; Eric as a fraudulent converter or a confidence trickster, or the publisher of prospectuses contrary to the terms of the Companies Act. Eric, even, as the perpetrator of some small larceny which did not involve any element of bodily violence or any undue risk of detection to the larcenor. But Eric as a murderer, by force: Eric as a ruthless strangler and a disposer of bodies in boxes. No. The picture did not convince.

"There he goes," said John Cove, who had stationed himself where he could see out of the window. "Look at him. Wearing a cavalry greatcoat. A relic, no doubt, of his front-line service in the Pay Corps. And an Old What's-is-name scarf. An Anthony Eden on his head and a brief-case in his hand. That is to underline the point that as well as being an officer and a gentleman he *is* also a professional man. The precious little snake. Let's find out what his alibi is this time."

Miss Bellbas, summoned to take a letter from John, informed them that Mr. Duxford was going out to search the register at the Patent Office.

"Funny he should be making for Lincoln's Inn Fields, then," said John. "Unless they've moved it, the Patent Office is the other side of Chancery Lane. However: Dear Sir, With reference to yours of the sixteenth…"

Half an hour later the telephone rang. The call was for John.

"Oh, Mr. Cove—Mr. Brown speaking."

"Carry on," said John. "Any luck?"

"I followed up the subject, sir," said Mr. Brown, with professional caution. "I traced it as far as Suffolk Street, in the Strand."

"What happened to it then?"

"I'm afraid I mislaid it, sir—I had to keep some distance from it, you understand—"

"Up-wind, too, I expect," said John. "All right. I was just thinking aloud. What are you planning to do now? Where are you speaking from?"

"From a box on the Embankment, sir. I am fairly confident that the subject is located in one of the larger buildings at this end of Suffolk Street or Devonshire Street."

"So much for the Patent Office," said John to Henry. "All right. Press on regardless. When do I hear from you next?"

"I'll ring you at the office not later than six o'clock."

"Fine," said John. "Keep trying." He replaced the receiver. "Are you going to wait to hear the second instalment?"

"Not me," said Bohun. "I've got better things to do with my evenings. Also I still think you ought to tell Hazlerigg."

"I expect I shall, eventually," said John. "But I might as well find out first just what it is I'm going to tell him. I can't draw back now. The hunt is up. From a view to a chase, from a chase to a kill. Yoicks and likewise Tallyho!"

It was a quarter past six before the telephone rang again.

"It's me, sir," said the hoarse voice of Mr. Brown. "If you'd like to come along now—"

"Where are you?"

"Come down to the end of Suffolk Street, sir. First right, and then right again. It's a little place off Somerset Court. Merriman House. First door on the left and I'll meet you in the hall."

"Right away," said John.

The office by now was almost empty. In the secretaries' room, Anne Mildmay, who was putting on her hat, gave him a surprisingly friendly "good night". Miss Chittering was hammering out the first lines of what was evidently a very lengthy engrossment. In the basement, Sergeant Cockerill could be heard putting the muniments to bed and singing in a remarkably tuneful voice the tenor part of one of his favourite hymns. "All are safely gathered in," sang Sergeant Cockerill. "Safe from sorrow, safe from sin."

John stepped out into New Square, turned into Carey Street and made his way through the precincts of the Court and into the Strand. It was cold, by the standards of an English April, though still quite light. But down under the arches of Somerset Court there appeared to reign an everlasting twilight.

John found Merriman House without difficulty. The approaches were muted and depressing. Age and grime had worked their will. What had once been red was now the colour of old blood: what had been white was black.

Mr. Brown was waiting for him in the half light of the entrance. He spoke in a professional whisper.

"The party," he said, "is up on the second or third floor. I have not as yet been able to ascertain which office he went into. I thought perhaps you might know."

"Haven't the least idea," said John. He found himself whispering too. "It might be almost anything from an abattoir to a den of coiners, mightn't it?"

"It isn't very cheerful," agreed Mr. Brown. "There's a board here, sir, with the names on. Wait whilst I strike a match. You can just make them out. There's Makepeace and Holly on the second floor, and Holdfast Investments Limited. Would it be either of those?"

"I've no idea," said John. "What's wrong with the light?"

"I think it's an electricity cut," said Mr. Brown. "It went dim about ten minutes ago. Now, on the top floor there's Bannister and Dean, Accountants, and Smith and Selverman, Solicitors."

"Let's have a look at that," said John. He, too, struck a match. "Smith and Selverman (H. V. Selverman)." It seemed to strike a chord—yes, of course! Those were the initials in the diary. H.V.S.

"All right," he said to Mr. Brown. "I think this is it. I haven't the faintest idea what it's all about, but I'm going up to see. You'd better hang around in case there's any violence."

"I'm not a violent man," said Mr. Brown doubtfully.

"That's all right," said John. "I'm quite violent enough for two when I get going. You stay on the stairs so that you can double off and phone for the police if I yell."

Up on the third floor the gloom was even thicker. Messrs. Bannister and Dean had plainly finished their accounting and shut up shop for the night, but in the offices on the other side of the landing lights still showed.

There were two doors. On one was painted "Smith & Selverman, Solicitors and Commissioners for Oaths". The other simply said "Enquiries". After a moment of hesitation John Cove tried the latter door. It opened. He walked in quickly without knocking.

The only occupant of the room was a sharp-nosed, red-haired boy. His hands and cuffs were black with copying-ink, but from a white face looked out a pair of remarkably intelligent eyes. He did not seem to be surprised, either by the lateness of John's arrival or the unceremonious nature of his entry. Indeed, he looked a difficult sort of boy to surprise.

"Well, mister, what is it?" he said.

"I've got an appointment," said John.

"Which of 'em are you seeing?"

John was visited by an inspiration. "I'm seeing Mr. Duxford," he said.

"All right," said the boy. "Wasser name?"

"Mr. Robertson, of Robertson, Robertson, Levi and Robertson."

"You'll have to wait. There's someone in with him."

"It's all the same to me," said John. He sat down on a chair and crossed his legs. "Mr. Duxford very busy these days?"

"So, so," said the boy. "Of course, he isn't here always—he's got his other businesses."

"Of course," said John. "One of the world's workers, our Mr. Duxford. Come to think of it, you know, I don't think I will wait. Perhaps I'll come some time when he's less busy."

A bell sounded.

"Please yourself," said the boy. "He's just finishing."

"As a matter of fact," said John, "I fancy I've found out all I wanted to know. Good night to you, sir. Give my best wishes to Mr. Duxford. Tell him Mr. Cove called, but was unable to wait." He backed out, leaving the boy staring.

IV

Back in New Square, in the offices of Horniman, Birley and Craine, Miss Chittering typed doggedly. She ought to have told Mr. Birley that she couldn't *possibly* complete the engrossment that night. She should have said that eleven o'clock the next morning was the earliest that it could be ready. But the truth was that few people had the courage to say things like that to Mr. Birley. Miss Chittering least of all.

Therefore, though the clock on the Inn Chapel had, some time ago, struck the half-hour past six; though the electric light had gone suddenly and unaccountably dim; though her eyes watered and her wrists ached, Miss Chittering continued to type.

Outside, in the dusk, the Square emptied and grew quiet. The office cleaners came and went. The porter locked the Carey Street gate and retired to light the lanterns which hang in festoons from the chains under the library arch. The red post-office vans rolled into the Square and clip-clopped out again, heavy with the correspondence of fifty offices.

As it grew darker, Chancery, the one-eared black cat, moved from his hiding-place in New Court Passage and drifted silently across the roadway on to the grass plot in the centre of the Square. He had long had his eye on a particularly stupid pigeon which roosted in the plane tree at the south end of the garden. He had noticed that lately it had formed a habit of making its evening toilet perched on the lowest branch of the tree. Chancery had given a good deal of thought to the possibilities of this situation.

In the office Miss Chittering looked at her watch. Sergeant Cockerill, she knew, was coming back to lock up at seven o'clock. She had only one more page to do. She should be able to manage.

The office and the street outside and the Square were all silent. The light was so dim that she found on looking up that she could hardly read the names on the deed boxes which stood, black rank on black rank, at the far end of the room.

Quite suddenly Miss Chittering felt frightened.

It was quiet. Yet, she knew her ears had not deceived her, a soft foot had moved in the passage outside. For a moment she sat paralysed, her muscles refusing to obey the panic-stricken messages from her brain. Then, wrenching herself to her feet, quietly but with desperate speed, she flew across the room. The door had a slip lock and it was the work of a moment to thumb down the catch.

Then she stood in the dim light, her heart bumping uncomfortably. She told herself not to be a fool. She forced herself to listen calmly. There wasn't a sound. It was all her imagination.

Then something really rather horrible did happen.

In front of her eyes, and only a few inches away, the handle of the Yale lock started to turn, softly, checked at the catch, and turned as silently back again.

Miss Chittering had suddenly no doubts at all. Murder stood outside in the passage. Yet, even in that moment, her overmastering feeling was more curiosity than fear. There was a chair beside the door. She stepped up on to it, steadied herself for a moment, and peered out, through the dusty fanlight, into the passage.

What she saw brought an almost hysterical cackle of relief to her lips.

"Heavens," she said. "It's you? You did give me a fright."

Stepping down from her chair she slipped up the catch and opened the door.

v

Seven o'clock was striking as Sergeant Cockerill turned into Lincoln's Inn from Chancery Lane. Outside Stone Buildings he encountered an old friend, one of the porters of the Inn.

"Good evening, Mr. Mason," said the sergeant.

"Good evening, Sergeant. Working for your overtime?"

"Just going to lock up. One of our girls staying late."

"I'll walk across with you, Mr. Cockerill," said Mason. "How's the fuchsias?"

"It's early to tell," said the sergeant. "They look healthy enough. It's not too late for a last frost, though. A late frost could take them all off."

"We shan't have any more frost now."

"With a Government like this one," said Sergeant Cockerill, "you could expect a frost in August." They stopped in front of the office. There was no light showing and both the inner doors seemed to be shut.

"I expect she's gone," said the sergeant. "Better make sure. You never know with girls nowadays. Probably left the fire on." He disappeared.

Mason was about to move on when something caught his eye. Something white in the dusk.

"Why, bless my soul, if that cat hasn't got one of the pigeons."

He stopped and prodded with the butt-end of his staff at the darkness under the plane tree. Chancery swore at him then backed a few reluctant paces into the tangled safety of a laurustinus. The front of the flower-bed was a mess of grey and white feathers.

"Cunning old devil," said Mason. "If he hasn't clawed that bird too much I might see what the missus can make of it. It's off the ration, and that's something these days."

As he was stooping down he heard a cry. It came from the building behind him. Then silence. Then footsteps running. It was Sergeant Cockerill and Mason, startled, saw that his face was white.

"What is it?" he said. "What's up?"

"Have you got a telephone in your lodge?"

"Yes, what—"

"Come on. No time to lose. Got to get the police."

He set off at a lumbering trot and Mason, after a moment's hesitation, followed him.

Chancery crept cautiously from his retreat under the laurustinus and retrieved the pigeon.

CHAPTER TEN

"De Minimis Non Curat Lex"

It sometimes happens that a valid requisition on title receives an evasive reply, viz.: "This is a matter of record" or "This should be within the Purchaser's own knowledge" or "The Purchaser must search". Such an answer must never be accepted without further enquiry—

I

UP TO THAT POINT, BOHUN REALISED, IT HAD BEEN JUST POSsible—not easy, but just barely possible—to treat the affair impersonally: to regard the discovery of Mr. Smallbone's body as a problem; an affair which could intrigue and puzzle without directly affecting.

Now it was different. The discovery of Miss Chittering, her sightless eyes protruding, her lips drawn up in a parody of agony, her neck indented with the deep mark of the wire noose which had killed her; that had changed things, for good.

Looking at their faces next morning, Bohun saw this very clearly.

From now onwards, until the matter was ended, one way or the other, they were never going to trust each other again, because they were never going to be quite certain.

II

The news had reached Hazlerigg within five minutes of the discovery of the body.

A lesser man would have departed at once for the scene of the crime. Instead, after a short moment of thought, Hazlerigg pulled up the office phone and started to give orders. As a result of which, three county police forces received urgent requests for co-operation; two North London squad cars were stopped on patrol and diverted to new destinations; and several members of the Metropolitan Force spent an active evening.

"With the least luck in the world," said Hazlerigg to Sergeant Crabbe, "we should be able to alibi half of them clean out of it this time. It looks as if six-thirty to seven is the important time. All virtuous office workers are home by seven."

"They *should* have been home," agreed Sergeant Crabbe, who was a notorious pessimist. "Things don't always work out the way they should do."

How tiresomely right he was became apparent the next morning, by which time the reports had come in. Hazlerigg read them through quickly, said something unkind on the subject of the Electricity Board, and then read them through again.

The first one was typical.

"At approximately seven-twenty I arrived at the address which had been indicated to me, in St. George's Square, Pimlico," it said, in that stilted manner which is encouraged in police reports, no doubt with the idea that they will sound more convincing when read out in court. "I was informed by a lady whose name I afterwards understood to be Miss Birley, that her brother, Mr. Birley, had not yet returned home. I asked if this was unusual, and Miss

Birley said that it was most unusual. She said that her brother was normally home by a quarter to seven, and would always telephone if he was going to be late. As I was interrogating Miss Birley, Mr. Birley arrived. He seemed surprised to see me and appeared to be considerably upset and was in an excited condition. He stated that owing to an alleged electricity cut he had been forced to wait for fifty-two minutes on the platform of Charing Cross Underground station. Such a thing had never happened to him before. After waiting approximately twenty minutes he had tried to get out and take a bus, but the crowd had been so dense that he had been unable to move. He stated that in his opinion the Government..."

From the Surrey Constabulary, P.C. Rook of Epsom: "I went to the house indicated, but was informed that Mr. Craine had not yet returned. I said that I would wait. Mr. Craine arrived home at eight minutes to nine. When asked why he was so late he said that he had got tired of waiting for his train to proceed from Surbiton where it had been stationary for nearly three-quarters of an hour. He had therefore got out and tried to hire a taxi but without success. That would have been at about seven-fifteen. He had eventually obtained a lift from a commercial traveller as far as Banstead cross-roads and had walked home from there. He considered that the Electricity Board..."

"Miss Bellbas, when interrogated, stated that she had entered a Northern Line train, on the Edgware branch, at Tottenham Court Road station. The train had come to a halt somewhere between Mornington Crescent and Camden Town. The carriage was very full, but she had managed to obtain a seat. When the train had been stationary for some considerable period the lady next to her had asked her what she thought would happen if there was a fire. Miss Bellbas had replied that if there was a fire they would all be burnt to death. The lady had thereupon uttered a number of hysterical screams. Fortunately at this point the train had restarted. Miss Bellbas was of the opinion that people who were unable to control themselves should not travel in Underground trains…"

"It's all too utterly bad to be true," said Hazlerigg to Bohun. "The people we aren't really interested in at all—Mrs. Porter, Mr. Prince, Mr. Waugh, and so on, seem to have got home safely and in good time. On the other hand, out of the members of List Two, five seem to have got stuck at unidentifiable spots round the London Transport system and the rest don't seem to have gone home at all."

"John Cove and Eric Duxford—" suggested Bohun.

"Yes, I heard about them," said Hazlerigg. "That's almost the only satisfactory aspect of the whole evening. Cove seems to be clear. And there's no doubt at all about Duxford. He's out."

"If he isn't he soon will be," said Bohun grimly.

"What do you—oh, that. Yes. I suppose it was a bit irregular. I can't help his private troubles. Whatever else he's guilty of, he isn't guilty of murder. Not this one, anyway. I only wish we could be as definite about everybody else. You might be interested to hear the score to date. Mr. Birley—Left the office at six o'clock. Arrived home in Pimlico at twenty-five past seven. Fifty minutes spent in a crowd on an Underground platform. Mr. Craine—Left the office at five to six. Caught the six-fifteen from Waterloo. Arrived home at about ten to nine. Some of his story should be checkable. I'm having an enquiry made at Surbiton station. Bob Horniman didn't go home at all. It seems he never does go home on Tuesdays. It's his landlady's night off. So on that night he eats out."

"Well, that should be easy to confirm."

"I'll believe it when it happens," said Hazlerigg. "Miss Cornel—Had to walk to Charing Cross owing to crowds trying to go by bus. Missed the six-ten for Sevenoaks. Caught the six-forty. Train didn't start till seven-twenty. Reached Sevenoaks at a quarter past eight. Stood all the way and saw no one she knew. Miss Bellbas—You've heard some of that. We might be able to get hold of the hysterical type who sat next to her. Or we might not. People aren't always keen to come forward and admit they made fools of themselves. Miss Mildmay—Left the office at about six-twenty. Waited for twenty minutes in Holborn for a bus, but the buses were all full of disappointed train-goers. Gave it up and walked home to Kensington. Arrived at eight o'clock. That's about the strength of it. And I'll tell you what it all adds up to. It adds up to a hell of a lot more work."

Bohun said diffidently: "I suppose you've not—er—you haven't overlooked Sergeant Cockerill."

"No," said Hazlerigg. "I haven't overlooked Sergeant Cockerill." He turned over the last of the statements. "Sergeant Cockerill finished locking up at about twenty-five past six. He saw Miss Chittering and she told him that she had an important engrossment for Mr. Birley which had to be completed before she left that night, and offered to lock the outer door for him. He said no, he would come back and lock up the outer door at seven, by which time Miss Chittering hoped she would have finished. Sergeant Cockerill walked round to the Fall of Troy which is a small public house—you may know it—on this side of Fetter Lane. Here he spent thirty minutes, drinking gin and warm water and talking to the landlord. At seven o'clock he returned and, happening to meet one of the Inn porters, walked round with him to this office. The rest I think you've heard…"

"And is all that—?"

"Oh, yes," said Hazlerigg. "It's fully corroborated. The landlord of the Fall of Troy and three of his saloon-bar cronies. Completely corroborated."

III

Very little legal work was done in the office that morning. Mr. Birley appeared to have passed the point where shocks could affect him further. This may even have been providential because he really had got quite a lot to put up with. For a start there was practically a Press siege. The police kept them out of the office itself, but anyone coming or going had the gauntlet to run. John Cove had already told the crime reporter of the *Nation* a quantity of startling facts about the firm, quite a few of which had got into the Lunch Edition. The *Daily Monitor* had a picture of Mr. Craine standing on the top step with his umbrella grasped sword-like in one hand and his hat over his eye, and Miss Bellbas had given an interview to the *Woman's World* in which she had attributed everything to the influence of the stars.

On top of the Press, Mr. Birley had other worries. A number of clients had already been on the telephone, needing to be placated. As the Duke of Hornsey had put it, with that penchant for expressing the obvious which had made him a pillar of the Lords for a quarter of a century: "You know, Birley, you'll have to stop it. There are some things which are not *done* in a good solicitor's office." Then there were the police, even more offensive than formerly. And that curious business about Duxford. And the aftermath of bilious indigestion from the postponement of his dinner the night before.

What with one thing and another Mr. Birley found that by twelve o'clock he had had enough. Seizing a moment when most of the journalists were away in search of sandwiches, he had slipped out and made for home.

IV

"I say," said Bohun, "what did happen last night? About Eric Duxford, I mean."

"If you hadn't been so damned snooty," said John Cove, "you could have come along and seen the fun. And fixed yourself up a nice alibi at the same time," he added.

"So I could. Pity one doesn't think of things like that at the time. But, tell me, what happened?"

John told him.

"I see," said Bohun, "and what does it amount to?"

"Well—breach of contract."

"What contract? Oh, you mean his implied contract of service with Horniman, Birley and Craine?"

"Yes."

"Sounds rather a technical offence."

"It isn't so damned technical when it comes to pinching clients from this firm and carrying them off to his own outfit and collaring the costs."

"Did he do that?"

"Yes. I thought I recognised some of the initials in that book of his. I expect he offered them reduced fees if he could do the work himself."

"I see. Are you going to tell Birley?"

"I haven't made my mind up," said John.

"You wouldn't object to Birley finding out, I take it, but you don't want the onus of having to tell him?"

"That's about it. I say, Bohun." John was suddenly completely serious. "Who's doing these things?"

"I don't know." Bohun got to his feet and looked down at John Cove from his greater height. "I don't think anybody knows. But the field is narrowing down a bit, isn't it?"

v

Inspector Hazlerigg was saying much the same thing in different words, and at greater length, to the Commissioner.

"I'm sorry for the girl," he said. "That goes without saying. I don't suppose she even knew why she was killed. And I'm sorry that it had to happen right under our noses like that. The papers are bound to take that up—"

"They have," said the Commissioner.

"Nevertheless, sir, I can't be wholly sorry it's happened. Because I think it means that now we shall be pretty certain to catch the murderer."

"How do you make that out?" said the Commissioner.

"I look at it like this, sir. The first murder was a prepared murder. The murderer was able to choose his opportunity and his place as carefully as he liked: and he had plenty of time to work out the angles. There are people with minds like that. The sort of mind that can cope with a double-dummy bridge problem and work out all the variations—you know, if South ducks the third round of trumps then West must put up his queen and throw away a small heart at round six instead of a small diamond."

"Hrrmp!" said the Commissioner.

"But you face the same man with a snap decision in the actual play of the hand: something that's going to mean the difference between making his contract and going down: with everybody watching him and waiting for him to play: that's when expensive mistakes get made."

"Well," said the Commissioner, who was not a bridge player, "I hope you're right. Because, make no mistake about it, we want this murderer."

VI

The checking of alibis is neither an easy nor a certain business. There are too many unknowns to make it a mathematical process. And even the known facts have a way of varying themselves in the process of verification.

Sergeant Plumptree visited a large catering establishment at the Wellington Street end of the Strand. He had in his pocket a statement by Bob Horniman who, it appeared, had had his evening meal there the night before. "I got there at about half-past six," the statement said, "I went into the first dining-room you come to. I can't remember which table I sat at. It was somewhere on the right. I left at about half-past seven."

Sergeant Plumptree had some difficulty, to start with, in making up his mind which of the many rooms answered the description of "the first dining-room you come to". There were three at almost the same distance from the main entrance. He got on the telephone and spoke to Hazlerigg who had another word with Bob Horniman.

"It's the one straight ahead," he reported.

"There are two straight ahead," said Sergeant Plumptree.

"Then check them both," said Hazlerigg.

Sergeant Plumptree then interviewed, in turn, a junior floor-walker, who clearly knew nothing, a senior floorwalker, who had something of the look of a rural dean, and finally an attractive woman of about thirty who seemed, despite her youth, to be a senior executive. She proved surprisingly helpful, and organised Sergeant Plumptree's search for him. "It can't have been the Minervan Room," she said, "because that closes when the teas are finished. So it must have been the Arcadian Salon. On the right, you said. Well, there are three or four waitresses who might have served a table on the right. The shift is from midday to eight, so they should be available now." She rang a number of bells, pressed two coloured buttons on her desk and spoke into a house telephone—presently Sergeant Plumptree was showing a photograph to one thin blonde, one stout blonde, one brunette and one nondescript waitress. None of them recognised it.

"Perhaps if you could tell me which table...?"

"Well, that's exactly what I can't do," said Sergeant Plumptree. It had occurred to him previously that it might have been simpler to have brought Bob Horniman along with him, but apparently police etiquette forbade it.

As he was going the manageress said:

"I see that this gentleman states that he was at his table for about an hour. I'm sure that the girls would have remembered that. Six-thirty or seven-thirty is a very good time for tips and if anyone sits on for too long after their meal they'll get up to almost any dodge to get rid of them. Why, I've even known them spill a whole pot of hot coffee."

The girls were summoned again and the point was put to them. They were all quite certain that the young man in the picture had not sat at any table for which they were responsible for anything like an hour. "He might have been in and out for a quick snack," said the thin blonde, summing it up, "but not an hour." The others concurred.

Sergeant Plumptree came away thoughtfully.

VII

"I caught the six-forty from Charing Cross," Miss Cornel had said. "I had to hurry to do that. Not that I need have worried. It didn't start till about twenty past seven. It was absolutely full, so I had to stand. It's an electric, non-corridor train. You *can* get a steam train to Sevenoaks. Why didn't I? Because I didn't know it was an electric breakdown, of course. And by the time I'd grasped that, the steam train had gone. Did I speak to anyone in the carriage? I expect so. What did I say? Well, we all said 'Thank God' when the train started. There wasn't anyone in the carriage I knew—none of the regulars. They'd all got away on the earlier train, I expect. The only person I saw to recognise was the ticket collector on duty. I don't know his name, but he's got a face like a duck—"

Sergeant Plumptree found the ticket collector with surprisingly little difficulty. As soon as he mentioned Miss Cornel's description the stationmaster laughed and said: "That'll be Field. Face like a duck. That's him. Donald, the other men call him. Donald Duck, you see."

Field, who really did look quite startlingly like a duck, picked out Miss Cornel's photograph without any hesitation.

"She's one of our regulars," he said. "Been coming up and down on this line for fifteen years. We get to know our regulars, specially during the war, what with the raids and one thing and another. Very friendly we got. She's a golfer, isn't she?"

"That's the one," said Sergeant Plumptree. "Now can you tell me what time—about what time—I don't mean the exact minute—that she got here last night?"

"Last night?"

"Yes—at about twenty to seven."

"You know what happened here last night, chum, don't you?"

"Yes," said Sergeant Plumptree. He had a sinking feeling that success was going to evade him again.

"What with one thing and another," said Field, "what with the people who was on the trains trying to get off and the people who was off trying to get on, if my own mother had come up to me and spoken to me, I shouldn't have remembered it. And she's been in her grave these ten years and more."

Sergeant Plumptree finished a hard day by interrogating the taxi-drivers who ply for hire outside Surbiton station. Here he scored his first positive success.

Mr. Ringer, who owned and drove an ancient Jowett, immediately picked out Mr. Craine's photograph from half a dozen others.

"Stout little party?"

"That's him," said Sergeant Plumptree.

"Came out of the station 'bout quarter past seven. There was a train stopped there—something to do with the current. Had been there more than half an hour. Some of the langwidge the gentlemen were using," said Mr. Ringer virtuously, "wooder surprised you."

"And this person asked you to take him somewhere?"

"Epsom," said Mr. Ringer. "I wooder obliged, but I was waiting for a lady I always pick up. Pity. Offered me a quid. Woody be a lawyer, by any chance?"

"Well, yes," said Sergeant Plumptree. "If this party is the party we think he is, he was certainly a lawyer. How did you know?"

"Norways tell a lawyer," said Mr. Ringer.

VIII

Meanwhile, Inspector Hazlerigg had had two visitors.

The first was a Miss Pott, of North Finchley. She had been unearthed by a mixture of luck and imagination. Hazlerigg had put in an enquiry with the London Passenger Transport Board on the subject of complaints received as a result of the electricity cut. One of these seemed promisingly near the right time and place.

"I understand," he said to Miss Pott, "that you made a complaint as a result of your experiences last night on one of the Northern Line Underground trains."

"That's right," said Miss Pott, "and between you and me I'm sorry I ever opened my mouth. I was a bit upset at the time, or I'd never have done it. I can see now it wasn't the railway's fault. I mean, they couldn't help it, could they? It was that awful girl sitting next to me—"

Hazlerigg slid a photograph in front of her.

"Yes. That's the one. Every time I said anything, she just agreed with me. I said, 'I expect we might be here all night,' and she said, 'Yes. We might'. Then I said, 'Supposing the train catches on fire—'"

"Yes," said Hazlerigg sympathetically. He felt that Miss Bellbas would probably not be the ideal companion for a long hold-up in a crowded Underground train.

"What time would it have been when you first got on to the train? About six-fifteen? I see. And when you got off it?"

"Well, I wasn't home till seven-thirty, and I live almost opposite the station."

"Thank you," said Hazlerigg. He made a note of Miss Pott's address. He had never thought of Miss Bellbas as a terribly likely murderer. But it was nice to be sure.

When he read the short note which Sergeant Crabbe had written, introducing his next visitor, Hazlerigg experienced a sudden sinking feeling, but before he had time to take any decisive action Herbert Hayman was in the room.

Herbert was a neat little man. He dressed neatly, and walked neatly, and Hazlerigg did not need to be told his calling.

"I work for Merryweather and Matlock," he said. "You may have seen our shop. It's about half-way down the Strand, opposite the Tivoli Cinema. We sell leather goods and luggage. We specialise in hikers' and campers' stuff."

Hazlerigg said he knew the shop.

"I read in the newspapers about Miss Chittering being murdered in that lawyers' office. We were going to be married."

Hazlerigg said nothing. Construing his silence as a demand for further explanation, Mr. Hayman went on hurriedly:

"She was a little older than me. Well—six years, to be exact. But she was a wonderful girl. She had a wonderful mind. She used to surprise me, Inspector. The things she told me about the law."

"Well, now," said Hazlerigg. "Perhaps you can tell me one or two things. When did you see Miss Chittering last?"

"Last Saturday. She used to come up from Dulwich every Saturday. When she wasn't working at the office she'd come in, and we'd have a talk—I'm in charge of the campers' department, you know." (He said this with all the pride of a colonel announcing his first command.) "Then she'd go out and get a cup of coffee and wait till I was finished—we shut up at half-past twelve on Saturdays—and we'd have lunch and go somewhere in the afternoon; we were both very fond of pictures."

"You went to the cinema?"

"No, no," said Mr. Hayman. "Real pictures. The National Gallery or the Tate. Hours we spent there—we were both very partial to the Dutch School. On Sundays I would usually go over to see her at Dulwich, after lunch, and we'd go for a hike."

It seemed an innocuous courtship. Hazlerigg could not say what he felt—that no marriage with a woman six years one's senior would be likely to thrive on a sole bond of intellectual admiration. That was not the sort of thing you said to witnesses. Therefore he contented himself with the usual formula.

"Well, Mr. Hayman. It was very good of you to come forward. If there's any way in which you can help us, I'll be certain to let you know. We have your address, haven't we?"

"There's one thing," said Mr. Hayman diffidently. "Perhaps I oughtn't to say this. But I think she was afraid of the man she worked for. What was his name—Birley. She didn't say so in so many words, you know."

"I think he bullied her," said Hazlerigg gently. "But, of course, that's no proof that he—"

"No, of course not," said Mr. Hayman. "I just thought I ought to mention it."

He departed, and Hazlerigg sat, for a long time after he had gone, quite motionless. Only the blinking of his eyes showed that he was alive. Curiously enough he was not thinking about Mr. Hayman at all. He was searching for something. A single, tiny, unrelated fact, in the storehouse of his memory.

It was almost eight o'clock, and quite dark, before he got back to Lincoln's Inn. He found Mason, the porter, in his lodge.

When he had introduced himself, and broken the ice by admiring Mason's collection of pewter jugs, he said: "I wanted to hear again from you, if you wouldn't mind, exactly what happened last night. It might be easiest if we went outside and walked over the ground."

Mason was agreeable. As they went out the Chapel clock started striking.

"There, now," said Mason. "That's just how it was—only seven o'clock, not eight. I'd just finished locking the library and I came out in front of Stone Buildings here as Mr. Cockerill came in the gate. He and I walked together, down towards the Square. I can't remember what we talked about. We didn't hurry—but we didn't dawdle either. The lights were all out in the office—like it is now..." He pointed. The premises of Horniman, Birley and Craine were as dark as the tomb.

"I see," said Hazlerigg. He stared at the blind façade. "Then Cockerill went in, and you walked on."

"That's right. No, of course, I forgot. That was when I saw the cat."

He explained about Chancery and the pigeon.

"Was that before Cockerill went in?"

"No," said Mason. "After. Just when I was walking off."

"Then you were looking at the dead bird, and prodding about in the flower-bed—and then you heard Sergeant Cockerill cry out?"

"That's right."

"And that would have been—how much later?"

"Oh. Not very long."

"Two or three minutes?"

"Yes. I expect so. What's it all about, Inspector?"

"Just a matter of routine," said Hazlerigg. He looked at his watch before he put it back in his pocket. It showed seven minutes past eight.

IX

When Hazlerigg got to bed that night he did not go to sleep immediately. Ordinarily, he had the professional's ability to shutter his
thoughts: he left his work and his worries behind him at his desk.
If it had been otherwise, he could hardly have slept at all.

Tonight, however, a current of thought got through the
insulation.

It started with this proposition. "The murderer could not have
anticipated the electricity failure." The first deduction from this
was that the murderer had to be a person whose late arrival home
could cause no comment. Someone who lived alone. Or someone
who was dining out. But was that a sound deduction? Had the
murderer not very possibly prepared an ingenious alibi, some
watertight excuse for being home late, *which they had never had to
use*. The heaven-sent and unexpected gift of the electricity failure
had served instead.

Having disposed of that one, Hazlerigg turned over once more
in his search for sleep.

But at the back of his mind, like the particle of sand in the
oyster, lay one hard grain of fact. It was a fact which he had learnt
in his talk with Herbert Hayman, Miss Chittering's fiancé. And it
matched up with something he had heard: something, he rather
thought, that Bohun had once told him.

The street lamps outside formed patterns on the white ceiling.
They would be turned out soon after midnight.

"I'll go on thinking about it till the lights go out," he said to
himself. "If I haven't got it by then I'll give it up."

The next thing he was aware of was the clamour of his alarm-
clock calling him to another day.

CHAPTER ELEVEN

—THURSDAY A.M.—

Capital Appreciation

> Years passed and he sat in the same place, wrote out the same
> documents, and thought of one thing, how to get back to the
> country. And little by little his distress became a definite disorder,
> a fixed idea—to buy a small farm somewhere by the bank of a
> river or a lake.
>
> CHEKHOV: *Gooseberries*

I

"I SAY," SAID JOHN COVE, "HAVE YOU HEARD?"

"No. What?"

"Eric's going."

"Then you did—"

"No," said John. "I didn't. That's the scrumptious part about
it. My conscience is absolutely clear. But Eric was so convinced
that I should split on him—judging others by his own shocking
standards—that he came to the conclusion it would be more digni-
fied and grown-up if he got his own say in first. So he demanded
an interview with Bill Birley and handed in his resignation all
gentlemanly-like."

"What happened then?"

"Well, I only got this part from Charlie—you know what those basement stairs are like—so you mustn't take it for gospel. But apparently Bill Birley was suffering from a number-nine hangover from this Chittering business and the police and what with one thing and another he definitely wasn't at his mental best. When Eric stalked in and said: 'I wish to resign,' Birley just gazed at him in a suffering way for a moment and said, 'All right, when?' and the whole scene fell a bit flat. Eric, apparently, in an endeavour to waken a flicker of interest, said, 'And I don't mind about notice. If it's all the same to you I shall leave tomorrow.' However, even this didn't stir the great man, who simply moaned and said—Oh, hello, Eric. We were just talking about you."

"I expect you were," said Eric Duxford. He was obviously in that uncomfortable state of mind when one is spoiling for a row without knowing quite who to have it with. "I hear you called round at my office on Tuesday night."

"Well, I didn't actually know it was your office," said John, tilting back his chair to a dangerous angle. "It seemed, from the information painted on the door, to belong jointly to a Mr. Smith and a Mr. Selverman."

"Smith's retired," said Eric shortly. "Henry Selverman's my partner. And a damned good business man."

"A one-man firm?"

"And what of it?" said Eric. "He knows more about the law than any two of the stuck-up ducal bootlickers in this office."

"No doubt," said John. "I should say he must have a very close—almost a personal—acquaintance with certain branches of the law. Breach of contract, for instance, or that lovely, old-fashioned tort, seduction of servants—"

"Look here," said Eric. "If I thought you'd gone and told Birley—"

"You know damned well I didn't," said John coolly. "And if it's any consolation to you, I never intended to. However, since you have chosen to award yourself that order of the boot which, in my opinion, you so richly deserved—"

"You filthy cad."

"Control yourself," said John. He tilted his chair to an even more impossible angle. "You're too fat for fighting and, in any case, we are both long past the age when exhibitions of personal violence have anything to recommend them."

"I have no intention," said Eric, "of demeaning myself by laying hands on you."

"That hissing noise you heard," said John to Bohun, "was me sighing with relief."

"But I will say this"—Eric paused at the door—"I'm bloody glad I'm not staying in this place. It makes me sick. Day after day: 'Yes, me lord, no, me lord. May I have the honour of blacking your lordship's boots for you.' You're not solicitors. You're flunkies. I can tell you, I shall be glad to get into an office where we do some real work. It mayn't be as swanky as this, but we are our own masters…"

Bohun listened, fascinated. Excitement was rubbing all the careful gloss off Eric's speech, and the brass was showing through in increasing patches.

"That's the boy," said John. "I should slam the door, too. It's almost the only way of rounding off a good sentence like that."

Eric gave him a final annihilating look and stalked out.

"Do you know," said John, when he had gone, "if he'd had the guts to say that whilst he was employed here—actually on the pay-roll, I mean—I'd almost have been forced to applaud him. There was a good deal of truth in it. As it is, however, it seems a bit like spitting and running away."

II

Hazlerigg, at this moment, was considering a series of reports. They dealt in great detail with the letter which had been found under Miss Cornel's desk.

"The exhibit," said the first, "corresponds in twelve distinct instances with the test sample supplied. Texture, colour, weave, depth of impress, colour of impress, etc. etc. etc."

"I have examined the two samples of handwriting under a magnification of one hundred," began the second. "The number of characteristics which correspond in each sample is too high for me to come to any other reasonable conclusion than that they were written by the same person at about the same period."

And then a very interesting note from Mr. Allpace, stationer, of Belsize Park. "I supply Mr. Smallbone with writing paper and have in my possession the die-stamp for heading the same. Mr. Smallbone wrote to me early in February ordering a new supply and stating that his present supply was nearly exhausted. I had five hundred sheets stamped, but they have never been called for. I have written twice to Mr. Smallbone reminding him that his notepaper was ready, but have had no reply."

Sergeant Plumptree said: "That's quite right, sir. When I went up to get a sample of Mr. Smallbone's notepaper, on your instructions, I had some difficulty in finding a piece. There was none in his writing-case or desk. In the end I got a bit from Mrs. Tasker. Apparently when he paid his rent he used to fasten the cheque to a sheet of notepaper and leave it on the table outside her sitting-room, so luckily she was able to produce a piece."

"Then it looks," said Hazlerigg, "as if the notepaper was genuine, and it looks as if the signature was genuine. And yet—was there any sign of a typewriter?"

"No, sir. He never had a typewriter. Mrs. Tasker said she thought he used to type his letters in a friend's office. She didn't know the name of the friend or anything else about him—"

"Well, it's feasible," said Hazlerigg.

He said it absent-mindedly. In fact, his thoughts were far away. When Sergeant Plumptree had gone he sent for Miss Cornel.

"Something's just occurred to me," he said without preamble. "Should have thought of it long ago, but what with one thing and another... However, here it is. Where are the papers and files and books and things which ought to have been in that deed box? All the Ichabod Stokes stuff. It must have added up to something fairly bulky. Not the sort of thing you could take away under your coat. Well, where is it?"

"I can tell you one thing for certain," said Miss Cornel slowly. "It's not in the office."

"What makes you say that?"

"In any other solicitor's office," said Miss Cornel, "a bundle of papers, a couple of account books, a folder of documents, might get pushed away and overlooked—not here. Not in a Horniman office."

"I see," said Hazlerigg. "How much was there—roughly I mean?"

Miss Cornel made a vague gesture with her hands.

"It's difficult to say," she said. "The box was about half full. There were all sorts of odds and ends. More than anyone would care to have to lug around with them."

"Yes," said Hazlerigg. "Yes. That's just what I was thinking."

III

Bob Horniman, exiled from his own office and driven for the time being to work in the deed examination room, a dismal apartment in the basement, had got into the habit of spending a good deal of time in dropping in on other people, and Bohun was therefore not surprised to receive a visit which corresponded with the arrival of his eleven o'clock tea.

"You can have John Cove's cup," said Bohun. "He's out at a completion."

"Thanks." Bob sat on the edge of John's desk, swinging his legs, until Miss Bellbas had removed herself, and then said: "I'm glad Cove's out, because there's something I've been wanting—well, to tell you the truth, something I've been plucking up the courage to ask you for some time."

"Yes," said Bohun cautiously.

"Oh, it's nothing to do with this police business," said Bob, noting his reserve. "It's—look here, your father's got money, hasn't he?"

"A pound or two," admitted Bohun.

"I'm sorry. I'm not doing this very tactfully. I remember being told that he was something in the City, and I've always heard of him as a sort of mystery financier with millions at his fingertips."

"I don't think it runs to that," said Bohun. "I don't think anyone really has millions nowadays. He has certain capital resources which he is free to invest—"

Bob seized on the word. "That's it. That's just what I meant. It would be a sort of investment."

"Perhaps," said Bohun patiently, "you would explain exactly what it is you have in mind."

"I want to sell my share in this firm," said Bob. "I thought you might like to buy it," he added.

"Are you serious?"

"Oh, absolutely." Now that Bob had got it off his chest he seemed much happier. "It's not a thing I'd offer to anybody, but—well. I know you, and Craine seems to cotton on to you all right, and Birley—well, quite frankly, if he gets a few more shocks like he's had lately, I don't think he'll last out much longer."

"Yes, but why do you want to do it—why are you getting out? Dash it all, you can't just throw everything up as if..." Bohun, looking round helplessly, happened to catch the eye of a large photographic portrait of Abel Horniman which glared back at him. "It's your vocation."

"Vocation, my foot," said Bob. "Look here, I've never told this to anyone in my life, but you might as well know exactly where you stand. I hate the law. I loathe and detest all this pettifogging round with words and figures, and hours and days and weeks spent mangling bumph and sitting on my bottom worrying about whether Lady Marshmoreton's annuity should be retained in Consolidated Mines or shifted to 3½ per cent Non-Cumulative Preferential Fish Paste, and whether Lord Haltwhistle has got the power to appoint an eighth part of the fifteenth part of the funds in his great-aunt's will trust to his nephews and nieces in equal shares, and if not why not."

Bohun grinned. For the first time since his arrival in the office he remembered Bob as he had last seen him at school, with a serious inky face, broken glasses, and a pair of black boots two sizes too large for him.

"I think maybe you've got something there," he said, "but what do you want to do?"

"Sailing," said Bob, "and farming. I know of just the place in Cornwall where you could run a small stock farm with one cowman, and there's a creek runs up actually through the farm. It's deep enough for a small sea-boat. It would only cost six thousand, and perhaps another three or four thousand to stock it. I'd have to have a reserve, because I don't suppose I should make it pay at first."

"I see," said Bohun. "And how much did you—how much were you expecting to get for your share in the equity of the firm?"

"Twenty thousand," said Bob. "And it ought to bring in an absolutely safe four thousand a year."

There was a short silence. Bob Horniman thought of a meadow, knee-deep in the first pasture of early summer; of a silver river running through the meadow; of the murmur of flies; of mighty udders, rhythmically a-swing. Bohun thought of the Duchess of Southend's Marriage Settlement.

"I'll see my father at lunch-time," he said. "Where money's the question he usually makes his mind up quickly. I'll probably be able to give you an answer by tomorrow evening."

IV

Mr. Bohun (senior) had for his offices the third floor of one of the noble buildings on the east side of Lombard Street.

His offices were almost spartan in the simplicity of their arrangements. On the right, as you came out of the elevator, a door invited your enquiries. On the left was a similar door, without anything on it at all. Henry opened this door and went into an anteroom, in which sat an old-looking young man, who earned a four-figure salary by insulating Mr. Bohun from the outside world.

He looked up as Henry came in, nodded, and returned to the study of an elaborate graph which he was plotting in six different coloured inks.

Mr. Bohun, who was sitting in a leather arm-chair beside an open fire (the only one allowed in the building), got up, said "Hullo, Henry" in an absent-minded sort of way, and sat down again. He didn't click switches or talk into boxes and tell people he wasn't to be disturbed, because there were no switches or boxes in the room, which looked like a smoking-room or study. Anyway, the young man outside would see to all that.

"Hullo, Dad," said Henry. "You aren't getting any thinner."

"No exercise," said Mr. Bohun. "No excitement. In this firm we don't go in for excitement. Not like you lawyers. We keep papers in our deed boxes. By the way, I see you've been having more trouble lately."

"Yes," said Henry. "That's really one of the things I wanted to tell you about. Here's how it is…"

By the time he had finished, Mr. Bohun had allowed his pipe to go out. He showed no other definite sign of interest.

"What do you think about it yourself?" he said finally.

"I'd like to do it," said Henry. "They're not a very happy firm at the moment. You could hardly expect them to be. But I think they're sound enough at heart. They've got a first-class connection and a lot of business. Perhaps they'll lose some of it over this tamasha, but it'll die down. People don't change their solicitors very easily."

"What about the price?"

Henry grinned. "I know quite well," he said, "that you've got your own means of finding out anything you want to know in that line. You don't need my opinion."

"Perhaps not," said his father, "but let's have it."

"I think," said Henry slowly, "that it would be a fair gamble. They're not gilt-edged. If they were you wouldn't get four-tenths of the equity being offered for twenty thousand."

"No," said his father. "I don't think you would. All right. I'll have a look at it. One of the conditions, of course, will be that you stay in the firm. I shall be investing the money in you as much as in Horniman, Birley and What's-it."

"Very handsome of you," said Henry. "I'm going to get myself some lunch. I suppose it's no good asking you to come out."

"Never have lunch," said Mr. Bohun. "Waste of time. By the way, I suppose you haven't got any idea who did these murders? Not," he added hastily, "that I'm being inquisitive but it might make a difference to my offer."

"I've no idea at all," said Henry truthfully.

v

"Well, now, Mr. Hoffman," said Hazlerigg. "I understand that you've finished the first part of your work and can give me a general report on the financial position."

"An interim report," said Mr. Hoffman. "Then, if you consider that any particular aspect of it wants detailed analysis—"

"Let's start with the general picture, if you don't mind."

Thereupon Mr. Hoffman spoke for an hour, with very little interruption from Hazlerigg. He had a sheaf of notes but he did not refer to them much. It was in his head.

He spoke of capital assets and of invisible assets, of fixed assets and floating assets; of goodwill and the professional index; of the solicitor-client relationship; of the ratio of incomings to outgoings; of over-all balance; and of the law of diminishing returns.

And every point which he established was nailed to the table with figures—pounds and shillings, and years and months, and percentages and fractions.

When he had done, Hazlerigg said: "Thank you very much." Then he said: "I take it you will be letting me have the gist of that in writing." Mr. Hoffman nodded. "Absolutely off the record and without prejudice, what does it add up to?"

Mr. Hoffman considered the question. Then he parcelled his papers neatly back into his brief-case, screwed on the top of his fountain pen, replaced his pen in his inside pocket (where it lived with three coloured propelling pencils) and leaned back in his chair with a relaxed smile; a parting of the lips which, in a man less austere, might almost have been called a grin.

"I always think," he said, "that starting a business is very like lighting the drawing-room fire. First, you stack up the sticks and paper and coal in the grate, and then, at the favourable moment, you apply your match. There's an immediate and beautiful blaze. The paper burns away and the sticks crackle and you put on more and more coal—that's your working capital—and you get precious little real heat by way of return. Then, in every fire, and in every business, there comes a moment when you know if the thing is going to go or not; and *if* the fuel is dry and *if* the draught is right, and *if* you've laid the thing properly, you'll get a decent fire. If anything's wrong, then you can prod it and puff it and pile on fuel till you're black in the face. You'll get nothing but smoke, stink and a hearth full of charred paper. But once the thing's alight there's nothing more to it. The office boy can keep it going. He's only got to drop an occasional lump of coal on. Incidentally that's one of the things people don't think of when they moan about the boss sitting back and taking the profits whilst they do all the work. Anyone can look after a fire *when it's alight*."

"Agreed," said Hazlerigg. "What then?"

"That's all obvious, isn't it," said Mr. Hoffman. "Anyone who thinks about it can see it. But what people don't always realise is that it works the other way round as well. A good fire, you know, will go on burning and glowing and giving out heat for a long time *after* you've stopped putting on any fuel. And if you put on a little from time to time—not enough to replace what's being burnt, but a lump or two—well, it'll go on burning for a very long time. That, as nearly as I can explain it, is what was happening in Horniman, Birley and Craine in about 1939 and 1940. I don't think anyone could have spotted it from outside—but the fuel supply was giving out. Partly," went on Mr. Hoffman, "I expect it was the war. Partly the fact that the system they use here, though an excellent one, isn't productive of very quick or profitable returns. It would be admirably suited"—Mr. Hoffman did not intend this satirically—"to a government office. But chiefly, I think, it was the fact that whilst the incomings were decreasing the liabilities were increasing—especially Abel Horniman's liabilities. They must have been. He had his big house in London and his country house and farm in the country, and he was beginning to attain a certain position, a position which needed money to keep it up; money, and then more money."

"I thought his bank account was rather a modest document," said Hazlerigg.

"I'll give you one example of the sort of thing they were driven to. This building is leasehold. Not a very long lease. Every well-run business which operates on leasehold premises puts aside a fund against the day when the lease expires—for repairs and dilapidations, to say nothing of the premium that they may have to pay to get the lease renewed. Horniman, Birley and Craine had been building up a leasehold depreciation fund for a great many years.

Well, in 1939 they stopped adding to it. In 1940 and 1941 they drew it out and spent it." Mr. Hoffman paused for a moment to marshal his thoughts, then went on: "What happened next is the most difficult of all to explain. But sometime, about the end of 1941, the firm had a blood transfusion."

"Yes," said Hazlerigg. There was no doubt about his interest now. "Please go on."

"Abel Horniman got his hands, somehow, on quite a large capital sum. It isn't obvious—but when you look for it you can see it. That leasehold depreciation account was built up again. The very heavy mortgages on both of Abel's properties were reduced. And more than that, certain expenditure which should normally have come out of income, was made out of capital, which meant, of course, that what income there was went further, and everything looked much more healthy all round."

"A blood transfusion, you said?"

"That was the metaphor that occurred to me." Mr. Hoffman sounded apologetic, as if he realised that an accountant had no business to dabble in metaphors, let alone mixed metaphors. "But it really does explain in the simplest way that I can think of exactly what happened. Somewhere—and I may say that I haven't the very least idea where—Abel Horniman got hold of this money. I can only tell you one thing about it. It came from outside. Maybe someone died and left it to him—only you'd have imagined we should have known about it. Possibly he robbed a bank."

"Well, he may even have done that," agreed Hazlerigg without a smile. "This sum of money—can you estimate how much it was?"

"Oh, quite a lot," said Mr. Hoffman. "Ten thousand pounds, at least."

VI

"After all," said Miss Bellbas. "Murder's a serious thing. It might be one of us next."

"Even so," said Anne Mildmay. "It seems to me rather like sneaking."

"Oh, be your age, Anne," said Miss Cornel crossly. "This isn't the sixth form at St. Ethelfredas. I agree with Florrie. This is serious."

"Well, you can tell him, if you like," said Miss Mildmay. "It just doesn't seem to me to be any of our business."

"I think we should," said Miss Bellbas.

"I'm going to," said Miss Cornel.

Hazlerigg was on the point of leaving when Miss Cornel came in. He was on his way back to the Yard for an interview with Dr. Bland, the pathologist.

"Look here," she said. "I won't keep you long. It's about that letter. The one that was found under my desk."

"Yes," said Hazlerigg.

"I might as well admit," said Miss Cornel, "that there's been a certain amount of difference of opinion about telling you this. But the general idea was that we ought to. It was something we all noticed at the time."

"Something about the letter?"

"Yes. This mayn't seem much to you—but if you remember it started 'Dear Mr. Horniman'. Well, that wasn't the way Mr. Smallbone ever wrote to Abel Horniman. It was always 'Dear Horniman', or 'My Dear Horniman'. There's quite a nice etiquette about these things, you know. When you get friendly, you drop the 'Mr.' and when you get more friendly still you add the 'my'. It's not a thing you'd be likely to get wrong."

"No," said Hazlerigg. "I appreciate that. Well, thank you very much for telling me. I don't really see," he added with a smile, "why you should have been so reluctant to let me have this information."

His mind must have been working at half-speed that morning. It wasn't until he was half-way to Scotland Yard that he saw the implication.

CHAPTER TWELVE

£48 2s. 6d.

Cloud rolls over cloud: one train of thought suggests and is driven away by another: theory after theory is spun out of the bowels of his brain, not like the spider's web, compact and round—a citadel and a snare, built for mischief and for use, but like the gossamer… flitting in the idle air and glittering only in the ray of fancy.

HAZLITT: *The Plain Speaker*

I

"YOU'RE ASKING ME," SAID DR. BLAND, "TO BE SCIENTIFIC about something that has no real scientific basis."

"In other words," said Hazlerigg, "we're asking you to perform the impossible."

"That's it."

"And, as usual, you are going to oblige."

"Soft soap," said Dr. Bland. "All right. So long as you don't expect me to get up in court and explain it all to a jury."

"That's the last thing I shall ask," said Hazlerigg. "All I want you to do is to narrow the field. If you can indicate that certain Saturdays are more likely than other Saturdays, then we can concentrate, first, on the people who were in the office on those days."

Dr. Bland raised a tufted eyebrow at the chief inspector.

"So long as you're not arguing *ex hypothesi*," he said.

"What the devil do you mean?"

"You wouldn't perhaps have some particular person in mind already?"

"James Bland," said Hazlerigg, "you've got a damned diagnosing mind. Yes. I am thinking of one particular person."

"Then this may be helpful."

He unfolded on to Hazlerigg's desk an enormous sheet of graph paper ruled with the usual axes and traversed by nine or ten very attractive apical curves, each one of a different colour.

"They all start," explained the pathologist, "from the zone of maximum improbability—that is zero on the vertical axis, and move upwards towards maximum probability. The horizontal line is a time line, covering the four weeks in question."

"I see," said Hazlerigg. "I think. What are the different colours?"

"Different parts of the body deteriorate, after death, at different speeds. The speed of deterioration of any part depends on a number of constant factors, such as the temperature and the humidity of the atmosphere and equally on a number of accidental circumstances. For instance, if the stomach happens to be full at death—"

"All right," said Hazlerigg hastily, "you can skip that one. These lines, I take it, are the various items you have selected—"

"Test points, yes. The mauve, for instance, shows the degree of separation of the finger-nails from the hand. The yellow is the bladder-wall."

"What's the purple one?"

"Toe-nails."

"I see. And the positioning of the curve enables you to see the likeliest time of death according to each individual symptom."

"That's about it," said the doctor. "As I said at the beginning, there's nothing very scientific about it all. I've just represented, graphically, the points which have influenced me in coming to a certain decision. Generally speaking, I have been helped a great deal by the fact that the body remained—or so I have assumed—in the same very confined place and at a fairly constant temperature."

"And your decision?"

"From the moment of discovery, not less than six weeks, not more than eight."

Hazlerigg took up his desk diary and ran a finger back through the pages.

"It's April twenty-second today," he said. "We found the body on the fourteenth. Just over a week ago. Six weeks back from there brings us to—yes. And eight weeks—hum!"

"Does the answer come out right?" said Dr. Bland.

"Yes," said Hazlerigg. "Yes, I do believe it's beginning to."

II

Chaffham is on the coast of Norfolk. It is not a very large or a very prosperous place, and its principal feature, indeed the chief reason for its existence, is the deep-water inlet which affords anchorage here for a hundred or more craft great and small.

Inspector Hazlerigg, who had travelled down by police car, arrived at Chaffham at half-past three that afternoon. The sun would have done no discredit to a day of June. The water sparkled, as a light wind chased the clouds, and the grey, flat unlovely land did its best to simulate a smile.

Hazlerigg stood in the single main street which sloped to the jetty and the "hard". He looked at the grey-walled, grey-roofed shops, and behind them at the whale-backed hill where only the thorn trees seemed tough enough to outface the savagery of the North Sea. And he felt, deep down inside him, the contentment which even the most unpromising county can bring to her own sons. For he was a Norfolk man; and thirty-two hard years in London had not served to overlay it.

A telephone message had gone ahead of him, and a sergeant of the Norfolk Constabulary was in the main street when the car stopped. Five minutes later Hazlerigg was seated in Chaffham police station, which was, in fact, the front room in Sergeant Rolles's cottage, studying a large-scale map of the district.

"If he's a visitor," said Sergeant Rolles, "a summer visitor, or a yachtsman, he'll not live in Chaffham. He'll have one of the houses along Station Road or Sea Wall."

The sergeant ran his thumb-nail along the two roads, roughly parallel, which joined the station to the village street, following the south bank of the inlet, and forming the crosspiece of a "T" to which the main street was the upright.

"You know all the people who live up and down this street, I expect," said Hazlerigg.

"And their fathers and their grandfathers," said Sergeant Rolles. "But the visitors—well, they come and go. I know the regulars. Let's see that name again. Horniman. Young chap, would it be? Dark hair, wears glasses. Was in the navy—the R.N.V.R., I should say. That's him, then. Keeps a little place almost at the end of Sea Wall. Comes down most weekends. It's shut up now, I expect."

"Has he got local help?"

"Mrs. Mullet does for him," said the sergeant. "Cleans the place, and gets in his stores. He telephones her when he's coming down and she opens the house. I call it a house. It's a bungalow really. The Cabin, or some name like that."

"What's she like?"

"Mrs. Mullet? A most respectable woman. Her father used to keep the Three Lords Hunting. But he's been dead fifteen years. Fell down his cellar flap on New Year's Eve and cracked his skull. She's all right, sir. Her husband's as deaf as a post. He's a wicked old man."

"I think I'll have a word with Mrs. Mullet, if you're agreeable," said Hazlerigg.

"Help yourself," said the sergeant.

Mrs. Mullet received the inspector, with proper Norfolk caution, in a dim kitchen. Her husband sat in a high chair beside the range. His bright eyes moved from speaker to speaker, but he took no part in the opening formalities.

"It's like this, Mrs. Mullet," said Hazlerigg. "I'm very anxious to check exactly when Mr. Horniman arrived at his cottage each weekend. More particularly"—he took a quick glance at his notebook—"on the weekend of February 27th."

"Well, now, I don't know," said Mrs. Mullet.

"Does he come down here every weekend?"

"Oh, no. Not every weekend. Not until the summer. He was down here at the end of February—like you said. That was his first visit this year. Then again at the end of March, and last weekend."

"Well, then," said Hazlerigg. "If February 27th was his first trip, surely that's some reason for it to stick in your memory."

"I can remember it all right," said Mrs. Mullet. "The thing I don't know is whether I ought to tell you anything about it."

Hazlerigg said: "Well, ma'am, I need hardly remind you that it's your duty—"

"If I'm brought to court," said Mrs. Mullet, "that's one thing. If I'm brought to court I shall say what I know. But until then—"

Mr. Mullet swivelled his bright eyes on to the inspector to see how he would play this one.

"I must warn you," said Hazlerigg, "that you may be guilty of obstructing—"

"It's not a thing I approve of," said Mrs. Mullet. "But yooman nature is yooman nature, and all the divorce courts in the world can't stop it."

A sudden warm glow of comprehension irradiated the inspector. It was as if the sun had come out in the Mullet kitchen.

"I don't think you quite understand," he said gently. "I'm investigating a murder."

This got home all right. Mr. Mullet sat up in his chair and said quite sharply: "What's that? Murder! 'As Mr. 'Orniman been murdered?"

Mrs. Mullet said weakly: "Are you a police detective?"

"Well, yes," said Hazlerigg. "I'm not a private detective, if that's what you mean. And I'm not trying to get evidence for a divorce."

"Well, then," said Mrs. Mullet. "I'm sure I'll tell you what I can."

Chaffham, it appeared, though difficult of access by road, had the advantage of being less than a mile from the direct London-Cromer railway line, and an excellent afternoon train left King's Cross at two o'clock and reached Chaffham Halt at four. Bob Horniman, said Mrs. Mullet, used to catch this train, which was met by a single-decker bus (the Chaffham Bumper) driven by a one-eyed mechanic (the Chaffham Terror). This bus, barring enditchment and like accidents reached the cross-roads nearest to The Cabin at ten past four.

"Nice time for tea," said Mrs. Mullet.

"And that was always how he came?"

"That's right. I'd have a fire in and a meal ready. And not before he could do with it, I expect. After tea he'd go and look at his boat. He keeps it in Albert Tugg's yard, when he's not using it. Then he'd have a drink at the Lords. Highly popular, he was, with the gentlemen there. Then he'd go to bed. Sunday, he'd go sailing, and catch the six o'clock train from the Halt. He'd leave the key with me as he went past to catch his bus. Then I'd go in on Monday morning and clean up."

It sounded a harmless and indeed rather a pleasant weekend. Hazlerigg reflected that you never really know a man until you meet him on holiday. He would not have visualised the quiet, bespectacled Bob Horniman as the life and soul of the public bar at Three Lords Hunting.

After a few more general questions he took his departure.

As soon as he had gone Mr. Mullet, who wasn't half as deaf as he liked to make out, surfaced briskly and hobbled across to the cupboard. From the top shelf he took down a much-folded copy of his favourite Sunday newspaper and turned to the centre page.

"It be that Lincoln's Inn murder," he observed. "Thought it must be the same 'Orniman. A firm of lawyers. Found a body in a box. Fairly rotted away, it says."

"Well, I never," said Mrs. Mullet. "What will they do next! Such a nice-looking young man, too."

"Lawyers," said Mr. Mullet. "Good riddance if they all killed each other, I say. Snake eat snake."

At about the same time that Mr. Mullet was making these uncharitable remarks, Inspector Hazlerigg had reached the end of the Sea Wall and was taking a quick look at Bob Horniman's weekend cottage.

It was shuttered and deserted. Over a strip of sand-blown garden and rank lawn he saw the jetty, and the halyards of a little flag-staff. The sun had gone, merging sea and land in uniform unfriendly grey. With the evening a cold wind had arrived.

Hazlerigg walked back to the police station. It occurred to him that he had an urgent telephone call to make.

III

Sergeant Plumptree sat at Hazlerigg's desk. In front of him he had a list. It had nearly three hundred names on it, and to almost each name was annexed a telephone number. Sergeant Plumptree looked at the list and sighed. He had already rung fifty-five of the numbers and he was feeling very tired. His ear-drums were buzzing with infernal dialling tones and his throat was sore with enforced bonhomie. He recollected a story he had once read about the wife of the President of the United States who had shaken hands with three thousand guests at a State reception and, when her husband said "Good morning" to her at breakfast, had started screaming hysterically.

He understood exactly how she had felt.

He dialled the next number. "Mrs. Freestone? Oh, it's Mrs. Freestone's maid. Could I have a word with Mrs. Freestone? I'm speaking on behalf of Horniman, Birley and Craine. Oh—hello, Mrs. Freestone. I'm very sorry to trouble you. We are trying to trace a telephone call which the firm had some time ago—at the end of February. Saturday, February 27th, to be exact. Can you remember if you rang the firm up about that time? Yes, it is rather a long time ago—but being a Saturday morning we thought it might have stuck in your memory—No—Yes—No, of course you couldn't be expected to remember every telephone call you made two months ago. Very sorry to have troubled you, Mrs. Freestone."

Another tick on the list.

"Hullo. Is that Sir Henry Rollaway—Oh, it's Sir Henry's man. Would you tell Sir Henry that Horniman, Birley and Craine…"

IV

That same afternoon, Bohun put down the draft will he was perusing and hit the desk softly with the open palm of his hand.

"Of course," he said. "I knew it meant something."

"Knew what meant something?" asked John Cove.

"Forty-eight pounds, two shillings and sixpence."

"Don't be silly," said John.

"That's because you haven't had an actuarial training," said Bohun. "Every figure has a meaning. To the discerning eye there is all the difference in the world between a seductive little multiplicand and a sinister prime."

After a few minutes' thought he went to look for Mr. Hoffman, whom he found at a table in Mr. Waugh's room. Mr. Hoffman was thumbing through a batch of cancelled cheques with absent-minded enthusiasm.

"Inspector Hazlerigg told me," said Bohun, "that when you were examining Abel Horniman's private bank account, you could only find one item which you couldn't explain. As I remember, that was a quarterly payment of £48 2s. 6d."

"That is quite correct."

"It just occurred to me to wonder," said Bohun apologetically, "—it seems such an obvious suggestion—but have you tried grossing it up at 3½ per cent?"

Mr. Hoffman looked surprised. "With or without tax," he said.

"Adding on tax. In view of what you said, I thought it was rather a coincidence."

Mr. Hoffman's pencil moved across the paper. Then he clicked the tip of his tongue delicately against the roof of his mouth and said: "Tchk, tchk. Yes, indeed. How very surprising. To think that I never noticed it."

It was the grudging salute of one mathematician to another.

Henry went slowly upstairs, and across into the partners' side of the building.

It seemed to him that circumstances were conspiring to force decisions on him; decisions which he had little desire to face.

"Yes," said Mr. Birley, "what is it?"

"I wondered if I might have a word with you and Mr. Craine."

"All right," said Mr. Birley. The thought struck him that Bohun also might be going to give notice. Nothing would surprise him now.

"Certainly," said Mr. Craine. "What's the trouble?"

"No trouble really," said Bohun. And without further preamble he told them of Bob Horniman's surprising offer made to him that morning. It occurred to him that he might be committing a breach of confidence, and it also occurred to him that in the circumstances it could not matter much.

When Mr. Birley had grasped what was going on he said explosively:

"Bob can't do that. Really, Bohun. I'm surprised at you."

Mr. Craine said nothing. He looked thoughtful.

"I should have thought you would have known enough about the Law of Partnership," went on Mr. Birley, "to know that one partner can't transfer his share just as if it was so much personal property. His other partners have got some say in the matter, you know. It was different with Abel. He was the founder of the firm and he reserved the right to transmit his share to his son. That was agreed. I never entirely approved of it, but that's neither here nor there. But Bob's got no more right to hand it on to you than to Miss Bellbas. I don't mean to be rude," continued Mr. Birley—who clearly did—"but you've only been here a week. And you've hardly been qualified a month."

He looked to Mr. Craine for moral support, but Mr. Craine, who had been looking at Bohun speculatively, remained silent.

"Of course, in a few years' time," said Mr. Birley, "when you've—er—proved your metal—we might perhaps consider a salaried partnership."

"Quite," said Bohun. "And I much appreciate the confidence in my abilities which inspires the offer. A moment ago you said that you might just as well have offered a partnership to Miss Bellbas. Now I don't suppose you meant that seriously, but it enables me to put what I have to put quite clearly. Considered as potential partners, the essential difference between myself and Miss Bellbas is that I am in a position to put twenty thousand pounds into the business—as an investment, of course."

"Why do you suppose," said Mr. Birley, "that the firm should be in need of twenty thousand pounds?" Curiously, he did not put the question in an offensive or rhetorical manner. He asked it as if he was genuinely in search of information; and Bohun answered in the same tone.

"You know as well as I do, that Abel Horniman borrowed ten thousand pounds from the Ichabod Stokes Trust, and used it to bolster up the finances of the firm."

"He put it all back," said Mr. Craine sharply.

"If he ever took it," said Mr. Birley. "It's never been proved."

"And never will be now," said Mr. Craine.

"I expect you're right," said Bohun. "If Mr. Hoffman can't spot the join, I don't suppose anyone will ever do any better. Particularly as the money was put back almost at once: and all the interim trust accounts seem to have disappeared into the limbo."

"Then what—" said Mr. Birley.

"But the fact that no one seems to know where it ultimately came from doesn't alter the fact that at some time or other this money will have to be paid back."

"How do you know that it was a loan," said Mr. Birley. "He may—well, he may have been left the money."

"I can't think you intend the suggestion seriously," said Bohun. "If the money had been left to him you'd certainly have known of it—but in any case, it doesn't arise. It's now quite certain that Abel Horniman was paying interest on the money down to the day of his death. The item appears in his bank book. Forty-eight pounds two and sixpence. Three and a half per cent per annum on ten thousand pounds, less tax. Rather a significant item."

"Who was the money paid to?" said Mr. Craine.

One of the oddest points of this odd conversation was that both the partners seemed unconsciously to be treating Bohun as an equal.

"The money was drawn by Abel in cash," said Bohun. "We've just found that out. I presume he paid the money for security reasons into a private account—at another bank. Then he could pay the interest by cheque—to—"

"To whom," said Mr. Birley and Mr. Craine in a grammatical dead-heat.

"Well, that's just it," said Bohun smoothly. "To whoever he got the money from, I suppose."

"The whole thing's inexplicable," said Mr. Craine. "Speaking quite frankly—since all the cards are on the table—Abel had no security he could borrow on. He had this business, of course. That produced a good income—but there was no equity in it. Certainly nothing he could pledge. His London house and his farm and estate were mortgaged to the hilt, and over."

"Where he got it from," said Bohun, "heaven knows. It's even been suggested that he took a gun and robbed a bank. One thing seems certain—or anyway highly probable. Smallbone found out the truth about it. And the truth, if it had been exposed—as Smallbone would have revelled in exposing it, he was that sort of person—would have resulted in ruin for Abel Horniman and disaster for his firm. That, it seems plain, is why he was killed."

He paused.

"Now that Abel is dead the first threat has lost its sting. The second one, of course, remains. That's why I took the liberty just now of suggesting that the firm might find itself in need of some ready capital."

v

"Major Fernough?" said Sergeant Plumptree. He wondered if he sounded as tired as he felt.

"Yes, this is Major Fernough speaking."

"I'm sorry to trouble you. I am speaking on behalf of Horniman, Birley and—that's right. Your solicitors. We are trying to trace a call made to the office on February 27th."

"Was that a Saturday?"

"That's right."

"In the morning?"

"Yes."

"Funny thing you should mention it," said Major Fernough. "Wait a moment whilst I look at my diary. Yes. You're quite right. I did ring the office that morning. Just after eleven o'clock. What about it?"

"Well—er—who did you speak to?" said Sergeant Plumptree cautiously.

"Don't be silly," said Major Fernough. "That's the whole point. That's what I complained about. I didn't speak to anybody. There was no one there. I rang up three times. Damnably slack. If you say you're going to have someone in the office on Saturday morning then you ought to have someone in the office."

"Quite so, sir," said Sergeant Plumptree, with heartfelt gratitude. "Thank you, sir. Thank you, indeed."

VI

As soon as Mr. Birley reached his house in St. George's Square that evening, he went upstairs to his bedroom. A glass-topped hospital table stood beside the bed, and above the bed was a large white cupboard.

Mr. Birley opened the cupboard and surveyed the solid array of bottles. He considered his latest symptoms with the earnest zest of a practised hypochondriac. Latterly he had been seeing dashes. Not dots or spots—these were common enough and could easily be dealt with by a dose of salts—but bar-shaped dashes sometimes flanking, sometimes superimposed upon the dots. The whole effect was not unlike a message in morse.

Mr. Birley weighed his symptoms against his powerful array of remedies, and finally selected a large green bottle and poured himself out a measured medicine glass of ruby-coloured liquid. He stirred it for a moment with a rod, then downed it in one. After this he inspected his tongue in the glass, felt his pulse, and closed his eyes again.

The dashes were still there, but fainter.

Mr. Birley repeated the dose twice and quite suddenly began to feel happier. (This was not actually surprising, since what he was drinking was, had he known it, very inferior port masquerading as a health tonic and sold in small bottles at a very superior price.)

Mr. Birley went downstairs to his study and sat at his desk. He thought with distaste of Henry Bohun and with active dislike of Mr. Craine. He thought of Bob Horniman and, with no very great charity, of the dead Abel Horniman. He thought of the future. Ahead of him stretched unbroken reefs of trouble. Endless shocks to his nervous system; endless assaults on his gastric fluids; endless nights when fear of insomnia would prove more potent than insomnia itself.

After all, he reflected, he had no need of his professional earnings. He had never spent half of them and the accumulation of years served only to excite the rapacity of the Chancellor of the Exchequer.

And lastly, and by no means least, if anything unpleasant did happen—and that damned fellow Bohun had sounded very confident—might it not be better if it could be shown that he had taken steps *before*…

He pulled a sheet of paper towards him and started to write.

VII

After supper that night Bohun put on his working clothes, told Mrs. Magoli not to wait up for him, and started out.

He wanted to think, and he had found that walking at night

through the streets of the City was one of the best ways of thinking. He was not due on his watchman's job until ten o'clock, so there was no need to hurry.

It was a lovely night, with high, packed white clouds and the moon playing hide-and-seek between them. Bohun made his way steadily eastwards, only dimly conscious of the route he was taking but certain with the certainty of a born Londoner that he could not stray very far from his bearing.

There were two distinct and separate problems. He saw that now. It was confusion over this prime fact that had created to date so much unnecessary obscurity. The first was the problem of who had killed Mr. Smallbone, and why had they done it—with the pendant to it, of why it had been necessary to remove Miss Chittering. The other problem was how Abel Horniman had managed to lay his hands on ten thousand pounds.

The two problems were connected, of course. Here Bohun felt himself to be on secure ground. The chain of causation, in outline, was as he had laid it before Birley and Craine. Abel Horniman had raised ten thousand pounds by some method on the windy side of the law. Marcus Smallbone had found out about it. Marcus Smallbone was the sort of man who was known to be untiring in nosing out scandals, indefatigable in his zeal for proclaiming them to the world. Therefore somebody who did not wish the facts to be known had removed Mr. Smallbone with a homemade cheese cutter. And seeing exposure threatened from some indiscretion of Miss Chittering, had removed her, too.

It was becoming increasingly and painfully plain who that somebody must be. Motive and opportunity were both evident. It was necessary now only to solve the fundamental problem behind Abel's acquisition of wealth.

Bohun had reached this point when he found himself at Aldgate Pump. He therefore turned south-east and devoted his thoughts for the next fifteen minutes to a consideration of methods by which a hardworking, systematic, professionally knowledgeable, not very active solicitor might manufacture ten thousand pounds.

The obvious solution would be to dip into a trust fund—some fund of which he was, in effect, the sole active trustee. And this, as a first effort, was no doubt what Abel had done. He had borrowed the money from the Ichabod Stokes Trust. That did not afford a final or satisfactory solution. The system of solicitors accounting is designed to reveal such illicit borrowings, and beneficiaries, even though charitable in every sense of the word, are certain in the end to raise objections to the disappearance of substantial portions of their income. Realising this, Abel had very promptly paid back into the Stokes Trust an equivalent sum of money which he had succeeded in raising in some other and more ingenious way. The repayment into the Stokes Trust had passed without detection and, in Bohun's opinion, would never now be proved, particularly since most of the relevant accounts were lost.

This left unsolved, however, the question of where the money had ultimately come from. It had been borrowed, he was fairly certain, but on what conceivable security?

VIII

"Thoughtful tonight, 'Enery," said the bald man.

"Something on my mind," said Bohun.

"A problem?"

"That's it," said Bohun. "A problem. What's this pitch like?"

"Oh, very snug. Very nice little business." The bald man waved a proprietorial arm round the shadowy warehouse. "Enough whisky to give us a hangover just for looking at it."

"Where do we sit?" said Henry.

"In here." The bald man showed him into a sort of porters' room, just inside the main warehouse. "Gas-fire, gas-ring for our cuppers." He demonstrated certain other arrangements. "All the fixings."

"Very nice," said Bohun. "What's the routine?"

"Ten minutes in the hour. We'll take it in turns. Takes eight minutes to get round, allowing two for extras. If the other chap's not back by the end of ten minutes, then you know what."

"Fine," said Henry.

He tilted his chair at a convenient angle and resumed his interrupted train of thought. Fortunately, the bald man was not talkative, and after a bit, silence descended on the little room, broken only by the purring of the gas-fire, and ticking of the gold-and-green time-clock in the corner.

Security—mortgage—lien—bill of sale—pledge—collateral. How could a man mortgage something which he hadn't got? That was what it boiled down to. What sort of security could he have offered? It must have been good security, thought Henry, if the borrower only had to pay three and a half per cent for his loan. You didn't get risky money at that rate of interest.

He took his problem with him when he went on his round at half-past three, down the corridors of crates and boxes, under the great unwinking night lamps. It was with him as he tested the automatic alarms on the two steel-roller-covered entrance doors; and it was still no nearer to an answer when he got back and found the bald man brewing one more in an endless series of cups of tea.

He put it to him. "How can you raise money on something you haven't got?" he said.

"Search me," said the bald man. "I'm not a borrowing man."

Bohun felt that he was reaching a stage of mental exhaustion and nullity. He took out a well-thumbed copy of the *Plain Speaker* and was soon adrift on the strong tide of Hazlitt's prose.

Out of the corner of his eye he saw the bald man leave the room and noticed that it was exactly half-past four.

"Cloud rolls over cloud; one train of thought suggests and is driven away by another; theory after theory is spun out of the bowels of his brain, not like the spider's web, compact and round, a citadel and a snare, built for mischief and for use—"

"'A citadel and a snare'," said Bohun, "'built for mischief and for use.' There's glory for you." He saw that the bald man was still absent, and the hands of the clock said nearly a quarter to five.

"Hell," said Bohun uneasily. "I do hate this sort of thing." He put the book back in his pocket and tilted his chair forward so that he could see the doorway reflected in the glass over the fireplace. He felt with his toe for the concealed, spring-loaded switch.

The door opened softly and a young man came in. They all look so alike, thought Bohun. Young, tough, white, boxer's face. Black hair, white silk scarf, old battledress. This one carried a gun and looked as if he knew how to use it.

Bohun let him get three paces in the room before he kicked the switch. A steel shutter came down across the door, thudding softly home against its counter-balance. Bohun got cautiously to his feet and said with almost ludicrous earnestness:

"Think before you do anything rash. I'm certain you wouldn't like the police to find you locked in here with a dead body."

"Open that unprintable door," said the young man.

"It's no good," said Bohun. "I can't, really. Here's the switch. No deception. You can see for yourself. It just works one way, to drop the door. It can only be opened now from the outside, with a proper key, when the police get here."

"*When* they get here," said the young man nastily.

"That's pretty soon, really," said Bohun. "The same switch sounds the alarm at Cloak Lane and Bishopsgate, and drops the outer doors. They can get cars here in three minutes. Your pals are all in the bag, too."

"Wonderful thing, science," said the young man.

Bohun saw that everything was going to be all right and sat down again.

"I've got a good mind to bash you, all the same," said the young man.

"It wouldn't do you any good really, would it?" said Bohun. "Look here, shall I give you a tip?"

"I'm not fussy," said the young man.

Bohun walked over to the window, which was heavily barred, and raised the sash. The young man came and stood beside him.

"I wasn't suggesting that you could get out," said Bohun, "but I happen to know that there's an old ditch down there—it's a drain really—six foot of nettles and then God knows how many feet of mud."

"Thanks," said the young man. He pushed his gun through the bars, and they heard the soft thud as it fell into the darkness. "It wasn't loaded. Very civil of you, all the same. Anything I can do by way of exchange." He sat down on the chair recently vacated by the bald man.

"Well," said Bohun, "perhaps you can tell me the answer to a question that's been puzzling me all evening. How can a man raise money on something he hasn't got?"

The young man thought for a moment. "That's dead easy," he said. "Pawn the same article twice. It's the quickness of the hand deceives the eye. My old man used to do it with cuff links. It's quite a lark... Oh, here come our feathered friends... Remind me to tell you about it some time."

It was half-past five when Bohun got home. A City police car gave him a lift as far as the end of Chancery Lane. As he walked up the Rents the answer came to him in all its stunning and beautiful simplicity.

"Pawn the same thing twice."

Bohun climbed into bed. For the first time in years he slept for a full three hours.

CHAPTER THIRTEEN

A Very Puisne Mortgage

But here a grievance seems to lie
All this is mine but till I die
I can't but think 'twould sound more clever
"To me and to my heirs for ever."

Lines inserted by Pope in Swift's
Imitation of the Sixth Satire of Horace

I

FRIDAY WAS QUITE A DAY.

Bohun spent the first hour of it down in the firm's strong-room. This was the kingdom of Sergeant Cockerill, and like everything about the sergeant, it was neat and well-ordered and artistically efficient.

The deeds and papers which, in a normal solicitor's office, lie about in insubordinate bundles loosely constrained with red tape, had been strait-jacketed into card and canvas folders; and these, in their turn, stood dressed by the right on shelves of slab slate. Occupying the serrefile rank, two paces to the right and two paces to the rear, stood the Ledger of Wills, the Ledger of Securities and the Ledger of Deeds. It was through this last book that Bohun was searching.

"Was there any particular deeds that you had in mind, sir?" enquired Sergeant Cockerill.

"Well—no. Not really. I know the sort of thing I'm looking for, but I don't know exactly what it is. I shall probably recognise it when I see it, if you see what I mean."

"If it's any help to you," said Sergeant Cockerill, "you'll find all the deeds indexed under the name of the client and cross-indexed under the name of the partner who deals with them."

"Yes, that should help," said Bohun. "I know it was Abel Horniman."

Sergeant Cockerill looked up rather sharply at this, but said nothing.

Bohun also paused in his search and for a moment there was silence in the vaulted tomb-like room with its door of eight-inch steel.

"You were very attached to him, weren't you?" said Bohun.

The sergeant did not pretend not to understand him.

"Yes," he said. "More than thirty years I knew him. He was a good man to work for. I'd say he was a great man."

This struck a chord all right. Bohun had to think for a moment, then he remembered that Miss Cornel had used almost exactly the same words.

"I was his batman in 1914," went on Sergeant Cockerill. "That surprises you. You didn't know that Mr. Horniman went to France in the Gunners. He was too old for such capers, really: but go he would. Lucky for him, I always thought, he got pneumonia on top of a sharp nip of muscular rheumatism. It was the damp and the cold. Between 'em, they nearly did for him. But I reckon they saved his life, none the less. He had a medical board and got taken out of the army. We were all sorry to see him go. Yes, a great man."

For all practical purposes the sergeant was now talking to himself.

"He was waiting outside the depot on the day I was demobbed. I hadn't told him. He'd found out. That was the sort of man he was. He stood me a drink and offered me a job. Well, that was longer ago than I care to think of." The sergeant turned about abruptly. "I must go and make them their teas. I can't trust that young Charlie with it. Sixteen years in this mortal vale and he still hasn't learnt to warm the pot."

When the sergeant had gone, Bohun did not immediately resume his search of the register. An illusive memory was teasing him. He thought it was something to do with Cockerill. He couldn't put his finger on it. After a bit he gave up trying.

Using the index it took him surprisingly little time to trace the deeds he wanted. He made a careful note of dates and parties on a piece of paper and then turned to the deed containers on the shelf. They were numbered to correspond with the ledger and he soon had his hand on the right envelope. It was empty except for an old deed receipt. Some minutes later he was upstairs in his room talking to John Cove.

"Do you remember the sale of Longleaf Farm?"

"It is inscribed on the tablets of my heart," said John. "It was the very first piece of conveyancing that I did in this office."

"I thought I made out your initials on the deed receipt. Can you tell me about it?"

"What do you want to know?" said John. "The vendor, if my memory serves me, was one Daniel Jedd. The purchaser, a Major Wright. If you're passionately interested I'll get out the file. Here you are. It was quite a straightforward title. Indeed, I suspect that's why Abel gave it to me as a first effort. It started with—yes—three straight conveyances. The first in 1880. Another in 1901 and the third to Ezekiel Jedd in 1920. He settled it by his will and died in 1925. Then there's a vesting deed—vesting it in his son Amos as life tenant. Amos died in 1935. Another vesting deed, in Daniel Jedd, who, without further ado, barred his entail and sold as absolute owner in 1938. Bob's your uncle."

"And it was the same property all the way through. All the way from 1880 onwards, I mean."

"To the last blade of grass."

"Then," said Bohun, "why weren't the first three conveyances handed over when it was finally sold out of this office?"

"Yes, I remember. Abel did say something about that. I can't remember what. The root of title we offered was the 1926 vesting deed."

"That was all right as far as it went," said Henry. "But you'd have thought that the earlier deeds would have been handed over too, or else"—he pointed to the draft conveyance—"the usual acknowledgment given for their safe custody."

"Now that you mention it, that does seem a bit odd. Are you absolutely certain they weren't handed over?"

"Absolutely. The conveyances of 1880, 1901 and 1920 were never marked out of the deeds register here at all. And look—here's a copy of the schedule. It starts with the vesting deed of 1926."

"So it does," said John, scratching his head. "Why do you suppose Abel wanted to keep the early deeds—he never struck me as the type who would go in for home-made lamp shades."

"I don't think he kept them for lamp shades," said Bohun slowly. "I think—oh, that's probably for me. Hullo. Yes, Bohun speaking."

"We've traced that bank account," said Hazlerigg's voice. "In view of what you told me early this morning I thought you might find it interesting. The quarterly payments were made to the Husbandmen's League Friendly and Loan Society. Their office is in Lombard Street."

"Fine," said Bohun. "I'll go straight along."

"I take it that hunch you had is working out then."

"Very nicely."

"Keep me posted," said Hazlerigg, and rang off.

"What's it all about?" said John.

"My idea, roughly," said Bohun, "is that Abel Horniman forged a set of title deeds. Well—not forged, really. That's the wrong word. He effected a little rearrangement. Something after this style. I think he got hold of three solid-looking and obviously genuine conveyances—just for the sake of argument let's say the three first conveyances of Longleaf Farm, that we've just been talking about. Those particular ones were very suitable because they hadn't got a plan on them—just a description. I think he took the last one—the 1920 conveyance, the one to Ezekiel Jedd, removed the last page, and sewed in a new one that he'd written out himself, in law script—that was the sort of thing he did rather well, wasn't it?"

"Oh, yes. He wrote a beautiful copperplate. The perfect practical conveyancer."

"It stuck in my mind that Mr. Birley said something of the sort at the firm's dinner. Well, I think the page he faked up *had* a plan on it. Furthermore, and here I'm guessing again, I think it was a plan of Abel's own farm—Crookham Court Farm. Then all he had to do was to draw up a conveyance purporting to be by Ezekiel Jedd to himself—again with a plan of Crookham Court Farm—perfectly open and above board—take it down to the Stamp Office and have it stamped, and there you are."

"It sounds like falling off a log," said John, "but—I may be being stupid—why did he want a second set of title deeds to Crookham Court Farm? He must have acquired a perfectly good set when he bought the place in 1936."

"Well," said Henry. "He had to hand over the real deeds to the National Provincial Bank when he mortgaged his farm to them, way back in 1937. Don't you think a spare set must have been quite useful when he wanted to raise the wind again in 1943?"

"Viewed in that light," agreed John, "a chap could hardly have too many sets of title deeds. Where are you going?"

"Down to the Husbandmen's League to make sure. Coming?"

"Might as well," said John. "I can see that I shan't be allowed to concentrate on my Final until everything has been cleared up in Chapter Sixteen. How did you get on to this particular swindle?"

"It's known as the cuff-link trick," said Bohun. "If we run we shall just get that bus. You pawn one cuff link twice. I started to have it explained to me by an expert last night."

II

The Husbandmen's League occupied a floor in the building that housed Mr. Bohun Senior. There was nothing markedly agricultural about them apart from their name and their seal, a design showing two blades of corn (thrift) crossed in front of a sickle (hard work). They were, in fact, a collection of long-headed believers in private enterprise who lent their money at three and a half per cent to farmers. Hazlerigg had already been on the telephone to them and Bohun and Cove were shown straight into the office of the general manager. Mr. Manifold was a baldish West Countryman, constructed basically on the lines of a barrage balloon. The worries of the morning had emptied a pocket or two of the gas out of his fabric.

"I hope," he began, "that there's nothing wrong. We heard, of course, of Mr. Horniman's death. Very sad." He assumed a mournful expression momentarily. "We had anticipated that probate would be exhibited in the normal way, and the executor would have continued the quarterly payments. The next one falls due on the first of June."

Bohun decided that brutality would probably get him through quickest in the end.

"I don't doubt," he said, "that the interest payments will be kept up, for the time being anyway. But I am afraid I must break it to you that the security for the loan is illusory."

"Illusory?" Mr. Manifold deflated sharply, then recovered and went rather red, exactly as if he had received a badly-needed replenishment of helium. "Perhaps you would be good enough to explain how the security of two hundred acres of freehold farming land can be illusory?"

"Have you got the deeds here?"

"I have asked for all the papers to be brought up," said Mr. Manifold stiffly, "and here is Mr. Fremlinghouse—our legal adviser."

Mr. Fremlinghouse, who was very tall, had a light moustache, and wore horn-rimmed glasses, advanced and laid a packet of deeds in front of Mr. Manifold. Mr. Manifold untied the red tape and shuffled them over to Bohun.

Bohun only needed to look at the first one to be certain. He pushed it across to John Cove. "February 15th, 1880. Indenture of Conveyance. Henry Balderstone and Others to John Pratt. Longleaf Farm in the County of Kent."

"The name was changed later, as I remember it," said Mr. Fremlinghouse.

"It certainly was," agreed Bohun grimly.

Passing over the next deed he opened the conveyance of 1920. It was engrossed bookwise, on clean-looking parchment, in the usual beautiful characterless law copperplate. Bohun looked carefully at the final page. John Cove and Mr. Fremlinghouse looked over his shoulder.

"You can see the join quite easily," he said. "The last page inside the back sheet. It's been sewn in behind the fold, and the hinge has been covered by that transparent adhesive stuff—map-makers' tape, I believe it's called."

"Gracious goodness," said Mr. Fremlinghouse. "Now so it has. I don't think I examined it particularly—not from that point of view at least. It's quite a common practice to repair deeds with that transparent tape. What is your idea—that the last page is an insertion—a substitution?"

"That's it," said Bohun.

"Now I do like that," said John. He had his finger on the clause describing the property. "Neat but not gaudy: 'formerly known as Longleaf Farm, but now and for some years past known as Stancomb Farm in the County of Kent'."

Mr. Fremlinghouse was examining the three deeds with a professional interest that almost bordered on enthusiasm.

"No plan in the first two deeds, I see," he observed.

"No. Just a schedule of tithe numbers with their acreages and the usual interminable descriptions: 'All those several fields or closes of arable and pasture land and land covered by water, together with the messuages hereditaments buildings etc. etc.' I wonder they troubled to write it all out. I'm certain no one ever bothers to read it."

"I imagine," said Mr. Fremlinghouse, "that it's a relic of the days when you got paid for your conveyancing by the yard. I see your man has simply carried on from the last page of the genuine conveyance—quite so—and inserted the words: 'As the same is delineated on the plan annexed hereto.' Then he supplied his own plan. Wait a minute, though. What about a comparison of the schedules?"

"The total acreage was about the same," said Bohun. "The old deeds gave tithe numbers. He changed them to Ordnance Survey numbers to correspond with his own farm."

"Beautiful. Beautiful," said Mr. Fremlinghouse.

"Really, Fremlinghouse," said Mr. Manifold. "Isn't this exactly what we pay you to protect us from."

"No conveyancer can protect you from deliberate fraud," said the solicitor. "On the face of it, these deeds confer a proper title to Stancomb Farm on one Ezekiel Jedd. They're properly stamped and appear to be properly executed. Then we have another excellent deed conveying the same property from Ezekiel Jedd to Mr. Horniman. What more could anyone ask for?"

Another thought struck Mr. Manifold. "What about our valuer?" he said. "If Stancomb Farm doesn't exist, what did he value? Or is his report a forgery, too?"

"I see you haven't grasped the full inwardness of the idea," said Bohun. "When your valuer went down to Kent to inspect the farm he would naturally get in touch with the owner—arrange an appointment and so on."

"Of course."

"Well, the owner of this Stancomb Farm—which we now know to be a figment of his own fertile imagination—was Abel Horniman. I've no doubt Abel met him with a car, took charge of him, and showed him round *his own farm*. That's why it was a plan of his own farm—Crookham Court Farm—and not a purely imaginary one, that he put on the forged set of deeds. Everything then tied up very neatly."

A gleam of hope appeared in Mr. Manifold's eye. He pointed to the last deed.

"If that's really a plan of Crookham Court Farm," he said, "can't we claim that our mortgage covers that farm—whatever it says in the deed?"

"I suppose you might," said Bohun. "Only it won't do you much good. It's already very heavily mortgaged to the National Provincial Bank."

"Why didn't you find that out?" said Mr. Manifold. He felt that it was intolerable that he should be able to blame nobody. "Didn't you search at the Land Registry? I take it you made the usual searches." This was a minutia of the law which he happened to understand, and he got it off his chest with some pride.

"Certainly I searched," said Mr. Fremlinghouse. "And I found Abel Horniman's mortgage of Crookham Court Farm duly recorded. Why should I worry about that? He was mortgaging Stancomb Farm to you. Of course, it really was Crookham Court Farm, too, but I wasn't to know that."

Mr. Manifold said something like "Tchah", and started to tear up a large clean sheet of blotting-paper.

"Look here," said Bohun. "It may not be as bad as it seems. I think there's every chance that the money will be repaid in full."

The telephone bell rang. Mr. Manifold ignored it for as long as he could, and finally picked up the receiver with a very bad grace.

"What?" he said. "Who? Oh! Wait a minute." He covered the mouthpiece and turned to Henry. "It's Scotland Yard," he said. "Chief Inspector Hazlerigg wants you to go round there at once."

"Tell him I'll be right along," said Bohun.

As he and John Cove left they saw Mr. Manifold and Mr. Fremlinghouse looking at each other with a wild surmise.

III

"I'm sorry to drag you down here like this," said Hazlerigg, "but things are moving quite fast and I wanted to hear your story."

Bohun told it to him.

"It seems easy," said Hazlerigg. "Ten thousand pounds for one sheet of writing. However, most great frauds look easy."

"I don't think," said Bohun, "that anyone except an expert conveyancer who also happened to be right on the spot, like Abel, could have pulled it off. Take one thing—supposing the valuer had been a local man, who knew the property. That would have blown it sky-high. I expect you'll find that Abel knew the Husbandmen employed a London valuer. He may even have known him personally. That would have made it easier still."

"One thing puzzles me," said Hazlerigg. "According to you he laid the foundations of this fraud as long ago as 1938. Did he know about the angina then?"

"Probably not," said Bohun. "He knew he was running short of cash, though. One of the real beauties of this method was that it was reversible. So long as he kept up the interest payments he was pretty safe. Then, if things looked up and he could repay the money all he had to do was discharge the mortgage. Then he would get the deeds back. He could burn them if he liked. The Husbandmen got their money. Everybody happy. No questions asked. Really, just like the office boy who steals from the petty cash and hopes to make it up next week on the pools."

"They're all the same," said Hazlerigg. "However, that part of the business is reasonably clear now. Thanks to your efforts," he added generously. "Here's what must have happened. Smallbone got to hear of Stancomb Farm, and something—we shall never know what—led him to suspect its non-existence. On February 17th—that was Friday—he went down to make sure. We ought to have paid more attention to that remark he made to his landlady: 'If I find what I'm looking for, that'll be the beginning of great things.' The nasty little man already saw a *cause célèbre*, dirty washing galore, himself perhaps in the witness box. Well, he found what he was looking for—or he didn't find it, which amounted to the same thing. He came back that same night to his rooms and the next day—"

"Yes," said Bohun. "How did he spend the next fortnight?"

"He spent the next week attending a sale of china and pottery at Lyme Regis. That's one of the items of information that's just come in. Ordinary routine. There's no doubt about it, perfect identification. He wasn't hiding or anything. He registered in his own name."

"And in the intervals between bidding for might-be Ming and dubious Chelsea, he was thinking about how to wring the most enjoyment out of the Horniman scandal?"

"Yes. I think he wrote at least two letters and I think he wrote them to Bob Horniman. He may have known by then that Abel was pretty far gone. Perhaps he didn't want the shock to kill him before he could get him into the dock. That was the sort of way his mind would work. The first letter would set out the facts he had discovered, and ask what the firm intended to do about it. Were they going to pay the money back? (He knew damn well they couldn't.) And even if they did, he was afraid it was his duty to go to the police—criminal proceedings, Larceny Act, etc. etc. Bob thinks this over and writes back making an appointment for the morning of Saturday 27th. Told him he could explain everything."

"Then," said Bohun, "I suppose he got busy manufacturing his cheese-cutter and clearing out one of the larger deed boxes. By the way, how did Smallbone spend the following week? At a sale of glass at Hemel Hempstead?"

"We don't know yet," said Hazlerigg. "We shall," he added with calm conviction.

"I don't doubt it," said Bohun, who was beginning to have a healthy respect for the results of routine. "What happened next?"

"Smallbone acknowledged Bob Horniman's answer and confirmed the appointment. Hoped what Bob had to tell him would be satisfactory. That was the letter we found, of course. It was written to Bob's private address. That's why it didn't go through the office filing system."

"Written to Bob?"

"Yes. It took a committee of typists to point out to me the difference between a letter starting 'Dear Horniman', and 'Dear Mr. Horniman'."

"And Bob had it in his pocket and dropped it at the office?"

"Something like that. This is only the rough outline. We'll fill in the details later. On Saturday morning, Marcus Smallbone comes up to Lincoln's Inn at twelve-fifteen, as arranged. Bob is alone by that time. He tries argument. Quite futile. So it has to be the other thing. Into the box with the body. Chuck away the key. Sit tight."

"It would need a bit of nerve that last bit. Sitting tight, I mean."

"Yes," said Hazlerigg. "You ought to read his citation," he added inconsequently. "Did you know he got a D.S.C.? It was quite a good one. He got it on Arctic convoy."

Bohun thought about this for a bit and then said: "Have you got any direct proof?"

"You don't often get direct proof of murder," said Hazlerigg mildly. "We're beginning to get quite a lot of indirect proof. It's starting to add up. That's all I can say. The time of that second murder for instance. Three or four people haven't got a firm alibi for the half-hour that matters. But Bob Horniman, so far as I know, is the only person who's troubled to offer us a false one."

"You're sure of that?"

"Morally certain. I'm prepared to put every single waitress in the restaurant he says he went to that night into the box to swear they've never set eyes on him. We've done a lot of hard work on that bit."

"Anything else?"

"One other thing to date. According to his story he and Miss Mildmay were in the office that Saturday morning together until after twelve o'clock. Say they were mistaken. Say they left at five to twelve. We wouldn't quarrel over ten or fifteen minutes. But how do you explain the fact that a client rang your firm up three times at *eleven* o'clock and got no answer?"

"H'm! What's your explanation?"

"I don't have to explain it. Bob Horniman has to do that. But let's suppose he got rid of Miss Mildmay almost at once—said there was no work for her—asked her to keep her mouth shut about it, though, afterwards. And supposing he was busy himself. He had to get rid of a lot of books and papers."

"Yes," said Bohun. He had just remembered something. He had remembered the way Anne Mildmay had looked at Bob Horniman, after the office party, on his first evening with the firm. That was ten days ago. It seemed a lot longer. It seemed...

Quite suddenly he got to his feet.

"If you don't want me for anything else at the moment," he said, "I'll be off."

"Can I get you a taxi?"

"No, thank you," said Bohun. "I'll walk."

"Quite sure?"

"Thank you. I'll be all right."

"Well, I'll ring you up if anything transpires. And you might keep in touch with me."

"All right," said Bohun. He went out quickly.

Hazlerigg watched him go and there was a thoughtful look in his grey eyes.

Bohun walked all the way home.

It had come to him quite suddenly: the monstrous idea that Bob Horniman really was a murderer and that he really was going to pay for it: was going to have his arms strapped to his side and a hood put over his head: was going to be made to stand on a chalked "T" on a trap; was going to have his neck snapped by the dead-fall of his own descending weight. Up to that moment he had been intrigued by the machinery of detection and had not cared to look beyond it.

Now he felt quite sick.

It was not that he knew Bob very well. He could hardly be described as a friend. But they had been at school together. And Bob had done well in the war, and had always shown himself very friendly to Bohun; and he was Bohun's sort of person.

"If only he had stopped after the first one," said Bohun. "That could have been forgiven. Not by the law perhaps—the law took an absurdly narrow-minded view of the sanctity of creatures like Marcus Smallbone—but by his friends. None of them would have moved a step in his detection. But to kill the pathetically stupid and harmless Miss Chittering. From motives of self-preservation—"

"I wouldn't step under that bus, sir," said the policeman at the Aldwych corner. "Not whilst it's actually moving. Fatal accidents, very upsetting to the schedule."

"I'm sorry, constable. I wasn't looking." Bohun proceeded more circumspectly, past the Law Courts and up Bell Yard. Another thought had occurred to him. What would *his* position have been as a partner, if Bob had completed the recently proposed deal? Suppose Bob had transferred his share in the partnership to him and removed himself quietly to a farm in Cornwall before anything had come to light. The demand from the Husbandmen for their June instalment of interest would, he imagined, have been the match which would finally have set off the powder keg. Suppose Bob had already extricated himself by that time?

"The man's a crook," said Bohun firmly. "Sympathy's wasted on him. He's also a particularly cold-blooded murderer." A further instalment of awful thoughts. Was there not one person who, if their theories were correct, held Bob in the hollow of her hand? Anne Mildmay. They didn't want to get back to the office on Monday morning and find that Anne had gone the same way as Miss Chittering.

Bohun, now back in his room, thought for a moment of ringing up Hazlerigg. Then he decided that this was a thing which he could settle for himself, with a little co-operation. There was at least one trustworthy ally to hand. He sought out Miss Cornel.

There was not much time for finesse.

"You're pretty good friends with Anne Mildmay, aren't you?" he said.

Miss Cornel looked faintly surprised, but confined herself to saying: "Yes."

"Good. Could you possibly have her to stay with you this weekend?"

"Friday night to Sunday night?"

"That should cover it."

"I could ask her," said Miss Cornel. "No, wait a minute. It's my Saturday morning on duty."

"We're not opening tomorrow morning," said Henry. "I heard Mr. Craine saying so."

"The firm's going downhill," said Miss Cornel. "I suppose it's no use asking what this is all about?"

"I'd much rather you didn't," said Henry. "Just for forty-eight hours."

Miss Cornel looked at him shrewdly.

"I see," she said. "It's like that, is it? All right, I'll do what I can. Maybe she'll have plans of her own, though."

"Try and persuade her," said Bohun. "Yes, Charlie. What is it?"

"Mr. Craine wants you, sir, right away."

"All right."

He found Mr. Craine reading a letter. The little man was as near worried as Bohun had ever seen him.

"We may need you yourself almost more than your money," he said.

"What's happened, sir?"

"Birley's quit," said Mr. Craine. "Here you are. It's all in this letter. Lock, stock and barrel. He's not even claiming his share in the equity."

"What happens now?" said Bohun.

He felt a little dazed. He had a feeling that the next time he opened his eyes the Duchy of Lancaster would have taken over the firm.

"His share reverts, I imagine, to the other partners," said Mr. Craine slowly. "You'll be getting more for your money, that's all."

"I see," said Henry. "Well, I ought to be in a position to let you have an answer one way or the other by Monday."

It occurred to him that quite a lot of problems were due for solution over that weekend.

IV

The oddest event of an eventful day was yet to come.

Bohun left the office at six o'clock, went home and did absent-minded justice to one of Mrs. Magoli's collations before setting out on his evening stroll. It was a night of low cloud, with rain behind the clouds, and he buttoned his mackintosh round his neck determined to keep his mind rigorously away from anything to do with Horniman and Birley and Craine.

It was outside the Temple Concert Hall that he saw a name. It was a poster announcing a performance that evening by the Equity Choir of Bach's St. Matthew Passion. The leading soloists were well-known singers. And there it was, in smaller letters: "Second Tenor, Eustace Cockerill."

"There couldn't be two people with a name like that," thought Bohun.

He pushed the door softly and went inside.

The small concert hall was packed, and as no one appeared to pay any attention to him he placed himself quietly behind a pillar and disposed himself to listen.

Part One of the performance was more than half over. The chorale, "Here would I stand," drew to a close, and Bohun locating himself by means of the Tenor and Bass Recitatives that followed, knew that he had come in at exactly the right moment. The second choir were on their feet and he saw Cockerill get up quietly to join them.

There was an unmistakable touch of confidence in the way he held himself and after the first two notes of the "O Grief", Bohun's impression was confirmed. The man had a more than ordinarily fine voice. It was not one of the great tenor voices of the world. It lacked perhaps the tight consonantal finish which die-stamps the work of the professional; but full compensation was offered; the tone and the good temper and the clear sincerity of the singing. "Oh grief, how throbs His heavy laden breast. His spirit faints, how pale His weary face." It was as if the singer was hearing the words for the first time. The mutter of the choir: "My Saviour, why must all this ill befall Thee?" The tenor voice spoke again: "He to the Judgment Hall is brought. There is no help, no comfort near."

The words set off a train of pictures, like an uncut cinema film, starting with an old and evil judge mouthing over the words of the death sentence and finishing in a small concrete shed in a high-walled yard at dawn.

When he brought his thoughts back, Cockerill was on his feet again for his second solo. "I would beside my Lord be watching." This is a difficult passage for any amateur, but the singer rode through it with a sort of innocent triumph, taking the long runs with perfect judgment, until it fell away into its final chorale.

"And so our sin will fall asleep. Will fall asleep. Our sin will fall asleep."

Taking a quick look round him as the last notes died, Bohun saw that he was not alone in his appreciation. The audience having paid the tribute of silence and stillness to a moving performance, broke into the momentary shuffle which is the complement of this sort of attention.

Bohun saw something else, too.

Three rows ahead of him was a head on a thickset neck, topping a pair of blacksmith's shoulders.

It was a figure that he had every reason to recognise.

It occurred to him to wonder what had brought Inspector Hazlerigg out at night to the Temple Concert Hall.

CHAPTER FOURTEEN

Preparations for Completion

A house may be habitable but entirely different to the house contracted for.

BICKERTON PRATT: *Conveyancing Practice*

I

"I SEE," SAID THE ASSISTANT COMMISSIONER.

He drew a truculent rabbit on the scribbling-pad in front of him: thought for a few minutes, then took out a four-colour propelling pencil from his inside pocket and dressed it in a Harlequin tie.

"The ball's in your court," he said.

"I can't see any way round it," agreed Hazlerigg. "The trouble is that all this recent stuff has come in so fast that I haven't had time to put any of it to him."

"He's been questioned, of course."

"On the preliminary matters—like everyone else—yes."

"I see." The Assistant Commissioner returned to the rabbit and presented it with a top hat, an eyeglass and, as an afterthought, a wooden leg. "He certainly had the opportunity for both murders. The means weren't beyond him. And he'd got plenty of motive."

"Too much motive, in a way, sir."

"Why do you say that?"

"Well," said Hazlerigg diffidently, "I've always believed that a certain type will kill in anger and another type for gain. In a sort of way he seems to have done it for both."

"Too much motive makes a nice change, anyway," said the Assistant Commissioner. "Look at Aspinall's chap! However, there's also the fact that he lied about his movements on both occasions. That's the sort of thing a jury can appreciate. By the way, I think Sergeant Plumptree might get a pat on the back for tracing that Saturday morning phone call. It was sound work."

Hazlerigg nodded.

"I don't see what else we can do," went on the Assistant Commissioner. "You're quite right. He'll have to be given a chance to explain this new stuff. Where is he now?"

"Somewhere on the North Sea, I imagine."

"Oh—yes, he's staying down at that weekend cottage, isn't he?"

"He arrived late last night. I've got the local sergeant keeping an eye on him. He rings me up from time to time. He's a good man, too."

"It mightn't be a bad thing—from our point of view—if he did try to bolt."

"He's not the sort of chap who'll lose his nerve easily," said Hazlerigg.

The Assistant Commissioner appeared to make up his mind.

"I can't see that we stand to gain anything by waiting," he said. "Take a warrant and go down this afternoon. Whether you use it or not is entirely up to you. You'll just have to see what you think of his explanation. I can't give you any guidance—you've had as much experience in that sort of thing as I have. I needn't remind you that once you *do* make up your mind—"

"I know, I know," groaned Hazlerigg. "I shall have to caution him. It's going to need the most devilishly accurate timing. How any police officer can be expected to decide at exactly what point in an interview he thinks the man he is questioning is the guilty party when the sole object of his questions is to arrive at exactly that proposition—"

"Save it for the Court of Criminal Appeal," said the Assistant Commissioner callously.

II

"I don't like the looks of it," said Sergeant Rolles.

He and Hazlerigg were standing together in the darkness of Sea Lane. Somewhere in front of them, a dim box, was The Cabin. Visibility was limited.

"Four o'clock he brought her in, sir. He's been up and down the estuary all afternoon—beating about and getting the feel of her, you might say. She's a thirty-two foot cutter, sir, with an Austin '7' Marine converted engine A two-berth boat really—but he handles her alone and it's wholly pretty to watch him."

"Didn't he come ashore at all?"

"He did. Came back to the house and had his tea which Mrs. Mullet had got for him. Then went aboard again. He's there now."

"What's he doing?"

"Just sitting on his bottom," said Sergeant Rolles. "One thing, she *is* still there. He hasn't taken her off to Rooshia."

"You've got better eyes than mine, then," said Hazlerigg handsomely. He could scarcely see the house, let alone anything beyond it.

"I've been standing here longer in the dark, sir," said Sergeant Rolles. "Now who's that? Oh—it's Mrs. Mullet." A heavily coated and skirted figure loomed up.

"What's this?" said Mrs. Mullet. "A police smoking concert?"

"You keep a civil tongue in your head, Mrs. Mullet. This is Chief Inspector Hazlerigg of Scotland Yard."

"We've met," said Mrs. Mullet.

"And he wants to know what your Mr. 'Orniman's doing in that boat."

"It's a free country," said Mrs. Mullet. "If you want to find out why don't you ask him?"

"I think that's quite a good idea," said Hazlerigg. "But I'd like you to do it, if you wouldn't mind."

"I could oblige," said Mrs. Mullet. For all the indifference in her voice, they could see her black eyes winking and snapping with curiosity.

She moved away down the path, and round the house. The two men followed discreetly.

Bob Horniman's voice hailed out of the darkness: "Is that you, Mrs. Mullet?"

"That's right, Mr. 'Orniman, it's me. And I've brought your milk for brekfus. Are you coming ashore?"

"Not yet," said Bob. The edge in his voice, which had been scarcely noticeable before was now more evident. "Leave it in the porch, would you. Has that wire come?"

"Not when I left the cottage it hadn't," said Mrs. Mullet. She walked back from the jetty. "You see," she said. "Non-committal."

"All right," said Hazlerigg. "I suppose we've got to take the chance."

He was liking the situation less and less. He could make Bob Horniman out, now, against the light reflected off the water. He seemed to be crouching on the low roof of the well deck, legs crossed, looking down, apparently oblivious to the cold night wind that was whipping off the foreshore. The boat, at stern anchor only, was ten feet or more from the jetty which itself ran a good fifteen feet out on to shelving beach. Certainly too far to risk a jump.

Ever since the Assistant Commissioner had asked him whether he thought Bob would bolt, he had an uncomfortable feeling that he knew the answer. He had said nothing.

It had seemed stupid to prophesy about something which would have to be answered one way or the other so soon.

He took a deep breath.

"Mr. Horniman."

"Hallo. Who the hell's that?" said Bob.

"Inspector Hazlerigg here. I wanted a word with you."

There was a very short silence.

"You've chosen a condemnation odd place for it, then," said Bob.

"I know," said Hazlerigg. "But what I've got to say happens to be rather important."

There was another rather longer silence.

"Then we'd better not stand here shouting at each other across the water." Bob was on his feet now. "Sound carries across water, you know." He had undone a hand rope and was kedging himself inshore against the pull of the anchor chain. When he had closed the gap sufficiently he stepped on to the jetty and tied the hand rope neatly through a ring. "Come up to the kitchen," he said. There was no expression left in his voice at all now.

Hazlerigg followed him up the little flagged path. For the life of him he couldn't say whether he was more relieved or surprised.

Ten minutes later he was still undecided.

Bob Horniman had not fenced with his questions. Neither, Hazlerigg was sure, had he answered them quite candidly.

The two men were facing each other across the table in the back kitchen. Under the strong unshaded light Bob's face looked whiter than ever, and his eyes behind his heavy glasses were wary.

Suddenly he broke in on what the inspector was saying. "Will you answer me one question?"

"If I can," said Hazlerigg.

"Am I supposed to have murdered Smallbone?"

Now this was the one question in the world which Hazlerigg wished to avoid having to answer. But before he could temporise, Bob went on, with a suggestion of flippancy. "Was I supposed to be sitting on deck debating whether or not to cast myself into the waters of self-destruction?"

"Well—"

"Look here, Inspector, if I were to promise you, on my most solemn word, that there *is* an explanation for the apparent discrepancies in my statement about Saturday morning and Tuesday night, but that it has got nothing at all to do with Smallbone's or Miss Chittering's death—would you be prepared to leave it at that?"

"No," said Hazlerigg steadily. "I shouldn't."

"Very well," said Bob, and his jaw came forward dangerously. "I suppose I can't prevent you nosing round and looking for what you can pick up in the way of information. Only don't expect me to help you."

"In that case," said Hazlerigg, taking a deep breath, "I have no alternative but to caution you—"

A sharp double rap made both men jump. Then, before either of them could say a word, the door burst open, and the aged Mr. Mullet appeared. He was out of breath and mauve with excitement.

"It's come," he piped. "I thought you'd like to have it at once, so I brought it." He was waving an opened telegram in the air.

Seeming to feel that some explanation was necessary, he added: "It's all right, m'dear. I looked."

Bob smoothed the orange form on the table and Hazlerigg read over his shoulder.

"A-Z negative. McNeil."

"Thank God for that," said Bob. "Excuse me a moment, I've got to use the telephone." He strode out of the kitchen into the hall and they heard the "ting" as he took off the receiver.

"Have you got any idea what all this is about?" said Hazlerigg. He found himself speaking to Mrs. Mullet, who seemed to have materialised behind her husband.

"Trunks," said Bob's voice in the hall. "Sevenoaks 07632."

"It's that young leddy," said Mrs. Mullet. "The ones he brings down here for the weekends."

"Good God," said Hazlerigg. "Of course. What a fool I've been."

"Ten minutes? Well. I'll wait for it." Bob came back into the room. He was holding himself straighter and seemed somehow to have grown in size. "Now," he said. "What would you like to know?"

"The truth would be helpful," said Hazlerigg. "That is, if you've no objection to—"

"Oh, Mrs. Mullet knows most of it," said Bob. "She thought you were a divorce sleuth the first time she saw you. However, I expect it would be easier without an audience. Would you mind taking your husband into the front room, for a few minutes, Mrs. Mullet. You might make the fire up, and open one of the bottles in the sideboard and get some glasses out. I think we might have something to celebrate."

"Bottles it is, Captain," said Mr. Mullet, who seemed to have a remarkable facility for picking up promising messages. "Leave it to me."

"Now, Mr. Horniman," said Hazlerigg. "Perhaps you'll explain what it's all about."

"It's Anne Mildmay, of course," said Bob. "I'm madly in love with her, and in about seven and a half minutes I intend to propose to her over the telephone."

"And that telegram was...?"

"Yes. I thought—we both thought—she was going to have a child. My child. Now we know that she's not. She had an Aschheim-Zondek a fortnight ago. That telegram was the result. Don't you see? If she's not going to have a child it makes it easy. I can ask her to marry me."

"I should have thought," said Hazlerigg doubtfully, "that if she *had* been going to have a child you'd have felt bound—"

"That's just it," said Bob. "I *should* have felt bound. So would she. It would have been a hopeless basis for marriage. Now everything's all right."

"If you say so," said Hazlerigg. "It's your marriage. Now perhaps you wouldn't mind explaining—"

"Of course," said Bob. "Well, that evening Miss Chittering was killed, of course, we were having dinner together. Not at that place in the Strand. At a little restaurant in Frith Street. I had a table booked for a quarter to seven."

"Do they know you there?"

"They ought to," said Bob. "I've been going there, on and off, for the last ten years. It's quite a tiny place—just the proprietor and his brother who does the waiting. They both know me."

Hazlerigg recognised the truth when he heard it.

"I'd better have the name," he said. "Now what about that Saturday?"

"Well," said Bob, "that really was rather awkward. You see, that was the day—well—that was when all the trouble started."

Hazlerigg stared at him for a moment, and then in spite of himself he started to laugh.

"Do you mean to say—" he began.

"Yes," said Bob uncomfortably. "I'm afraid I do."

"No wonder you were too busy to answer the telephone," said Hazlerigg.

"Yes," said Bob. "Well, as you can imagine, we neither of us felt like doing much office work. We pushed off at about a quarter past eleven, as a matter of fact, and caught the midday train for Chaffham. It gets in at two o'clock. I expect Mrs. Mullet would confirm—oh, there's the phone."

He jumped for the door. Hazlerigg got up and warmed the seat of his trousers at the hob. He heard Bob pick up the receiver and say: "Sevenoaks—Oh! Is that you, Miss Cornel? It's Bob Horniman here... Could I speak to Miss Mildmay?" Then a pause. Then Bob's voice: "Anne, darling, it's all right."

Hazlerigg shut the door, and returned to his place in front of the fire. He could no longer hear what Bob was saying, but he judged from the tone of his voice that everything was all right.

III

"God's fresh air," said the stout girl in hiking shorts.

"That's right," said her companion.

"God's free fresh air," said the stout girl. "That's what they say, don't they?"

"That's right."

"Like hell it's free," said the stout girl. "Railway fares up, purchase tax on walking shoes, four and sixpence for a so-called lunch."

"That's right," said the Yes-girl.

"Before the war," said the stout girl, "I walked through the Lake District. Right through it. I stayed at Youth Hostels. I took ten days and it cost me three pounds sixteen shillings and eightpence, including fares."

"Well, I never," said the Yes-girl. "You'd hardly credit it."

It was nine o'clock that evening. Hazlerigg was sitting in a third-class railway carriage, on his way back to London. When he had got into the carriage it had been empty, but he had been vaguely aware that two girls had got in at Ipswich. He was deeply engaged with his own thoughts.

He was reviewing the case to see how it looked without its central character. For Bob Horniman, in his opinion, was out of it. Not that his Saturday morning alibi was worth much. He could have murdered Smallbone and been in plenty of time to catch the midday train for Chaffham. Nor could you describe as strong corroboration the evidence of the girl with whom you were in love. But on one factor of certainty, on one base of the living rock, Hazlerigg rested his conviction of Bob's innocence. The same pair of hands had committed both murders. No one, be they never so crafty or calculating, could have reproduced that fractional left-handed pull which hall-marked both killings. And if Bob had been at his Soho restaurant at a quarter to seven he could not have killed Miss Chittering. The alibi had to be verified, but he was certain he would find that it was so.

It was true, also, that Bob's explanation had not covered everything. Any explanation would have been, perhaps, open to suspicion if it had. On the subject of the letter discovered in the typists' room, for instance. Bob had simply said that he knew nothing about it. He had never received it. If he was speaking the truth, it began to look very much as if the letter might be a plant. The possibility had been in Hazlerigg's mind all along; ever since he had noticed those pin-marks in the top left-hand corner of the paper. He had remembered that it was quite a common habit for a busy man to pin cheques or receipted bills to blank pieces of notepaper with or without the addition of a signature. Lawyers got them every day. Indeed, now he thought of it, had not Plumptree told him that Smallbone had pinned his last rent cheque to a piece of notepaper and left it on the hall table for Mrs. Tasker to find. Anyone in the office might therefore have received such a missive from Smallbone. They would only have to remove the cheque and they could then type in what message they liked in the space between the address and the signature. Forgery without tears.

"You see them going off from Paddington," said the stout girl. "Torquay, Paignton, and places like that. Piles and piles of luggage. I don't call that a holiday."

"Nor do I," said the Yes-girl.

"But take a nice large rucksack," said the stout girl, nodding down at hers, where it stood, bulging formidably, on the seat beside her.

With a sweet click the last tumbler fell into place.

"God in heaven, what idiots we've been," said Hazlerigg loudly.

Both girls jumped. Hazlerigg, who was a bit of a lip-reader, saw the stout girl forming the word "Drink". Her companion, for once, had an opinion of her own: "Barmy."

"When does this train stop next?" he demanded.

The stout girl felt for her alpenstock and estimated with a quick glance the distance to the corridor door. "It doesn't stop," she said. "It goes straight through to London."

"Then stop it we must," said Hazlerigg. Out of the window he saw the lights of a fair-sized town approaching.

He got to his feet and before either of his travelling companions could guess his intention, he had reached up and jerked the communication cord.

He could not have timed it more perfectly. There was a momentary pause as the vacuum brake took charge: then a series of shuddering jolts, a sharp decrease in momentum. The dark world outside slowed down, the blur of lights separated out into individual windows, and with a long, indignant hiss, the train slid to a halt opposite the deserted platform of a fair-sized station.

Hazlerigg was out before it had fairly stopped.

A door marked "Stationmaster" flung open and a startled and indignant official appeared. Hazlerigg said a word to him, produced his warrant card, and fairly trundled him back into his office.

"I want to use your telephone," he said. "You've got some priority arrangement for up-calls to London. Use it, please, and get me Scotland Yard."

The stationmaster got busy.

Hazlerigg looked back on to the platform. Heads were out all the way down the train, and he could see the bobbing of a lantern as one of the guards climbed the ramp. He reckoned the situation was just in hand.

Five seconds later he was talking to Sergeant Plumptree.

"Look here," he said. "You'll have to listen and not ask questions. I've just stopped the Cromer Express and I reckon I've got two minutes. Get hold of that chap Hayman—the shop assistant in that bag shop in the Strand—yes—Miss Chittering's boy friend. I want to find out who bought a rucksack there on the morning of—let me see—Saturday, February 20th. A large green rucksack. Play fair. Show him all the photographs. Yes, I know it's Saturday night. I don't care how you set about it. You can ask for what help you like. If he isn't at home, put out a general alert and pick him up where you find him. At the cinema, at the pub, on the streets. This train is due at Liverpool Street at a quarter past ten, and I want you to get the information and meet me at the station with a police car and a good driver. I know it doesn't leave you much time, but that's the way it's got to be."

He rang off, thanked the stationmaster politely, and stepped out on to the platform into the arms of a deeply-suspicious guard. The time was nine-fifteen.

CHAPTER FIFTEEN

—SATURDAY NIGHT—

Completion

We cannot force our memories: they must come of themselves
by natural association, as it were; but they may occur to us when
we least think of them, owing to some casual circumstance or
link of connection, *and long after we have given up the search*.

HAZLITT: *On Application to Study*

I

A T ABOUT NINE O'CLOCK THAT EVENING BOHUN WAS SITTING
in his upper room, underneath the portrait of the severe lady
(who was his grandmother) and he was thinking about developments in automatic accounting machinery. He had seen an up-to-
date model demonstrated recently. Accounts were fed into it in
the form of cards, each card being punched with a combination of
holes and slots representing the figures of the account. The machine
would then perform any operation of addition, subtraction, proportion, collation or extraction which the abstrusest fancy of the
accountant might dictate. What had particularly amused Bohun
had been that on an incorrectly punched card being inserted, the
machine gave a most human scream, a red light shone, and the
card was ejected on to the floor. It occurred to him that this was

exactly what was wrong with the proposition of Bob Horniman as murderer. Every time he presented that particular card to his mental processes they as promptly rejected it.

Principally it was the matter of motive.

One of the suggested motives might be the correct one. Both together were impossible.

You could believe in an impetuous, hot-headed, warm-hearted type who came to the conclusion that if Smallbone was capable of tormenting a dying man then Smallbone himself was better dead. One or two people might reasonably have maintained such a proposition since it seemed that the late Abel Horniman, for all his faults, had been a man capable of inspiring both loyalty and affection. On the other hand you could believe in a cold-blooded type, one who calculated that, if he shut Smallbone's mouth and thus postponed the coming to light of the Husbandmen's Mortgage fraud, he might have a chance to sell out his share in the firm and get away with twenty thousand pounds.

It was when you made both of them the same person that you were talking nonsense.

Apart from this there was the consideration that if Bob Horniman had committed the murder on his Saturday morning at the office, then Anne Mildmay must almost certainly have been privy to it. Their statements proved this. They said they had left the office together at ten past twelve and had parted at about twenty past. Now with Smallbone due at the office at twelve-fifteen (vide his letter) either this meant that they were both lying about times or that Bob had not left the office at all, but had got Miss Mildmay to perjure herself and say that he had. In which case she must have had more than a shrewd idea all along that he was the murderer. This Bohun refused to believe. There was *something* between them—you didn't have to be very observant to see that. Anne Mildmay was angry and hurt with Bob, and there was a state of emotional tension between them. But it wasn't the tension of guilty knowledge shared.

And the night of Miss Chittering's murder: that seemed to be a singularly clumsy alibi that Bob had put up: quite out of keeping with the rest of a carefully-planned performance. And could anyone have been so incredibly careless as to drop that incriminating letter in the office by mistake? But if Bob was *not* the murderer, further vistas of speculation at once unrolled themselves. What about that letter? It was, more and more clearly, a plant. Put there to be found. Put there by someone who felt the breath of suspicion on their own neck and was becoming pretty desperate to avert it. Put there by...

It was possible. Yes. It was more than possible.

The clinching thought in this train of thought, the item which finally brought conviction was so trivial as to be ludicrous. It turned on nothing more nor less than the shape of an ordinary steel screw.

Feverishly, Bohun dragged back from his memory the events which had led up to the discovery of that letter. Miss Chittering had wanted to move a mirror. Miss Bellbas—he thought it was Miss Bellbas—had suggested putting it up beside the window. He had offered to fix it for them. Just at the moment when he had everything ready Mr. Craine had appeared and he had been obliged to hand over to Miss Cornel. He was not certain what had happened next, but when he reappeared—not more than thirty seconds later (Mr. Craine had only wanted to give him a letter)—everything seemed to have been dropped on the floor. Miss Cornel was on her knees looking for the screws. She had found one of them by the window and the other underneath her own desk, the middle desk of the three. That was it. And it was whilst they were trying to fish the screw out from under the desk that the letter had come to light.

In other words, shorn of all surrounding circumstances and in the plainest language, Miss Cornel had dropped a screw over by Miss Chittering's desk under the window and had purported to find it under her own desk in the middle of the room. Her explanation had been: "It must have rolled." He remembered that Hazlerigg had later measured the distance between the two desks. Ten feet. How on earth, said Bohun slowly to himself, how on earth could a screw have *rolled* for ten feet. Why, a screw couldn't roll one foot. It couldn't roll six inches. If you dropped a screw on the floor it went round in a circle. Even on a sloping surface it couldn't roll.

He got up and started to walk up and down the long room. An even more deadly question had sprung, fully armed, from the dragon's teeth of his thoughts. And one way or the other it was a question which had to be decided, and decided quickly.

Wait! There was just a chance—a very slender chance—that even now he might be wrong.

He looked up a name in the desk telephone book and dialled a number.

Perry Cockaigne, being a sports writer on a Sunday paper, was one of the few people who could be relied on to be found at his desk late on a Saturday night. He greeted Bohun with enthusiasm, and listened to him without surprise. It seemed quite natural to Perry that people should ring him up in the middle of the night with questions about the sport in which he specialised.

"Yes," he said. "I remember her. She doesn't play competitive golf now. No, old boy. You must be muddling her up with someone else. She was a right-hand golfer. Of course, I'm sure. I've seen her play dozens of times. Hits the strongest tee shot of any woman I know."

"Thank you very much," said Bohun, and hung up.

He was now certain.

II

When Bob Horniman's telephone call came through, Anne Mildmay was seated in Miss Cornel's living-room.

It was a comfortable, neutral sort of room. The enlargements of golfing photographs and the silver trophies gave it a masculine air which was contradicted by the Japanese flower prints and the *Lalique* work, and the large and carefully-arranged bowls of flowers.

Miss Cornel answered the telephone and came back and said: "It's for you. It's Bob Horniman. He would seem to be ringing up from Norfolk."

Anne was away for some time. When she came back into the room her eyes had the story in them for the older woman to read.

"He's asked me to marry him," she said.

"What did you say?" enquired Miss Cornel.

"I said Yes," said Anne. She stood outside herself for a moment, viewing herself in the new, exciting, exacting, terrifying role of bride and married woman.

"I shall make a rampaging wife," she said.

"In my day," said Miss Cornel, "that sort of thing was done in a conservatory, or a summer-house, at two o'clock in the morning, to the strains of the Vienna Woods Waltz. Not over the long-distance telephone from a friend's house."

"I'm sorry," said Anne. "There were complications. Perhaps I'd better explain."

She did so.

"I see," said Miss Cornel. "And what would you have done if the report had been the other way—excuse my frankness—would you have allowed the child to be born out of wedlock?"

"A bouncing little bastard," said Anne thoughtfully. "No. I hardly expect so. I don't know. Anyway, everything's perfect. Now."

"Allow me to congratulate you then," said Miss Cornel.

"By the way," said Anne. "There was one thing I couldn't quite make out. Apparently Hazlerigg was down there."

"Inspector Hazlerigg?"

"Yes. You don't suppose that he thinks—no, that's absurd."

"What's absurd?"

"He can't think," said Anne with a shaky laugh, "that Bob's a—I mean, that he did these murders."

"I shouldn't think so," said Miss Cornel slowly. A close observer might have noted the slight bunching of the muscles on the angle of the jaw, the very faint hardening of the grey eyes. "Is there any particular reason that he should?"

"Well, you know," said Anne, "we've both had to tell an awful lot of lies. Everything seemed to happen when we were—involved. That Saturday morning—"

She explained about Saturday morning with modern frankness and Miss Cornel said doubtfully: "You'd have to alibi each other then?"

"Yes," said Anne, "it wouldn't be awfully convincing, I know. But that Tuesday night, when Miss Chittering got killed. That's absolutely water-tight. We went to a little place in Frith Street. Bob's very well known there. And he booked the table by telephone for a quarter to seven."

"And you were there at a quarter to seven?"

"A bit before, I should say. The waiter—that is, he's really the proprietor's brother—said something to Bob about 'On time, as usual' and Bob said: 'Your clock's fast. We're early.' I should think we were sitting down by twenty to seven. We walked there from the office."

Miss Cornel, like Hazlerigg, recognised the sound of the truth. For a moment she said nothing and then she got up and went over to the cupboard. When she came back she had a dark, squat bottle in her hand.

"We must drink to the health of the happy pair," she said. "Can you pull the cork whilst I get the glasses?"

She was out of the room for a few minutes and came back with two green tumblers. She splashed in a generous three fingers and pushed the nearer tumbler across to Anne. "You mustn't desecrate this stuff by showing water to it," she said.

Anne drank and gasped. "It's strong, isn't it?"

"It should be," said Miss Cornel composedly. "It's genuine pre-war Glen Livet. I had this bottle given me when I won the Open Putter on the Ochterlony course in 1938."

Both ladies sipped in respectful silence.

"That one's to your address," said Miss Cornel. "One more for your intended."

"I don't think—" said Anne.

"It'll make you sleep," said Miss Cornel genially.

"The funny thing is," said Anne, "that I can hardly keep my eyes open—now."

III

"Scotland Yard?"

"This is Scotland Yard. Duty sergeant speaking."

"This is urgent. Can you put me through to—"

"Is this an emergency call?"

"It's not a nine-nine-niner, if that's what you mean," said Bohun. "I must speak to Chief Inspector Hazlerigg."

"I'll see if I can contact him, sir."

"It's to do with the Lincoln's Inn murder."

"One minute, sir."

There was a silence, a click, and a new voice said: "Can I help you? This is Inspector Pickup."

Bohun recognised the name vaguely as one of the inspector's colleagues. He said: "My name's Bohun. I must speak to Inspector Hazlerigg."

"I'm afraid that's going to be rather difficult," said Pickup. "The inspector was coming back from Norfolk tonight—"

"When does the train get in?"

"It got in fifteen minutes ago," said Pickup. "Apparently he stopped the train en route and telephoned for a car to meet him at the terminus. He didn't say where he was going."

"Is Sergeant Plumptree there?"

"Sergeant Plumptree went in the car to meet him."

"Damn," said Bohun.

"If you have any information," said Inspector Pickup, "perhaps I could take it. I'm standing in for Inspector Hazlerigg whilst he's away."

Bohun hesitated. He visualised himself trying to explain, over the telephone, to a complete stranger, the orbit of a steel screw on an inclined plane. Or the fact that people who play a lot of golf develop strong wrists. And that if they play right-handed the development of the left wrist will probably be greater than that of the right.

"No," he said at last. "It doesn't matter."

He rang off. He thought for a moment of trying the station-master's office at Liverpool Street, but abandoned the project before he had even reached for the phone. The train would be in by now and the passengers dispersed.

Direct action seemed to be the only answer.

Bohun kept his car in a private lock-up behind Bream's Buildings. It was a 1937 Morris, not one of the uncrowned kings of the road, but a steady performer if handled properly.

Over the Thames by Blackfriars Bridge, he thought, there won't be much traffic at this time of night. I hope the lights are all right. Bohun had never driven by road to Sevenoaks before, but he knew it lay to the west of Maidstone and he guessed that if he took the Old Kent Road to New Cross and forked right at Lewisham he could not be very wide of the mark. After that he would have to ask.

He crossed the river and ran through the Elephant and Castle roundabout, coldly deserted under its neon lights.

For the first time he spared a moment's thought to wonder what was going to happen at the other end.

Supposing he found the two ladies virtuously asleep. Could he order Anne Mildmay to leave with him and return to London? Ought he to give even that amount of indirect warning to Miss Cornel? Even if every supposition he had made was correct, still was Anne in any danger?

Look out! Oh, a cat.

Whether she's in any danger or not, said Bohun, following the tramlines round the Lewisham bend, it's my fault that she went down there, and it's my responsibility that nothing happens to her. The best thing I can do is to let them both know I'm there and I'll camp out in the garden until morning. I shouldn't think even Miss Cornel would dare make a move with me on her front lawn.

Where was Hazlerigg?

An A.A. scout, coming home from a late call, gave him some directions and he swung south through Bromley.

His thoughts reverted to Miss Cornel.

He wondered if everybody was always as slow and as stupid as they had all been, at seeing what lay under their noses. Of course, neither of her alibis was worth the paper it was written on. To start with, her companion at the office on that Saturday morning had been *Eric Duxford*. He could guess how much that meant. Eric no doubt arrived, put in a nominal ten minutes' work and then went straight away to his other office. In fact, now that Bohun thought of it, had there not been an entry in Eric's "private" appointment diary for eleven o'clock on February 10th—the very Saturday morning in question? Then, again, was it pure luck that Miss Cornel should have been at the office with such an accommodating partner? He rather thought not. It had originally been Miss Chittering's Saturday. Miss Cornel's story was that Miss Chittering had asked her to change Saturdays. What would Miss Chittering's version have been—if anyone had thought to ask her?

And was that one of the reasons why Miss Chittering had been—steady! Road fork. Sevenoaks, nine miles. He was getting on. That was the weekend they should have concentrated on from the start. They knew Smallbone was alive up till Saturday morning. Instead of trying to find out how he spent the next week they should have realised...

But did one ever realise that the obvious explanation, the simple explanation was the right one?

All that speculation about the key of the deed box! Of course the one person who could most easily lay hands on it was Miss Cornel. Or about the difficulty of getting Marcus Smallbone to attend at the office at a given time. Who would be more likely to fix such an appointment than Miss Cornel? Or as to how the letter intending to incriminate Bob got under Miss Cornel's desk? And why it wasn't found before it had to be? Then there was the Tuesday of Miss

Chittering's death. Miss Cornel really had no alibi at all. It was the very simplicity of the idea which had made it so difficult to get hold of. Probably she had not gone to Charing Cross that night. There was no reason for her to do so. She could catch the train just as well from London Bridge or Waterloo. There was the very slight risk of meeting a passenger who knew her. She lived alone. Of course, the confusion caused by the electricity cut had been a help.

Steady again! He must be near by now. He remembered that Sergeant Plumptree, describing his visit to Sevenoaks, had said that Miss Cornel's bungalow lay north of the town. He would have to take a left fork soon.

His headlights picked out a signpost; then he saw the policeman standing in the shadow of the hedge.

He braked sharply.

"Excuse me," he said. "I'm looking for a bungalow called Red Roofs. A Miss Cornel lives there."

"Five hundred yards along on your right, sir," said the policeman impassively.

Bohun thanked him. He was moving when it occurred to him to wonder if it would have been wiser to have asked the policeman to come with him.

Then another thought struck him. The policeman had answered his question very promptly. And, though he had looked for it, he hadn't seen the bicycle which he would have expected if the man had been on patrol.

He had more the look of someone posted...

Here it was.

A neat garden. A low hedge. Bohun cut out the engine and cruised the last hundred yards. Then he got out and switched off his headlights.

The moon, reflecting from the window-glass of the front room, made it difficult to see if there was a light behind the curtains or not.

He thought not. The house was very quiet.

As Bohun walked up the flagged path he had a sharp, clear picture of Miss Cornel coming out of the front door with a smile on her mouth and a heavy spade in one muscular hand.

Moonlight and imagination!

Then the front door did open quietly: but it was Inspector Hazlerigg who stepped out.

CHAPTER SIXTEEN

—LATER—

The Bill of Costs Is Presented

"E. and O.E."

I

THE CROWN, ON THE ADVICE OF ITS LAW OFFICERS, PREFERRED only one charge against Miss Cornel; the murder of Marcus Smallbone. To this charge, despite the strongest persuasion of her advisers, Miss Cornel pleaded guilty. After a formal hearing, therefore, Mr. Justice Arbuthnot pronounced the sentence of death. It was then represented to the Home Secretary that although the available evidence as to the prisoner's state of mind—her fanatical attachment to her late employer and the lack of any motive of personal gain in her crime—were not sufficient to support a plea of unbalance of mind, they might properly be considered in relation to the Crown's prerogative of mercy. The Home Secretary, after due consideration, commuted the sentence to one of penal servitude for life.

On the day that he announced his decision, three conversations of interest took place.

II

"Did you ever think that Sergeant Cockerill might have done those murders?" asked Bohun.

"Originally, he was fairly high up on my list," admitted Inspector Hazlerigg. "Why?"

"It's academic now, of course. But he had a motive—much the same sort of motive as Miss Cornel had, actually. You knew he used to be Abel's batman."

"Yes. We'd dug down as far as that."

"Did you know he was left-handed?"

"I most certainly did not," said Hazlerigg, considerably startled. "Are you sure?"

"Perhaps left-handed is rather a strong way of putting it. I mean that he's a man who does a two-handed job by holding the object in his right hand and making the movements with his left. A right-handed man usually does it the other way about."

"When did you notice this?"

"I noticed it," said Bohun, "when he came into my room on the Tuesday or the Wednesday—it was almost my first day in the office—and started mending a chair for me."

"I see."

"Then again, he had plenty of very good opportunities."

"Quite so. Might I ask when you decided that he was *not* a murderer?"

"When I heard him sing," said Bohun. "The fellow's an artist. No one who sings Bach like that could kill a man with a piece of picture-wire. That's a commercial, utilitarian way of killing. An artist would have too much respect for the beauty of the human neck. He might shoot a man in a fine frenzy, or stab him with a stiletto, or—you're laughing at me."

"Don't stop," said Hazlerigg. "It's a pleasure to listen to you. You know, you'd get on famously with our modern school. Pickup is always lecturing me on their theories. They think that all detection should be a combination of analysis and hypnosis."

"It's all very well for you to laugh," said Bohun crossly, "but if you think it's nonsense, what were *you* doing at that concert? I saw you."

"If you really want to know," said Hazlerigg, "I was doing something which might have been done a good deal sooner. I was finding out how Sergeant Cockerill spent his Saturday mornings."

"How he spent—"

"Yes. Did it never seem to you to be rather an odd arrangement that he should appear at the office for a few minutes at half-past nine or ten, then disappear for two or three hours, and turn up again at twelve-thirty. How did you suppose he spent the middle of the morning?"

"I don't think I ever really gave it a thought," said Bohun. "But I can see you're longing to tell me. What did he do?"

"Well, as a matter of fact," said Hazlerigg, "he used to rehearse. But I found there was a little more to it than that. One of his neighbours, who was also in the choir, used to give him a lift in his car, and wait for him afterwards and take him home. A Colonel Lincoln. A very respectable man and an unimpeachable witness. He used to park his car in New Square whilst Cockerill locked up. He says Cockerill never kept him waiting more than two minutes."

"That sounds pretty conclusive," agreed Bohun.

"I was fairly certain, even before that," said Hazlerigg. "That was only corroboration. As I frequently said, the sheet anchor of my faith all along was the conviction that the same person must have done both killings. Now I agree that on the face of it Cockerill could quite easily have killed Smallbone. But he could never have killed Miss Chittering."

"Well, do you know, it just occurred to me to wonder," said Bohun. "It's true that Mason, the porter, was with him when he was approaching the building—"

"I know what you're going to say. It occurred to me, too. You thought that Cockerill might have gone inside and quietly noosed Miss Chittering during the time that Mason was fooling around with that pigeon. I timed it the next night. He would have had about four minutes. I suppose it was barely possible—feasible, I mean, in a detective story sense. But apart from the improbability of it, there was one factor which I think ruled it out of court. I went along with Mason the next night to check up and he was quite emphatic about it. *All* the office lights were out. There's a fanlight over the secretaries' room and you can see at once if that light's on. According to Mason it wasn't. The reason for that's plain enough, of course. When Miss Cornel had finished with Miss Chittering she turned the lights out and pulled the door shut—she didn't *want* the body to be discovered at once. It would have made everybody's alibis far more confusing, in fact, if the discovery could have been delayed until the next morning."

"Yes. By the way, how did she get back into the building without being seen by anybody?"

"I don't suppose she ever left the building. She probably sat, in the dark, on the next flight of stairs and waited till the coast was clear."

"What a ruthless woman," said Bohun. "And, incidentally, what a nerve."

"A strong left wrist isn't the only thing you develop in a Women's Golf Championship," said Hazlerigg.

III

"Darling," said Anne Mildmay. "You remember that awful night."

"Which awful night?" said Bob, looking up from what he was doing. "Oh, at Sevenoaks—yes."

"Do you think I was drugged?"

"I don't know," said Bob. "You had a very advanced hangover the next morning."

"But what would have been the point of it?"

"If you ask me," said Bob, "it wasn't drugs at all. It was two glasses of neat whisky coupled with the excitement."

"And what was I supposed to be excited about?" demanded Anne coldly.

"The prospect of marrying a farmer," said Bob.

Silence fell again on the little room, with its French window which opened on to an uncut lawn running down to a quiet river under a silver September sky.

"The joke of it is," said Bob, "that I took up farming to get away from office work." He wiped the ink off his finger on to one of the tassels of the tablecloth.

"Never mind," said Anne. "Get on and finish that 'Milk Marketing—Cows in Calf—Feeding Stuffs—1950–51—Estimated quantities', and I'll take it down to the post after tea."

IV

That same afternoon, Bohun, back in the office, was drinking his tea (as a partner he now had it brought to him in a cup *with* a saucer) and watching Mr. Craine. No one, he reflected, would have thought that the cheerful little man had just completed a very trying six months. His reserves of vitality were amazing. He had paid off the Husbandmen and dealt firmly with their scruples about suppressing the details of Abel's most irregular mortgage. He had used the balance of Bohun's money judiciously to strengthen the finances of the firm. He had taken on three new assistants, and had snapped up the services of John Cove, now inexplicably qualified. He had undertaken the whole cost and the endless work involved in Miss Cornel's defence. He had smoothed down the susceptibilities of innumerable clients. He had engaged a new, even more ravishing and, at the moment, inexperienced secretary. She was learning quickly.

"If Miss Cornel was mad," he was saying, "then I'm mad, and you're mad. We're all of us mad."

Bohun nodded.

"I'm glad she didn't hang, though," he said. "After she'd killed Smallbone—and the real reason, the *inner* reason for that I don't suppose we shall ever know—everything else was self-defence. The killing of Miss Chittering and the efforts to throw the blame on to Bob. She was fighting for her life."

"Do you know," said Mr. Craine. "I'm not sure that even now I quite understand about that rucksack. And who was the little man from the Left Luggage Office that Hazlerigg was going to subpœna?"

"I think," said Bohun, "that that was the most truly remarkable thing about the whole business. The single thin, unbreakable thread of causation which joined the body of Marcus Smallbone to the Left Luggage Office at London Bridge Station. It turned on such a trivial series of events, and yet it was strong enough to cause the death of at least one innocent person."

"Strong enough to bring Miss Cornel into the dock," said Mr. Craine. "It seemed to me to be the only tangible evidence they had.

I admit it never came to the test, because she pleaded guilty—but all that stuff about rolling screws and left wrists—Macrea would have made pretty short work of that."

"I rather agree. Well, here's how it worked. Miss Cornel decides to kill Smallbone. She decides, for a number of reasons, that the best place to do it is at the office, on a Saturday morning, when she knows she will be alone. Then she must devise a hiding-place where the body may lie hidden for some little time. Eight or ten weeks will be enough. Fortunately, there *is* such a hiding-place. One of the boxes, so handy, so capacious, so fortunately air-tight. She selects the one least likely to be opened in the course of the day's work, and steals, or copies, the key. The fact that this box happened to contain the papers of the very trust of which the victim was a trustee was bizarre but coincidental. But it was these papers, you note, which constituted the first real snag. And this was where the Horniman office system signally justified its founder. In no other office—in no other solicitors' office in London, I think—would the disposal of a bundle of papers and files and account books have caused the murderer any embarrassment. There would have been a dozen places where they could have decently been laid to rest with other papers, out of sight and out of mind, collecting as the months and years went by only a further coating of black dust. In this office they would have been noticed in twenty-four hours—the fat would have been in the fire with a vengeance. Therefore they had to be disposed of *out of* the office."

"Well, that oughtn't to have been too difficult," said Mr. Craine. "She could have—let me see, now—dropped them into the Thames."

"In broad daylight?"

"Or taken them home and burnt them in her garden."

"She particularly did *not* want to arrive at Sevenoaks station—where she was well known and very likely to be noticed—carrying a bulky package. The fact could easily have been remembered."

"Then she could have—well, you tell me."

"It wasn't all that easy," said Bohun, "and she thought it out very carefully. On the Saturday morning in question, on the way to the office, she stopped and purchased a large green rucksack. She had it wrapped up, as a parcel, at the shop—explaining that it was a gift for a friend—and brought it to the office with her. Once Eric Duxford had departed on his private business and she was alone, she took all the papers out of the Stokes box and proceeded to cut out, with her nail scissors, all references in the papers to Horniman, Birley and Craine. It wasn't too bad, because it was mostly account books and schedules of investments—not letters. I expect she burnt the snippets then and there. The rest of the papers, now comparatively unidentifiable, went into the rucksack. After she had finished with Smallbone and left the office, she carried the rucksack with her—a little luck was necessary not to be seen coming out of the office with it, but Lincoln's Inn is a very deserted place on Saturday morning. When she got to London Bridge she deposited it in the Left Luggage Office. She knew that unclaimed packages were opened after six months, but she reckoned that even when that happened no one would be smart enough to connect a lot of old papers without any name on them with Horniman, Birley and Craine, and thus with the Lincoln's Inn murder. Ten to one they would have been sent for pulping without another thought. And further and more important even if the connection was noticed, there was no one to connect *her* with the rucksack. It was a common type. She had bought it at a large and busy shop and paid cash. And she had been careful that no one who knew her had seen it in her possession."

He paused.

"It was a bit of bad luck, so shattering that it seems to belong to the realm of reality rather than the realm of Art, that this particular rucksack should have been sold to her by the head of the Camping Department of Messrs. Merryweather and Matlock."

"Miss Chittering's fiancé?"

"Yes. He recognised Miss Cornel and remembers that he mentioned the transaction to Miss Chittering later—even described the rucksack."

"Yes, I see."

"Imagine Miss Cornel's feelings when, in the secretaries' room, in front of almost the whole staff—including myself—Miss Chittering suggested that Miss Cornel should lend Miss Bellbas 'her big green rucksack'."

"Good God," said Mr. Craine. "What did she do?"

"Kept her head. Turned the conversation. But I reckon she knew from that moment what would have to be done—and a week later she did it."

Bohun finished his tea and rose to go. As he reached the door Mr. Craine surprised him by saying:

"I wonder what she really thought of Abel."

"I think she was very attached—"

"Yes," said Mr. Craine. "It's funny when you come to think of it—the different way people see each other. I don't mind betting the Husbandmen think of Abel as nothing but a crook. I thought about him—when I thought about him—as a damned good lawyer and a bloody difficult partner. To her I suppose he was a sort of God."

"No," said Bohun. "I don't think he was quite that. She was too level-headed to have terrestrial gods. It was just that she saw all the better side of him. Do you remember that money she used to distribute to those poor old ladies, as almoner for Abel. When you come to reckon it up, that was a most revealing indication of their relationship. The money was entirely in his discretion. He might so easily and safely have stolen that. But he didn't. He was prepared to swindle a large corporation to the tune of ten thousand pounds but he wouldn't dip his hand into their shillings and pence. And Miss Cornel knew it. She carried his purse for him. She'd been his right hand and his left hand for nearly twenty years."

"Of course, he was a widower," said Mr. Craine thoughtfully. "You don't think—"

"No," said Bohun firmly. "I don't. I think it was one of those relationships which just happens. I don't suppose either side fully understood it."

Back in his own room he found Mrs. Porter with the afternoon post. He turned his thoughts resolutely towards the future.

"To the Whizzo Laundry—two z's, Mrs. Porter—West Street, Wirral. Sir, Our client, Lady Buntingford, instructs us most emphatically that she dispatched three undervests—"

BRITISH LIBRARY CRIME CLASSICS

Many of our titles are also available in eBook and audio editions